April S

Kathleen ... ...

BREWIN
BOOKS

Published by Brewin Books Ltd
Studley, Warwickshire B80 7LG
in August 2000
Reprinted October 2001

First published by Isis Publishing Ltd
Oxford
in large print

ISBN 1 85858 175 5

British Library Cataloguing in Publication Data
A Catalogue record for this book is available from the British Library

Typeset, Printed and Bound by
Heron Press, Kings Norton,
Birmingham

PART ONE

Darkness came early in many of Birmingham's Edwardian and Victorian densely populated back to back alleyways and court yards, where many poor uneducated large families lived in crumbling hovels they called their homes, which seldom saw the sun rays. Not everything turned out right for these people: poverty, hardship and living from hand to mouth often made them frustrated and angry, yet this kind of people who lived in these overcrowded hovels and bug infested, also had a sense of humour which often help them to survive.

These dilapidated slums faced each other across a narrow courtyard of broken uneven cobbles, where neighbours heard and knew each other's business, never missing a good gossip. At the end of the alleyway were three wooden dry closets, two dustbins (or miskins which they are often called), also two brewhouses. In the centre of the court stood a gas lamp, and built in the wall was an iron water tap where neighbours got their water for all uses.

There was no water laid on in their homes, neither was there any gas light inside the rooms, until later years. The only light and warmth was from a coal fire or a paraffin lamp hanging from the ceiling or a table lamp. Often candles.

These poor people were often called the "Have Nots" by the "Upper Crusts" who had plenty. Yet these "Have Nots" were the kind of people to help and share to anyone in need.

These people had large families to cope with, therefore there were many quarrels over children being a nuisance as they played outside someone's door, when a neighbour wanted a rest.

But children needed recreation, but there was nowhere else to play. There was no garden or a park for miles.

Esmerelda Rabone had never had much schooling, therefore she was brought up in ignorance. The only life she knew was helping her mother to do washing and mangling in the communal brewhouse, also ironing and helping to sort whatever was worth taking to the local pawnshop. The only other help her parents received each week was from the welfare state, and birthdays came and went like any other ordinary day for little Esmerelda.

It was a very sad day when she watched her two younger sisters die with whooping cough and measles. A few months later, her father died in the infirmary, then her mother to follow him four days later with that dreaded disease, consumption. She was now alone at that tender age of twelve.

Many kindly neighbours gave what little they could to help, taking her scraps of food and bits of coal for the fire, or whatever they could spare. But the neighbours were afraid to take her into their homes, for they had large families. Often two or three families in one house. The were also afraid she might be carrying that same disease that her parents had died with.

There was only an Uncle Rabone, her father's brother, whom she remembered, who came once a month and brought her mother a small sum of money to help the family budget. He was known as her Uncle Simon. He often brought her sweets, yet she couldn't understand why he never brought any for her two little sisters. One day she asked him why.

"Uncle Simon, why do you not bring any sweets for me sisters?"

"I'm sorry, I never thought they ate sweets."

"They do, because I share mine with 'em."

"I'll bring 'em some next time I come." As he began to stroke her face and her hair he said, "One day when you grow up I'm going to dress you up in silks and satins and take you on a long holiday."

"And me little sisters?" she asked as she gazed up at him. But he just nodded.

Little did she know then that her uncle knew she was going to lose them both, also her parents, within the next few weeks.

One day while her mother had gone to visit her father in the infirmary, she was left to tend to her little sisters, who were only three and four years old, when her Uncle Simon came and brought four bars of Fry's chocolates. "Two for you and one each for your sisters, my dear." As he gazed around the almost bare room he asked where her mother was. "She's gone to visit me dad," she replied, "at the infirmary, and I've gotta look after me little sisters till she gets back."

"Well come and sit on me lap and eat yer chocolate."

As she sat, she began to giggle as he started to rub his goatee beard up and down her neck. Then as his hand began to stroke her face his hand slowly began to stroke her chest. Innocently she thought he was being kind, but when he started to fumble with her frock and slide his hand along her bare thigh, she knew at once this was all wrong.

Quickly she pushed his hand away and jumped off his lap. Suddenly she glared at him. "I don't like yer doing that!" she cried out.

"Why, my dear?"

"It's wrong and it's dirty."

"I was not going to hurt you, Esmee dear. I only wanted to see what sort of underclothes you wore."

"But why?" she asked, still glaring at him.

"Because next time I come I'll bring some nice warm new underclothes and pretty, pretty things to wear."

These words to an innocent girl who had nothing but the rags she stood up in, believed him.

She said she was sorry for doubting him, yet she didn't like the way he slobbered when he kissed her goodbye.

"I'll come again in a few weeks time. Tell yer mother I've left some money on the shelf for her needs, but don't tell her about the nice things I've promised you. It's going to be a nice surprise."

After she waved goodbye, she thought how lucky she was to have a kind old man for an uncle, who brought her sweets and left her mother money to buy food.

But as the weeks turned into months, she didn't know that before she was much older she had a lot to learn about her father's brother, Uncle Simon.

A few weeks later he received a note to say that her father and mother had died. Two days later he arrived carrying a large cardboard box. As soon as he kissed her tears, he handed her the box. She forgot her sorrow for a moment. As soon as she saw its contents she threw her arms around his neck and kissed him. "O thank yer, Uncle Simon," she cried when she saw a new black tammy shanter, a black woollen coat edged with fur and a pair of lace up boots.

*

Esmerelda and her Uncle Simon were the only two relatives. With the four bearers to each coffin, also several neighbours at the graveside to watch with heads lowered with tears, as they watched the coffins lowered into the ground. As Esmerelda began to sob, her uncle put his arms around her and held her close.

"Don't weep any more, dear. I'll always take care of you now."

Little did she know he had other intentions.

As soon as the neighbours heard him, Winnie Green turned to her neighbour and whispered, "Wot a kind man 'er uncle is an' look 'ow lovely she looks in them clothes 'e brought 'er."

"Yes, I pray ter the good Lord she'll live long enough to wear 'em, but one never knows, does one, with 'er mom and dad dyin' sa young? God bless 'er an' guard 'er", Winnie Green replied, as she began to cross herself.

"I 'ad a chat with 'er uncle before the lids was screwed down," Mrs Fletcher replied. "He ses 'e's tekin' 'er to 'is 'ome ter live with 'im."

Suddenly Nora Townsend piped up. "Yer carn't believe all you 'ear! I don't like the man, never did. There's a fishy look about 'im."

"Oh, be quiet, Nora Townsend. Ya ain't got a good word to say about anybody," Susie Smart whispered.

"Alright! You wait an' see," Nora replied. "I alwis right. Don't ferget I warned yer wen yer lodger was gooin' ter run away with that married man, an' 'er only fifteen an' in the family way an' all."

"Oh cum now, Nora," Maggie Tarply replied. "This ain't the time ter bring them things up."

After the burial service, the bearers and the neighbours left soon after the funeral feast, when Simon Rabone began to pack what few belongings his niece required. As soon as they were ready to leave and say their goodbyes to the kindly neighbours, Esmerelda clung to Mrs Smart, as she remembered how she'd been to her parents, and began to weep again.

Taking out his black bordered handkerchief to wipe her eyes again, he put his arm around her waist and tried to comfort her.

As soon as they were now both ready to leave, Susie Smart whispered to him, "Take good care of 'er, she's 'ad a lot ter bear. I would've took 'er in meself, but I ain't got the room with all my brood."

"I'll take care of her," he replied, "and I'll write and let you know how she's getting along."

Several neighbours and their children, whom she had sometimes found time to play with, also shed tears as she waved them goodbye.

Soon they hurried to catch the train to uncle's home in the Black Country.

*

Esmerelda had had many dreams of her uncle living in a nice, big house with a garden full of flowers and children living near, whom she could play with. But, when at last, she was led into a narrow, cobbled, dismal, deserted street, her dreams were shattered. She only saw one old house with its front door blistered with dark paint peeling off, which opened out on to the edge of the narrow pavement. Either side of the narrow street was a derelict coal yard, a public house, a rag and bone shop, and a totter's yard and a pawnshop. But she noticed these were all empty.

As she gazed up at the rusty three balls that hung over the building, tears began to flow as she thought of the times she had to take her mother's place in the queue, until her mother could find something to pawn for food.

As her uncle turned the key in the lock of number seventeen, she cried out, "This ain't where yer live, is it Uncle Simon?"

"Yes my dear, but later on we shall be moving to a better district where you can go to school and dressed like other girls. Now come along inside," he added impatiently.

As soon as they entered the front room, she was surprised when he called out, "Maggie, I'm home".

"Who's Maggie," she asked suddenly.

"I should have told you, but I forgot to mention, Maggie is my house keeper. You'll like Maggie," he added. "Now sit yourself down while I go and talk to her."

As soon as he left her to go into the kitchen, she sat down on a ladder-back chair and began to take stock of all the room contained. It was cluttered up with all kinds of knick knacks, faded pictures hung on faded wallpapered walls. A well worn oval table stood in the centre of the room. There were also two leather chairs, an armchair and a horse hair sofa, which lay beneath the window.

Although everything was old, the room looked clean. A bright fire was blazing in the shining, black leaded range and on the hob stood a bright copper kettle and an enamel mottled tea pot. Around the mantle shelf hung a dark green, velvet bobble fringe, and arranged neatly were an alarm clock in the centre and several small crock animals each side. The floor was covered with faded brown lino, also a rush mat lay on the hearth, where the large ginger top cat lay asleep. She began to wonder what his name was.

She never heard her uncle had come quietly into the room and stand behind her, until she almost jumped from the chair when he whispered in her ear, "His name is Jimmy. I'm sorry I startled you my dear, but you was deep in thought. Now take off yer tammy and coat, while I lay the table for tea. Maggie will show you where you have to sleep."

While she waited for Maggie, she began to think about her own home she had left just a short while ago, with its bare, whitewashed walls and the bare floor boards she helped her mother to scrub, also the broken table top and chairs and orange boxes to sit on.

She wished now, as she gazed again around the room, that her parents could see this place and all it contained and the kind uncle who had brought her here.

But Esmerelda had a lot to learn before she was much older. As Maggie came into the room, Esmee couldn't stop staring at her. She had a ruddy complexion with large, smiling, blue eyes. Her hair was turning grey, which she wore tightly back into a bun at the back of her head. She reminded Esmee of a kind neighbour she had not long ago kissed and said goodbye to, before her uncle had brought her here. When Maggie asked her why she was staring, she replied, "Are you related to Mrs Green?"

"Who's Mrs Green?" Maggie asked.

As soon as Esmee explained, she replied, "No my dear, I have no relations living now, but I once had a young daughter who would have been about your age, only she ...."

Before Maggie could say more, Simon Rabone turned around and stared at her. "I advise you Maggie!" he shouted. "That matter is closed!"

She almost lost her temper. She wanted to remind him again about those many long, sad years ago. But she knew she couldn't. Not while the girl was in the room listening.

Esmee began to stare at her uncle. She had never seen this side of his temper before, neither did she like the way they glared at each other.

Esmee turned away to warm her hands by the fire, when she heard her uncle change his tune.

"Maggie, will you show Esmee where she has to sleep, and don't be long. I daresay we are each of us ready to sit down and eat."

As soon as Esmee followed Maggie up the stairs, she asked, "Why is Uncle Simon angry?"

"It's a long story, my child. Maybe one day I will tell you," she whispered.

As she followed Maggie up the first six flights of stairs, Maggie said, "That's my room, and the one on the right is your uncle's bedroom."

As soon as Esmee saw the small bedroom up the next four stairs, she cried out excitedly, "Oh Miss Maggie, is this my bedroom?"

"Yes, my dear, but you'll have to keep it clean and tidy, because it's often too much now to climb the stairs."

"Oh I will, Miss Maggie, I will," she repeated.

As Maggie was turning down the padded patchwork quilt, Esmee began to look under the bed.

Maggie knew what she was looking for. "The bathroom is through this other door. The chamber is for use in the night. Now I'll leave you to settle down and empty your case. Don't be long, your uncle gets annoyed if he's kept waiting." After kissing Esmee on her cheek, she left.

As soon as Maggie had gone, Esmee began to take stock of the small bedroom. The single iron green painted bedstead she noticed lay along the right side of the bathroom door. The opposite side of the bed was a dark green painted small iron grate. It reminded her of the one she had in her attic bedroom at home. Opposite was an old wardrobe, with a long oval embedded mirror, a chest of drawers and a wicker chair. On the floor beside the bed was a faded coloured pegged rug.

Everything she saw was old but clean, but to her eyes everything was a luxury, for she had never known what it was to have a bed and a room all to herself. She had had to sleep with her little sisters in a bed that was not much bigger than this one.

As she looked around the room again, she began to hum and dance and twirl around as she cried out, "I'm going ter love it 'here, Miss Maggie. I know I am."

As soon as she stopped to catch her breath, she cried out, "Oh, I'll have ter 'urry now or me uncle will get angry with me."

As soon as she entered the dining room she saw the table was already laid with cakes and wonderful things to eat. Her uncle never looked up: he was reading his letters and beside his plate she noticed a large bible. She was about to say something, when she saw Maggie frown at her and put her finger to her lips, and as she saw her shake her head from side to side, Esmee knew what she meant.

As soon as she sat down at the table, she watched her uncle close his eyes and mumble beneath his breath. She knew he was thanking the good Lord for the food they were about to partake. Then as he kissed his bible, they began to eat.

Esmee was surprised. She didn't know her uncle was a religious man. That was something else she didn't know about him.

As soon as the meal was over, he picked up his letters and bible and walked into the parlour, without another word.

Esmee began to help Maggie clear the table, and after washing up the crocks and arranging them on the kitchen shelf, they sat down beside the range, when Esmee began to ask, "Is my Uncle Simon religious, Miss Maggie?"

"Hush dear," she whispered, "he may be listening."

"Does he listen at keyholes then?"

"I don't think so, Esmee," she whispered, smiling, "but what he can't hear he guesses, and woe betide if you happen to cross him the wrong way. I know you'll want ter know what he's really like, but there's plenty of time for me to tell you later. Now don't ask any more questions, not while he's here. But in the meantime, I want you to help me patch some sheets. Can you sew?" she added.

"Oh yes, Miss Maggie," she replied eagerly to help. "Me Mom taught me how to mend, darn, knit and cook, but I've never made like cakes or bread like you do. But I'd like to learn."

"All in good time, Esmee dear," she replied.

Maggie knew she was going to love this young girl.

After talking about her parents and the little sisters she had lost, also the kind neighbours and the children she had left behind, it began to get dark.

"I believe it's time now for your bed, Esmee, but first I will show you where the sheets go, then I have to go into the kitchen and see your uncle."

"Come in!" he called out sharply, as soon as he heard her knock. As she entered, she saw him closing his large bible. "I think Esmee had better have an early night, as it's her first day here," Maggie said.

"Very well, send her in," he replied.

Esmee was stroking the cat on her lap when Maggie told her she had to go into her uncle and wish him goodnight. "And don't forget to knock before you enter," Maggie added.

As soon as she knocked on the door, she heard him call out, "Come along in, my dear."

As she entered, she was almost afraid to be near him. She was learning fast the other side of his nature, and didn't like the way he got up from his chair and came across to hug her. As soon as he felt her draw away from him, he asked what she was afraid of. When she didn't reply, he took her in his arms and pressed his lips hard on her mouth.

As soon as he released her, she pushed him away and wiped her hand across her mouth. "Don't kiss me again like that!" she cried out.

"Why dear? Don't you like me to kiss you?"

"No! Not like that!" she replied.

"Well come and sit on my lap and I'll rub my whiskers up and down your cheeks like I used to."

"No! Uncle Simon, that was a long time ago."

I'm sorry I've upset you, dear, but I don't mean to harm you, because I promised your mother and father I would take care of you and I must keep my promise. Now, am I forgiven?" he added.

She could only nod her head, as she ran from the room, yet she would never forget that look in his eyes and the perspiration that stood out on his bloated face and the pressure of his wet lips.

As soon as Maggie saw her tears, she knew at once there was something wrong, yet she dare not ask Esmee until they were in the attic.

As soon as Maggie led her upstairs with the lighted candle and entered the room and as she placed the candle on the narrow shelf, she sat on the bed beside Esmee and asked what had brought her tears.

"I don't think I'll like Uncle Simon anymore, Miss Maggie," she cried out tearfully.

"Why? What's he been saying to you?"

"It's wot he's tried to do," she sobbed.

"Come now, don't cry. If you want to tell me, I'll listen."

"Well, when I went in the room to wish him goodnight, he jumped out of his chair and squeezed me to him and he was trembling all over when he kissed me. I hate him, Miss Maggie, and if it wasn't for you being here I'd run away."

"I know how you must feel child. Now wipe your eyes and get undressed and into bed, while I fetch you a cup of hot cocoa." Maggie too had other plans.

But Esmee didn't get undressed, neither did she get into bed. She kept having thoughts that one night he would come into the attic while she was asleep.

Before Maggie left the room, she asked how she could get to the bathroom.

"I'll bring you the key up later. In the meantime, you can use the chamber. Now I won't be long, I'm just going to have a good talk to your uncle. You'll be alright while I've gone. You'll find some books in the chest of drawers till I get back."

Maggie kissed her cheek, then hurried down the stairs. As son as she reached the parlour door, she flung it open and burst in. Seeing him reading his bible, she cried out, "Yer need read that! Yer fornicating old hypocrite."

"What yer raving about?" he replied, as he stood up to face her.

"Yer know what I'm raving about, and don't laugh at me! You sniggering old fool! You should be ashamed of yourself trying to molest a young innocent child!"

"I wasn't molesting her, as yer call it. I simply just wanted to kiss her goodbye before I left."

"I know your sort of kisses and what they lead up to from bitter experience, Simon Bloody Rabone!" she exclaimed.

"I ain't got time to argue with you now, woman! I'm late already and I've got a train to catch."

"I don't care how late you are! But I can see you've got yer cases already packed, so before you leave here you'll hear now what I have to say! I don't know where you're going or who you're going with. I'm not interested in you any more, you killed the love I had for you years ago, when I was young and attractive. I'm only sorry I ever read your advert."

"Have yer finished?" he replied, as he faced her again. "If you have, let me remind you Maggie, I never really loved you, you knew that!"

"Yes, when it was too late and I realised that when I told you I was carrying your child, when you told me then you was already married, and I've known for a long time you visit whore houses on yer travels."

"I don't visit no whore houses!" he exclaimed.

"No? Well I suppose you've got some other man's leaves off when yer stay on yer travels."

"That's my business. Why, you ain't getting jealous in yer old age, are yer, Maggie?" he replied sarcastically.

"I'm past being jealous of a hypocrite like you! But let me warn you once and for all, if any harm comes to that child I'll kill you Simon, and I mean that!" she replied bitterly. "And remember this," she added, "it's only my allowance that has kept me here."

"I can stop it if I wish to."

"If you dare even to try, I'll have you up in the courts for bigamy and you know it! So don't you dare to forget that you still have a wife living in Ireland," she replied bitterly.

"Well if you've finished what you have to say, we'll talk about that when I return."

"When you do, I hope you ain't fuddled with drink as usual."

"I can't stop to argue any longer. I've got a train to catch and I don't know this time when I'll be back. This time it might be six months or twelve."

"I hope you never come back!" she cried out as she left the room, slamming the door behind her.

She never asked him where he was going, nor what took him all over the country, or sometimes abroad. She knew he often lied to her.

As she put the kettle on to make Esmee's cocoa, she sat down and wept, as she remembered those cruel years when he had flaunted his fancy women, whilst she was pregnant with his child.

When the cocoa was ready, she laid the cup on a tray with a couple of biscuits and carried them upstairs.

As soon as Esmee saw her she asked, "Does Uncle Simon 'ave ter come through my bedroom to go to the bathroom?"

"No, my dear," she replied, smiling at Esmee's troubled expression. "I'll take you through and explain."

As Maggie unlocked the door she cried out, "Mind the step, we don't want you falling down."

As soon as she entered, she lit the gas mantle, and as Esmee looked around, she noticed the bathroom was long and narrow. Just wide enough for one person to move in comfort. The walls were bare and white-washed. On one side was a small hand basin, above was a glass cabinet. In the sloping ceiling was a fanlight. At the other end of the room was the toilet, with its wooden seat, an iron cistern and a rusty chain. Next to the toilet was another door. As Maggie put the key in the lock, she began to explain.

"This door, Esmee," she said, "leads to a small balcony and if you look over the side you'll see another balcony which leads into your uncle's bedroom. That's the way he comes up when he wants to use the bathroom. He also has a key which he always keeps on his watch chain, and the bottom half of the steps is another way into the kitchen. These stairs are used for fire escape. Now we better go back in before you catch cold."

As Maggie sat on the side of the bed with Esmee, she began to explain why the rooms were so small.

"Many years ago, before I knew your uncle, I was told he bought this place to live in. It used to be a draper's shop. Your uncle, always having an eye for business, saw it was going downhill. He bought it cheap and made it his home. The other dwellings around here are more or less lock-up shops, and it gets very lonely at night. In the morning I'll take you around the house and explain everything you need to know."

"Is Uncle Simon rich, Miss Maggie?" she asked.

"Why do you ask."

"Well, when he used to come to visit me mom, he always left her money on the shelf for her."

"Well I really don't know if he's rich, but he's comfortably well off. He's got his fingers in all sorts of businesses."

"Is that why he goes on long journeys?"

"Yes dear, but I always know when to expect him back. Now your cocoa's got cold. I'll go down and make you some more," she replied, trying to change the subject.

"Let me, Miss Maggie."

"You just get undressed and into bed. There'll be lots of other jobs for you to help me with later."

As soon as she came back with the hot cocoa, Esmee was already undressed and sitting up in bed.

As soon as Maggie began to tuck her in, she cried out, "My goodness, where's your nightgown?"

"I've never had one. I've always slept in my shift."

"Well you'll have to manage with one of mine and tomorrow we'll go shopping and rig you out."

After Esmee snuggled into one of Maggie's flannel ones, she cried out, "Thank you, Miss Maggie. I feel warmer now."

As soon as Maggie began to tuck her in again, she saw tears in her eyes as she tried to say, "I love you, Miss Maggie, I truly do."

"I love you too, dear. Now lie down and go to sleep and if you need me during the night, you've only got to bang on the floor boards."

Suddenly Esmee shot up in bed and threw here arms around her and as Maggie bent to kiss her cheek, she stood up to turn the gas out.

"Miss Maggie, I don't like sleeping in the dark. Can you leave it on?"

"Very well, dear. I'll just turn it down low and later on I'll let you have Jimmy. It'll be company for yer." After she kissed Esmee again, she tucked the bedclothes around her and left.

As she entered the kitchen to make herself a hot drink, she began to weep as she thought of her child she had lost so tragically those many years ago. As she began to wipe the tears away, she wondered if the good Lord had sent Esmee to comfort her in her old age, or was it fate? Or was it a guilty conscience that had made Simon Rabone bring his young niece to comfort her in her lonely hours?

Although she knew he never really loved her, there were times they were happy in each other's company, but she knew he was a different person when he was besotted in drink. But when she gave birth to their daughter Pollyanne, he couldn't do enough to repay her for the unhappy times he had caused her. She knew he loved the child dearly. He was so proud of her, he took her everywhere he went, and for four years they were happy.

She began to weep again as she remembered when her daughter was four years old, he took her to see a circus. It was late and she couldn't understand why they were not back. It wasn't until two in the morning that he came home with two policemen. She could already smell the drink on him. When the policemen said the child was lost, she wouldn't believe them. She began to accuse Simon of leaving her while he went off with one of his floozies.

After searching all night and Maggie calling her name, the search was given up until daylight.

At daybreak, little Pollyanne's body was seen floating in the canal. Although there was an inquest and a lot of enquiries, no one seemed to know how it happened.

Maggie never forgave him. After that sad day, she began to despise him. She refused to sleep in the same room with him and didn't care any more where he went or how many women he went with. She had closed her eyes and ears a long time ago to the gossip that went around the district about how he was carrying on with women. She knew he had a wife in Ireland, also another he had bigamously married in Scotland. She had kept his secret for years. Now she didn't care any more. She had an allowance and a home, which was agreed between them and signed by solicitors, and now she had Esmee to love and care for.

*

Maggie and Esmee felt much happier when Simon was away on his long business trips.

She loved Maggie and did everything she was told without even a grumble. Although at times, helping Maggie with the washing and ironing and cleaning the whole house tired her at times, but never complained. Maggie also taught her how to cook, darn and knit and how to be thrifty.

When Esmee was nearly thirteen years old, Maggie noticed she was filling out and thought it as now time to rig her out.

"Esmee," she said one day as they were hanging out the washing on the line in the back yard. "I think it's about time I took you to the shops. You're growing up now and that frock you're wearing is much too short and the buttons will soon pop off."

"Oh thank you Miss Maggie. But can you really spare the money?" she asked, as she put another peg into the well patched sheet.

"Yes love. I've saved over the years, also from the housekeeping money, so as soon as we've finished pegging out the clothes, we'll get ourselves ready and go to the markets."

Esmee had never been inside shops or markets since she was a little girl of four years of age, when her mother took her to buy left-over stale loaves or cake or broken biscuits or herrings or scrag ends of meat to feed the family. Esmee still remembered those hungry days.

Maggie held Esmee's hand as they walked around the stalls, but Maggie couldn't see anything suitable and evrything was too expensive. She knew she had to look for something cheaper, but good, as she knew Esmee would grow out of them as she grew older.

As she stood gazing in the window of a secondhand shop, Maggie saw a notice in the window which she read. "Closing down sale. Almost new clothes. Going for a song."

"Can we go in, Maggie?" Perhaps if I sing a song they will give us what we want."

Maggie began to smile as she replied, "It doesn't mean what it reads. It means they're going cheap. Now come along, we'll go inside and see what they have to sell."

As soon as they entered the shop, a middle-aged, dowdy-looking woman popped her head up from behind the counter. "Can I help yer?" she cried out at once.

"Yes," Maggie replied.

As Esmee began to look around at all the lovely garments hanging around the room, they almost took her breath away, for she had never seen such a wonderful display of coloured articles before.

When Molly was asked if she had anything to suit for Esmee, she took them into another room. After showing her several frocks, Maggie said they were too old-fashioned and dowdy.

"How old is she?" the woman asked.

"She's nearly thirteen," Maggie replied.

"Nearly thirteen! I'm surprised, I thought she was older than that. She has quite a good figure and quite a good bust, but I think I can fit her out. Just follow me," she replied.

As soon as they entered the store-room, Esmee's eye caught a royal blue velvet dress with cream lace on the collar and cuffs. "I'd like this one, Miss Maggie," she cried out as she stood stroking it.

"Very well," Maggie replied, "you'd better slip off your dress and try it on."

Although it fitted perfectly, Maggie saw it was much too long. But she was satisfied to pay the price of nine shillings and eleven pence, including an under-slip and liberty bodice. But when the woman said she would have to charge for turning up the dress, Maggie replied, "I ain't paying for a job I can do meself."

"Very well. Shall I send it on to yer?"

"No, we'll take it with us. I don't trust delivery people," she replied, as she left with the parcel under her arm. "Now Esmee, we must hurry now before the other shops close."

After buying an everyday frock, some under-garments including bloomers, and flannelette nightgowns, a pair of shoes and fawn lisle stockings, they hurried home before it got dark.

As soon as they arrived home and when the table was laid with jam and cakes that Maggie had made, Esmee asked, "What will Uncle Simon say when he sees me all dressed up?"

"He won't be home for many months yet. Anyway, he should be proud of you."

"Thank you, Miss Maggie, for everything," she said as she threw her arms around her and kissed her, "and I hope one day I'll be able to repay you for all your kindness for looking after me and caring the way you do," she added.

When Maggie saw the tears in her eyes, she began to hug her. "Now my dear, there's no need for tears. We're here now to look after each other," she replied.

A few days later the sun came out. It was a lovely afternoon and while they were pegging out the washing, Maggie said, "We don't go out much, Esmee. When we're finished we'll take a stroll along by the stream. The fresh air will do us good."

As they were walking across the field they saw an old gypsy woman making her way towards them. As she came near she cried out, "Buy a bit of white heather for luck, lady, and I'll tell 'e yer fortunes free."

"No yer won't, you old hag. I've met your sort before now, so go away!" Maggie yelled at her.

As soon as they hurried back across the field, Maggie looked back to see her raise her fist and curse.

As soon as they got indoors, Esmee asked why she was upset.

"I didn't want to hear what she had to say."

"But why are you crying?"

"I can't explain now, but each time I see a gypsy I always think what they told me when I was a young girl. When you're older I'll tell you what she said and what really happened."

Esmee asked no more questions and Maggie was grateful she didn't ask, which she knew would be hard to explain.

After Esmee had gone to bed, Maggie let Jimmy out to do his business or whatever, and as she drew the chair up to the fire, she began to reminisce.

She remembered those many years ago when the gypsy caravans and wagons came each year after year to the fields near where she lived with her widowed mother, and the words the gypsy had warned her of. "You will have a long life," she remembered her saying, as though it was yesterday. "You will fall in love with a dark, handsome man, but you will never marry. There are also dark days ahead. Also I can see death and sorrow ahead, but not until yer reach middle age will you find happiness."

She had never given that gypsy another thought until now and now her past came flooding back. Thirty years ago, when she was just nineteen, when her invalid mother died and she had to turn out to earn some kind of living.

She trudged along day after day to find a suitable job, and knowing she only had a few pounds in her purse, which she knew wouldn't last long. Then one afternoon she happened to see a notice in a newsagent's window: Bachelor, aged 28, often away on business, requires young woman to be housekeeper. Apply Number 17 Jermyn Passage.

As soon as she knocked on the door, she heard a man's voice call out, "Come in, the door's open." As she entered, she noticed his eyes seemed to undress her, as he stood with his back to the fire. She wondered then if this was the dark, handsome man the gypsy had warned her about.

After lying about her age, she told him she was twenty four, not nineteen, she also told him she had kept home for her invalid mother until she died.

After asking her name, address and more questions, she was engaged. She did everything to please and satisfy him, and grew to like him. A few weeks later, after coming back from one of his travels, she began to fall in love. She hoped he hadn't noticed, but a few days later, when he took her in his arms and kissed her passionately, they made love.

Soon she began to realise she was pregnant, and when she told him he began to explain why he couldn't marry her, as he had a wife living in Ireland. But if she would still stay and have his child, he would make her an allowance.

It wasn't long before she realised he didn't love her, only lusted for her. There seemed nothing else she could do but to accept his terms. She knew she had nowhere else to go. From that day on she began to despise him.

Meeting that gypsy woman had brought back some of her true sayings, which she had hoped to forget. A few weeks later the usual letter arrived to say that he was on his way home. Maggie never looked forward to his home-comings, neither did Esmee, but everything had to be in readiness.

As soon as Esmee heard he was on his way home, she felt she wanted to show off in her best blue dress, and hurried upstairs to get ready.

"I'm home, Maggie," was his usual greeting. But whenever she heard him, she often shrugged her shoulders, not caring whether he ever came back or not.

As soon as he had washed and shaved and ready to sit down to his meal, Maggie brought in his dinner.

"Well Maggie," he said as she stood beside the table, "how's my little niece and why ain't she here to greet me?"

Before Maggie could answer, Esmee came into the room, twirling around all excited. "'Ow do yer like me new frock Miss Maggie bought me, Uncle Simon?" she cried out.

After staring at her for several seconds, he cried out, "Well, well, well, you've grown up a little beauty since my absence. Now come and give yer uncle a kiss."

As she nervously walked slowly towards him, he saw Maggie was watching him, so he just pecked her cheek.

"Now," he said, as he pushed her from him, "if you look through the window you'll see what I've come home in."

Outside the door stood an Austin Seven black car.

"So I see you didn't come by train then," Maggie replied sharply.

"No, now I can get to and from my business much quicker."

As Maggie began to give him a hard look she replied bitterly, "Yes, you'll need it wherever yer go, in more ways than one!"

After having their meal in silence, he went out to put the car into the shed at the side of the house, and while he was busy dusting it down she sent Esmee upstairs to change her frock.

As soon as he came indoors she cried out, "When's yer next venture?"

"What yer mean, ventures? My travels are for business only."

"Some business! You don't kid me, Simon, I know what your businesses are, but as long as you keep them from here, I'll say no more!"

He didn't answer. He very seldom did when he knew she would have the last word.

But Maggie knew where to hit him most. She watched him pick up his bible and leave the room. "Bloody hypocrite" was her last words to him until he came down to breakfast next morning. It was then when he told her that he would soon be off again.

As soon as he got in the car, she asked, "I suppose you'll be coming home more regular now?"

"More or less, Maggie, more or less," he replied as he slammed the door and drove away.

*

Maggie was now feeling her age. Although she was only fifty-five, she began to suffer with pains in her arms and legs, yet she never complained, but Esmee often noticed she was in pain.

One morning Esmee said, "Why don't you see the doctor, Miss Maggie? I can see you're in pain."

"I don't think he'll do me much good, Esmee. What he gave me last time only eased me for a short time. Just leave me dear to rest up and I'll feel better. Do you think you can manage without me today?" she added.

"You know I can, Miss Maggie. You just go back ter yer bed an' I'll bring yer a hot drink with a drop of Uncle's whisky in, an' if yer like, I'll sit with yer awhile."

"You're a good girl, Esmee. I don't know what I'd have done without you," she replied, as tears came to her eyes.

Next morning Maggie felt much better and when she came downstairs, Esmee cried out, "Oh Miss Maggie, you should have stayed in bed. I was bringing up yer breakfast an' a drop of Uncle's whisky."

Maggie began to smile as she replied, "That's a kind thought, but we'd better not touch any more. Your uncle always knows how's he left it. Now let us sit down and we'll have breakfast, then I'll put my feet up for half an hour."

During the afternoon Maggie said she would like to go for a walk to get some fresh air. As soon as they wrapped up warm, they were ready to go.

They hadn't walked far across the field when Esmee saw Maggie lagging behind. "Are you alright, Miss Maggie?" she cried out.

"Yes dear, but I'll rest on this tree trunk."

"But you look awfully pale. Let us go back home and I'll send for the doctor."

"No Esmee. I know you mean to be kind, but I think if I go back and lie down I'll be better after a few hours."

As soon as they got in the house, Esmee took out the hot oven plate and hurried upstairs to put it in the bed and when she came down, she helped to undress Maggie of her hat and coat and shoes. She followed her upstairs to help her undress and into bed.

Esmee felt she couldn't do enough. She often cried at night when alone in her bedroom, thinking about Maggie, whom she knew was the only person whom she ever loved. She had loved her mother and father, but not in the same way. Maggie was kind and considerate.

After a few days in bed she was looking and feeling more herself and Esmee was glad to see her downstairs again, but she was still worried about Maggie's health.

"Now you're up and about again, Miss Maggie, I want you to take things easy. I'm quite strong and capable to take care of you, and the chores. I love you, Miss Maggie, an' I want you to get well again," she added.

As Maggie threw her arms around her, she replied, "I love you too, dear. Now let's sit down and have a nice cup of tea."

A few weeks later it was Esmee's fifteenth birthday and Maggie had promised to make her a special cake. As she was stirring in the fruit, Esmee saw how pale she was, as she flopped down on to a chair. Esmee ran to fetch her a drink of water, but when she put it to her lips, she was unable to swallow, and when she tried to talk, Esmee couldn't understand what she was trying to say.

Esmee began to weep as she tried to lift Maggie off the chair and help her upstairs, but Maggie couldn't move a limb. There were no neighbours where she could get help. There was only the postman and the coalman, and they had already been the day before. Neither was there a 'phone in the house where she could ring for the doctor.

Tears began to run down her cheeks as she tried once more to listen to Maggie, as she sat mumbling words Esmee couldn't understand. After wrapping a shawl around Maggie to keep her warm, Esmee knew there was nothing else she could do to help her, but said she was going to fetch the doctor.

After sorting over many letters in the chest of drawers, she found the doctor's 'phone number, with tears streaming down her cheeks.

It was a bitterly cold day. She didn't think of putting her hat and coat on, but kissed Maggie and said, "I won't be long." Esmee almost flew out of the door and down the passage. She knew the nearest 'phone box was in the village, about a mile away.

When she eventually arrived at the 'phone box she realised she had forgotten to bring any coppers. As she stood there, she began to weep again, when she saw a young man making his way towards her. Suddenly she realised he was one of the gypsies she had seen in the village stores. As soon as he saw her tears he asked if he could help.

"Yes please," she answered quickly. "I wanta phone the doctor for Miss Maggie. I came without any pennies."

"Come inside then out of the cold and if you'll give me his number, I'll phone him for yer. There you are," he replied, as he handed her the phone, "it's ringing."

Soon she explained to the doctor who she was, what had happened, and after giving her address he said he would come straight away.

As she hung up the phone, she went outside to thank the handsome stranger. "If you'll come back with me, I'll give you back your pennies."

"I don't need the pennies back, dear, but perhaps I could come along and help until the doctor comes."

"That's very kind of you," she replied, thinking she needed somebody to help.

"You better let me put my overcoat around you before you catch cold." As he gently placed the coat around her shoulders, he felt the desire to put his arms around her and kiss her tears away, but he knew it was too soon. He didn't want to frighten her.

They hurried along. When she thought it was time to hand him his coat and thank him for his kindness, he asked, "How far do you live?"

"It's around the next bend. Jermyn Passage."

"Oh yes," he replied, "I know where it is, I remember that old place well. Is that where you live? In that old drapery shop?"

"It's not a drapery shop any more. My uncle had it turned into living quarters when he bought it."

"But don't you find it very lonely, with all the other shops boarded up and condemned?"

"I wouldn't know about 'em being condemned," she replied. "Now I have to hurry," she added.

As soon as they reached the bottom of Hill Lane towards the "Passage", they slowed down as he asked her name.

"It's Esmerelda, but I'm always called Esmee."

"Mine's er ... Jake." She didn't notice the hesitation, but he had no intention of telling her his real name was Ramon Lee.

"Thank you for your help, Jake. I think I can manage now," she replied. But the gypsy was reluctant to leave. He felt he wanted to see and know more about this pretty fair-haired girl with large blue eyes. Suddenly he asked, "Would you like me to come and help until the doctor comes?"

She accepted his offer. She was beginning to like this handsome, dark skinned stranger with black, wavy hair and large brown eyes.

He followed her into the kitchen, where they both saw the doctor attending to Maggie.

"Is there anything I can do, doctor?" he called out.

"Yes, young man, you can help me lift her on to the couch where I can examine her, and you, young lady, get me some blankets and build up that fire! It's like a bloody ice-house in here! Then when I've finished, I want you to give her a strong cup of tea."

"Shall I put a drop of Uncle's whisky in?" she asked.

"No! No! Just tea, no milk and plenty of sugar!" As he was still staring at her he asked, "How long has she been drinking whisky?"

"I've never seen her drink any, only once, doctor, I gave her a drop when she was feeling cold. Anyway it was only a drop because Uncle Simon knows. He marks the label."

"Very well! Very well!" he cried out impatiently. "Just do as I ask and hurry. I have other calls to make."

As soon as the examination had finished, Esmee went over to speak to Maggie, but the doctor said she couldn't talk, but would be able to listen. She was to keep her warm until the ambulance arrived.

Esmee cried out, "Why are you taking her away?"

"Your Miss Maggie has had a stroke. We'll do what we can once we get her in the infirmary. Now don't let her see you weeping. I quite understand how you feel," he replied more kindly.

As soon as the gypsy went into the kitchen to put the kettle on the fire, the doctor whispered in her ear, "And who is this young man?"

"He came to help me to phone you."

"And when do you expect your uncle?"

"Day after tomorrow."

"Then as soon as he arrives, tell him to get in touch with me. Here's my card."

Staring hard at the gypsy as he came into the room, he asked, "Do you live here?"

"No, I only came to help."

"Very well. I wish you both good day and don't forget to give your uncle my message as soon as he arrives home."

"I will doctor, and thank you for coming so quickly."

"You just stay with her and give her plenty of tea until the ambulance arrives. Now I must hurry, and take care of yourself, young lady," he replied as he stared again at the gypsy. He knew there was something he didn't like about him, yet it was none of his business. He was only there to attend to Maggie. As he picked up his top hat and bag he stared again at the gypsy. "Can I give you a lift?" he asked.

"Thank you, doctor, but I'll stay with them 'til the ambulance comes."

"Very well," he replied.

Esmee saw him to his car and before he drove away he told her again to take good care of herself and should she need him at any time, she could always call or ring.

As soon as he drove away and went back indoors, she saw the gypsy trying to pour the tea through Maggie's half open lips, but the more he tried, the more she glared at him, making peculiar noises. This seemed to upset Esmee more. She too tried her best to give her drinks, but Maggie still couldn't take it, only to stare and mumble words that Esmee couldn't understand. Suddenly she began to weep again.

"Don't cry, Esmee dear," he said, but as soon as he put his arms around her, Maggie stared and gave a terrible shriek.

"She's trying to tell me something. Oh, if only I could understand what she's trying to say."

"She'll tell you when she gets better, but seeing you weep will only make her worse."

"But I don't want her to die," she sobbed.

"She's not going to die! Now wipe your face, she'll soon be well again, you'll see. Now I must be going soon and perhaps you'll let me call again."

She was beginning to like this handsome young gypsy, especially when he put his hand beneath her chin and pecked her cheek.

As he wished her goodnight, he said he would like to stay a bit longer but his ma would be wondering where he had got to. "Now you'll be alright 'til the ambulance comes?"

"Yes, and thank you for helping."

As soon as he left, Maggie tried to focus her eyes again on Esmee as she tried to mumble and make strange noises.

Esmee tried hard to understand her, thinking she was trying to tell her she wanted another drink, but she still spat it out from the side of her twisted lips, and when Esmee tried hard to understand the noises she was trying to make, tears began to run down Maggie's cheeks when she gave up and closed her eyes and gave up trying.

Little did she know that Maggie was trying to warn her about the gypsy. If only she could have understood, but Esmerelda Rabone was ignorant of the ways of man. The gypsy was the only man she had ever spoken to since her uncle had brought her to his home when her parents had died three years ago, and loving Miss Maggie, who was her only friend, she had felt content with her lot. Yet now, she had mixed feelings for this handsome gypsy, with his big brown eyes and dark wavy hair. She hoped he would soon call again.

The ambulance came about twenty minutes after Doctor O'Brien had left. Esmee kissed Maggie and said she would come to visit her with her uncle and not to worry, she would take care of everything.

As she saw the ambulance leave, she went back inside the house. Little did she know that the gypsy had not gone back to his caravan, but had stood near one of the empty premises and watched her go indoors.

He had second thoughts whether to go back to the house or leave his intentions for later, but he thought it would be better to bide his time. He didn't want to rush things yet. With these thoughts he made his journey back across the fields.

As Esmee let the cat out to do his business or whatever, she remembered the birthday cake that Maggie had been mixing that morning when she collapsed. Tears again ran down her cheeks as she picked up the mixing bowl and carried it outside the door and left it on the narrow pavement for some mongrel dog or sparrows. She knew she couldn't face seeing it.

After calling Jimmy indoors, she locked and bolted each door and went to bed, but she knew she couldn't sleep and prayed that her Miss Maggie would soon get well again.

She felt so lonely with only Jimmy to talk to, but Jimmy was only a tom cat and couldn't understand how she was feeling. Yet she wasn't afraid of being in the house alone. She had only to wait now and do what was needed until her uncle came home.

As she cuddled Jimmy, who lay beside her purring, she began to think of her mother and father who had died when she was twelve, also the loss of her two little sisters. She began to wonder why God always took away the people she loved, who had done no harm to anyone. Sadness overcame her once more. It was not until the early hours when she cried herself to sleep.

Next morning, Esmee was up early and after going around the side of the bed to unlock the bathroom door, she used the toilet and had a quick wash. She was just finishing dressing, when she heard the postman knock. She hurried downstairs to be greeted at the door with, "Letter fer your Miss Maggie," as she slipped the letter into her pocket. She knew it was from her uncle who always addressed the envelope "Miss Maggie".

She thought it was best to open it to see if there was an address inside where she could write and tell him what had happened, but when she began to read it, it was just a small note to say he would be home later that same day.

Esmee hustled and bustled, eager to get everything ready for his arrival. When an hour later she heard his car pull up outside the house, quickly she put the kettle on the fire to make him a welcome cup of tea, when she heard his usual call, "I'm home, Maggie."

"Maggie's not 'ere now, Uncle Simon," she blurted out.

"What yer mean she ain't here?" he exclaimed as he stared at her.

"She was taken to the infirmary an' the doctor said she had had a stroke and you have to go there straight away."

As he hurried towards the door, she asked if he would like a cup of tea before he went.

"No dear, I'll hurry and see how she is," he replied.

"Can I come with you Uncle?"

"No love, I think you'd better wait until I have news from the doctor and I'll ask for a pass when you can see her while I'm away."

"But you've only just come," she replied.

"I know, but I have business to attend to, when I shall be leaving again in the morning," he exclaimed. "Anyway," he said, "get me a glass."

"What yer want a glass for?"

"I need a drop of whisky! And don't ask stupid questions!" he replied angrily.

As he took the bottle he'd brought with him, she noticed he drank a glassful and left without another word.

While he was away she began to busy herself around the house, hoping he wouldn't be long before he brought her good news, but it seemed to Esmee he was away hours.

But at last she heard him put the car inside the shed. As soon as he stepped indoors, she knew by the look on his face it was bad news. When she asked how Maggie was, she saw tears in his eyes.

"Maggie died early this morning, and the doctor said it was for the best," he managed to say.

"For the best! For the best!" she screamed out at him, "But why?"

"Sit down, Esmee, and calm down! There's a lot to be done now," he snapped at her.

Soon he reached down from the cupboard his bottle of whisky and as he helped himself to another glass she yelled out again, "You Uncle Simon, can read yer bible until doomsday, but I don't or carn't believe there is a God above any more!"

"You may believe what you wish, Esmee," he replied more calmly. "If she had lived, the doctor said she wouldn't have been any use to anyone."

"How can yer say that! I carn't believe it, and what's ter become of me in this lonely house all alone while you're away?"

"After the funeral I'll think of something. Now leave me, I have some important letters to write. And leave that whisky there!" he added as she went to take the whisky bottle away.

Esmee left him with his empty glass beside the whisky bottle and went upstairs to be alone with her grief. As she sat down on the edge of the bed, she began to think about her mother and father, also the two little sisters who had died only three years ago, and now her kind and loving Miss Maggie. Now she felt left only with an uncle she couldn't like or understand his ways. She knew she never would.

Suddenly she cried out aloud as she gazed at the sky through the window, "If you are up in the heavens, tell me God, why you let people suffer and die when they are always good and kind? Please answer me, or give me a sign if there is a God up there."

*

Four days later Maggie was buried in the local cemetery. There were no other mourners: just Simon and Esmee and the six bearers.

As Maggie was lowered into her place of rest, Esmee began to weep again. As she wiped her eyes she happened to glance up and saw the gypsy standing watching some distance away, but when she looked again he was gone. She wondered if she should tell her uncle about the kindness that young man had shown her, yet she knew in his hour of grief, it wasn't the time.

She despised him when he drank too much. The bottle was now three parts empty, but she knew if she spoke to him about his drinking, he would flare up at her. So she just sat down and watched him as he emptied his glass.

As he looked across the table towards her he kept thinking, I wonder if I can tempt her now to have a drop? "Would you like a drop. Esmee, it'll warm you up?" he managed to say.

"No! No!" she cried out. "I'd rather have a cup of tea and something to eat. Can I get you something?" she added.

"No! Just leave me," he exclaimed.

Esmee was always wary of him when he was in one of these kinds of moods, but she always kept her distance, she didn't want him ever to kiss her again. She often remembered the night when he tried to put his tongue in her mouth and slobbered all over her. But she knew what she was going to do if he tried anything like that again. She didn't feel afraid of him any more.

While she was busy making a cup of tea and something to eat, she heard him call out, "Esmee, will you come in here, I want to talk to yer."

As she walked into the parlour, she noticed his eyes were red with weeping, and as she stood there he cried out, "Sit down, I ain't goin' ter bite yer."

As soon as she sat opposite he asked, "Did Maggie ever talk about me and how we came to meet?"

"No, I don't think so, Uncle Simon. She did say she was going to tell me lots of things, but she never got around to it."

"Well now, I feel I want you to know. Although Maggie and I quarrelled often, I still loved her. You must remember that."

"I know, Uncle. I often heard you quarrelling, but I could never understand what about."

"Years ago Maggie answered my advert for a housekeeper. Later we fell in love and she became pregnant."

"Why are you telling me this?" she asked.

"Because I want you to know I really did love her, but I couldn't marry her, because I was already married and my wife wouldn't divorce me. And when my little daughter was four, I took her to see the circus. On the way home I bought her an ice cream and told her to sit on a bench outside "The Brown Lion" while I went in for a drink, but one drink led to another and another and when I went outside to take her home, I couldn't find her anywhere. I was afraid to go back and tell Maggie, so I called at the police station. Although I helped to search for my child, it wasn't until the next day she was found drowned in the canal. Maggie never forgave me and during all these years since we rowed and snapped at each other. She despised me."

As Esmee saw his eyes fill with tears, she felt sorry for him. She would have put her arms around him to try to comfort him, but she wondered if he would take advantage of her. She hadn't forgotten the last time when he kissed her and tried to put his tongue in her mouth. She shuddered to think he might do it again, for she still didn't trust him.

After listening to him she cried out, "Well Uncle Simon, what's to become of me? Am I supposed to stay in this house while you're away on your travels?"

"Well I could write to my wife and ask her to come."

"If she does I shall leave and go into service," Esmee replied.

"There's no need for you to leave, Esmee. I promised your parents to look after you until you're twenty-one. Now there's no need for you to leave. Anyway I'm tired now and I'm off to me bed and in the morning I shall be off travelling again."

"How long for this time?" she asked.

"About three months. In the meantime I will leave you with the same monthly housekeeping the same as I gave Maggie. Will you promise you'll stay until I return?"

After some hesitation, she promised.

As he came forward to kiss her goodnight, he saw her put her cheek forward. He just smiled: his thoughts were elsewhere. He knew now he would have to treat her with respect until such time he could have his way with her and she could become his second Maggie.

After he'd gone to bed, she put the cat out and sat beside the fire. As her thoughts turned to the gypsy, she didn't seem to care about her uncle now. She hoped he would come to visit her or she would visit him while her uncle was away on his travels.

After a while she opened the front door to call in the cat, but the more she kept calling "Jimmy" the more she became angry. "Alright, stay out! See if I care!" she yelled out as she locked the door.

As she went into the parlour, she noticed that her uncle had emptied the whole bottle. "He must be drunk by now and snoring his head off," she said to herself.

It was eleven thirty when she undressed and got into bed. As she lay awake she kept thinking of her handsome gypsy and hoping that he was thinking of her too. Eventually she fell asleep.

It was almost dawn when she awoke to the sound of scratching on the bathroom door, followed by a few miaows. She sprang out of bed and as she took the key to unlock the door, she cried out, "That's the third time this week! Next time I'll let yer stay there!"

As she opened the door, suddenly she saw her uncle. As he threw the cat inside the room, she tried to close the door, but he had already put his foot there. "Wot yer want?" she managed to yell at him.

"Open the door, I want to come in to tell you something important."

"You're drunk an' yer not comin' in my bedroom! Not now, nor never!" she yelled at him.

"We'll see about that!" he replied.

As he pushed his whole body against the door she almost fell backwards. Quickly he made a grab for her and as he wedged her against the wall and the bed, he pressed his heavy body against her.

She stood there screaming for all she was worth, knowing what his intentions were. She began to struggle, but he held her fast. She could almost taste the whisky as he slobbered all over her. Soon he began to force her lips open and when he tried to put his tongue in her mouth, she opened her mouth wide. As soon as she felt his tongue, she bit it as hard as she could.

Suddenly he yelled out, "You bloody vixen!" and slapped her face hard as he let her go. As she jumped across the bed, she spat the blood in his face. Then quickly picking up the enamel chamber pot, she struck him twice: once in his face and again on his head. When she saw him fall across the bed, she ran downstairs, grabbed her coat and shoes and ran out of the house. There was only one place where she could look for help: across the fields to the caravans.

It was almost daylight when she stopped to get her breath, when suddenly she almost screamed out as she heard a voice behind her asking where she was going. As she turned around she was surprised to see it was the gypsy.

"Wot's 'appened to you?" he asked when he saw her shivering. When she tried to explain, he said, "You better come inside the wagon while I make you a hot brew. Then you can tell me what's happened."

As she did, and handed him the cup, she asked if his ma was in the caravan.

"No," he replied, "she's three caravans away delivering one of the gypsy's babbies. Now come, tell me why you're here."

As soon as he heard all the details, he asked at once if her uncle had raped her.

"Oh no! No!" she cried out. "But I believe that was his intention until I bit his tongue."

Suddenly he began to smile. "Well, good for you. Where is he now?"

"I don't know, unless he's still sprawled out on me bed."

"Well we better hurry back and find out." He knew he had to get her out of the wagon before his ma came back and found her sitting there weeping.

"Can I stay a bit longer, Jake, and meet your ma?" she almost pleaded.

"No, Esmee, we'd better go back and help him," he replied quickly.

Reluctantly she let him take her hand and hurried her across the fields. As soon as they arrived at the door, she looked surprised to see it was still open. Then looking into the large shed along the side of the house she cried out, "Jake, his car ain't here! He must have left!"

As soon as they walked into the living room, she saw a note lying on the table which said that he was sorry for what he had tried to do, and hoped she would forgive him when he returned in a few weeks time.

"What's it say?" he asked when he saw she was ready to put it in the fire.

"You'd better read it," she replied as she handed him the note.

As they went into the parlour, she quickly slung off her coat, forgetting she still only had on her see-through nightie, until she saw him gazing at her almost naked body. Suddenly she began to blush and feel ashamed. Snatching up her coat, she ran upstairs. Whatever will he think of me, she thought.

But he was thinking how well developed she was for one so young. Dare he take a chance and go up to her? But he thought it was better for him to wait until another time when he would get to know her more. As soon as she came downstairs fully dressed, she couldn't face him, she felt so embarrassed, but when he put his hands on her shoulders and turned her to look at him, she began to blush again.

"Look at me, Esmee," he said as he put his hand beneath her chin.

"There's no need to be ashamed. I've seen more naked bodies than you'll ever see. Sometimes I have to help my ma deliver babbies."

"Are you a doctor then?" she asked, as soon as she overcame her embarrassment.

"No dear, but I do help when one of the clan have a bad time. Now don't feel ashamed, and listen to what I'm going to say. I love you, I have loved you since the day I first saw you, when you stood outside that phone box weeping."

Esmee believed all he said and when she let him take her in his arms and kiss her, she returned his kisses. He had the urge to make love to her there and then, but he controlled his feelings again. He knew he could bide his time until she was willing to give herself. His excuses again were that he must hurry away to his ma, whom he said was often ill.

As she stood on the doorstep to wish him goodnight, she clung to him saying, "I love you too, Jake."

After kissing her once again, he hurried away calling out he would call the following night.

That same night as she lay in her bed, she began to have mixed feelings for this handsome gypsy and wondered if these feeling she had for him were really love.

She often remembered her mother's words when she asked her why she had so many babies. Her mother's simple answer had been, "Yer fell in love, yer wed, then you 'ad babbies an' that's all a girl wants."

Now she felt she was in love, but Esmerelda Rabone was ignorant about sex and the facts of life. She had yet to learn that life and love were not so simple.

*

The following day Esmee went shopping in the village, when she saw him coming out of the grocery shop just as she was going in. Her face lit up. "Hello Jake," she cried out, "I didn't know you came here to do yer shopping."

"Yes," he replied, "me ma carn't walk this far. If you'd like me to wait for yer, we'll walk together."

"I'd like that," she replied, smiling up into his face.

As soon as her purchases were bought, she caught up with him. She didn't hear what the old man behind the counter said as he turned to his wife. "See that, Sarah? 'er an' that gypsy."

"Yes Paddy, there's summat goin' on theea an' more than meets yer eye. Foolish young wench! Did yer see 'ow she smiled an' looked at 'im like they was lovers?"

"P'raps they are secret lovers, if yer ask me."

"But no good'll cum of it, 'im bein' a gypsy an' all," the old woman replied as she began to wipe her nose on her apron.

"O well, it's none of our business, Sarah, wot people around 'ere do with their lives, as long as they spend their money with us. Anyway, they'll be movin' soon as the pea pickin's finished."

On the way across the fields he carried her basket, as he told her he was taking a short cut. Little did she know he didn't want the other gypsies to see him.

"Shall we sit on the grass for a while?" he asked.

When she nodded in reply, he took off his coat and lay it down for her to sit on. As soon as they sat close together, he took her in his arms and kissed her passionately. She returned his kisses and as he tried to fondle her breasts, she snatched his hands away.

"Don't do that, Jake. Please."

"But why? I love you dear, and one day soon I'm going to marry you. You do want to marry me, don't yer, Esmee dear?"

"Yes Jake, but you must first meet and talk to my uncle."

"I will my dear; as soon as he arrives home we'll see him together. Now I hope you'll forgive me," he added. "I love you too much to take advantage and I'm sorry for what I did."

But he wasn't sorry. He had hoped she would let him fondle her all over, then have his way with her there and then.

By now it was getting dark and he was feeling disappointed, and as she picked up her basket ready to go, he told her he would see her to the bottom of the hill and then he must hurry home.

As soon as he said goodbye, she felt disappointed that he hadn't taken her in his arms but just pecked her cheek as he said he would call and see her in two day's time.

*

As he slowly walked towards his wagon, he kept thinking about the tribe and the gypsy Rhoda and his ma, and what he would say if Esmee should happen to meet her. As he got near the wagon to bed down for the night, he was surprised to see a light on in his mother's caravan. He still thought she would be at young Nancy Floyd's, who was expecting her first baby at any time. Suddenly he heard his mother call out, "Where 'ave yer bin, I've bin waitin' up fer yer?"

"I've been trying to trap a couple of rabbits but the farmer was about, so I took a long walk instead," he lied.

"I don't want any of yer lies, 'cause I was down in the village meself an' I was told yer was making eyes to a fair haired wench, an' yer was seen arm in arm carryin' 'er basket, so I don't want any more of yer bloody lies, Rammon."

"Yes, I did carry her basket. She was going my way, so what harm was there in that?" he exclaimed.

"'Ow long 'ave yer known 'er?"

"I've only met her once. Anyway we'll be moving camp soon," he added.

"Very well, but let me remind yer, you've still gotta marry Rhoda. I don't want any more scandal. I 'ad enough with that rogue of a father of yours."

"But Ma, I don't want to marry one of the gypsy clan. You know I hate this kind of life."

"It's too late now. Yer should 'ave thought about that before yer put 'er in the family way"

Suddenly he stared hard. "She carn't be!" he cried out. "She carn't be! I've only been with her twice."

"Twice is one too many times, so I'm warning yer, if yer don't marry Rhoda an' do yer duty by 'er I'll disown yer, an' yer well know wot that'll mean! Now get ter yer bed an' think over wot I've said, an' keep off that cider yer got 'idden away!" she added.

He didn't want to marry a gypsy girl, but he knew if he didn't before his mother died, he would lose all she owned. He always knew his mother had money hidden away somewhere. She also owned two caravans, two wagons and several ponies she loaned out.

As Rose walked up the steps and entered her caravan, she felt sad. Tears filled her eyes as she picked up her clay pipe, but decided she would smoke it later. After laying it down on the table, she sat down in front of the iron pipe stove and wept as she began to think about those past sad years so very long ago when she had sent her one and only son away to be educated. She knew it had been a waste of time and money for she was now realising he was so much like his father in looks and ways she did not like. Through the years she had become a lonely, bitter woman.

Gypsy Rose Lee, as she was often known, was not a true gypsy. She remembered the tribe had adopted her when she was ten years old. Therefore she knew no other life. She was now forty-five years old and still an attractive woman. She had many admirers and chances of marriage, but she had often said, "Once bit, twice shy."

Rose also remembered her mother, who had run away when she was four years old and left her with her mother's sister, her Aunt Polly. Polly often hoped that one day her sister Nelda would return and take the child off her hands, but nothing was ever heard from her. Polly never loved the child. Often she was left alone for hours.

When Rosie was six years old, her Aunt Polly fell in love and was married to a travelling salesman. When she started to have children of her own, Rosie became a little drudge, unwanted, neglected and often hungry. She was not even allowed to play or even touch her two little cousins, and always being reminded she was a bastard and often beaten, and as she grew older she began to rebel.

Often she was left alone when her aunt took the two girls away for weekends. Therefore Rosie found what happiness she could sitting in the woods about half a mile away. She loved these quiet jaunts, listening to the bird calls and watching the squirrels chasing each other up the trees. Sometimes she would paddle her bare feet in the running stream nearby.

One afternoon she saw some watercress growing on the edge of the stream. After picking some to eat, she thought she might please her aunt by taking some back to the cottage, but when her aunt saw what she had brought, she snatched it from her and threw it through the kitchen window. Rosie vowed she would never try to please her aunt again.

One warm, sunny afternoon as she was cooling her feet in the stream and eating the watercress, she happened to look across the other side of the bank, where she saw a chubby little red-faced girl about her own age. She noticed too she wore no shoes. She also wore a red, ragged frock and in her hand she held a large crust of bread and jam.

As Rosie feasted her eyes on the bread and jam, the girl called out, "Can I 'ave some of yer watercress fer me ma?"

"Yes," replied Rosie, "but you'll 'ave ter paddle over ter get it." While she was picking the cress, Rosie was feasting her eyes on the crust that she'd laid on the bank. As soon as the girl saw her staring at it she cried out, "Yer can 'ave it fer the cress."

"It ain't my cress, it grows wild," Rosie replied.

"Thank yer anyway. Can I cum agin?" she called out as she paddled across to the other side.

"Yes," Rosie replied, as she quickly snatched up the crust and began to eat it.

How happy she felt that afternoon for seeing her and being able to talk with someone her own age, and she hoped she would come again to ask her name and where she lived.

Rosie didn't know then that she was one of the gypsies' children who lived in caravans, until she went again to the stream.

As she was cooling her feet in the water, she saw a large buxom woman coming along the path carrying a bundle. Rose began to get nervous. She was ready to fly out of the water when suddenly the woman cried out, "Don't yer be afraid of me, me dearie. I've only cum ter do me bitta washin' in the stream. Do yer be the little girl wot give Martha watercress?"

"Yes," Rosie replied nervously.

"She couldna' cum with me terday she's got a cold, but if yer like ter cum with me when I've finished me washin', I know she'll be 'appy ter see yer."

"Yes, thank yer Mrs ....."

"Me name's Ruth, Ruth Kelly. I'm Martha's ma. An' wot's your name an' where do yer cum from?" she added.

"Me name's Rosie Lee. I live with me Aunt Polly in Briars Lane."

"That's a lung way from 'ere. Do yer aunt know yer cum 'ere?"

"No," she replied. As she chewed on some more watercress, Ruth could see she was hungry. "No, me aunt never bothers about me, nor where I go."

"Are yer 'ungry?" Ruth asked, as she saw her put more watercress in her mouth.

"Yes, yes," Rosie replied. "Me aunt only leaves left-overs fer me wen she goes away."

"Well yer betta cum back with me an' 'ave some stew with me an' Martha."

As soon as the gypsy finished washing the clothes, they were ready to leave. Rosie was now beginning to like this buxom woman with the smiling eyes and kindly face.

Soon as the wet bundle was slung over her shoulder, Ruth took hold of Rosie's hand and hurried across the narrow bridge on the other side of the stream, where Rosie saw several caravans parked on some waste ground where several children of all ages were playing hide and seek. Rosie had never seen gypsy children before and when they stopped to stare at her, she became nervous again.

Suddenly Ruth cried out, "Wot yer starin' at? Scat!"

As they ran away, Ruth led Rosie inside the caravan, where she now felt safe. She was amazed at all the bright brassware and different brightly coloured hangings that hung from the walls, for Rosie had never seen a caravan or inside one before.

As Ruth drew one of the curtains aside she cried out, "I wundda where she's got to, I left 'er in bed? Martha! Martha!" she called out from the top of the steps. "Where are yer?"

As Martha came running, her mother cried out, "Where 'ave yer bin?"

"I felt betta Ma. I went ter see me granny."

"Well you better see who I've brought 'ome with me."

Both girls were pleased to see each other and after asking each other their names, Ruth said it was time to set the table and put out the dishes while she went to fetch the pot from her mother's caravan.

As soon as they both laid the table, Martha began to show Rosie her picture books about "The Water Babies" and "The Ugly Duckling".

Soon her mother came, carrying a large iron pot of rabbit stew and dumplings. "Cum on, get this down yer before it gets cold."

Rosie had never smelt or tasted anything so delicious, and when she began to lick her plate dry, Ruth dished her out a second helping.

After the plates were washed and put away, Ruth settled down and when she lit her clay pipe she began to ask Rosie about her aunt and what she was like.

Rosie told her how her mother had run away when she was four years old and left her with Aunt Polly, and how she and her cousins often went away for long weekends, and how she was often beaten.

When Rosie showed her bruises on her arms and legs, Ruth couldn't believe what she was seeing. "I'll 'ave ter cum an' 'ave a werd with this aunt!" she cried out. "Yer poor child an' 'alf starved an' all." She added. "No! No! Please don't go! If she knows I've bin tellin' anybody she'll whip me some more. Now I'll 'ave ter 'urry back before I'm missed."

"Very well dearie, but yer can cum any time."

As Martha and her mother stood on the steps to wave her goodbye, Ruth had every intention to make it her business to pay a visit to this aunt.

As Rosie arrived at the cottage and saw no lighted lamp in the window, she knew her aunt and cousins had not arrived home.

She didn't feel hungry now for the stale scraps that were often left. She went straight upstairs, undressed and crawled into her makeshift bed, soon to fall asleep.

She was up early the next morning, starting her usual chores; riddling the ashes to save the embers. After setting the paper and sticks ready to light the fire, she went out into the yard to fill the kettle from the pump, with a lighter heart, knowing she could always go to the caravan while her aunt was away.

The following weekend her aunt and cousins were off again, but it was more than she dare to ask where they went. She always thought they went to visit their father. Rosie seldom saw him when he came to the cottage, but when he did come he often ignored her.

One day Rosie overheard snatches as they quarrelled.

"I don't know why you keep yer sister's bastard here for!"

"But where can she go?" she heard her aunt reply.

"Put her into service where she can earn her keep, or the bloody workhouse!"

Yes, Rosie thought, anywhere will be better than here.

*

One afternoon while Rosie and Martha were playing happily with the other gypsy children, Ruth came to say she wouldn't be long. As soon as she slung her bright plaided shawl around her shoulders, she picked up her basket of pegs, heather and curing herbs and set off at once to the lonely cottage.

As soon as she arrived she knocked on the door, and when she saw the curtain move, she heard a voice cry out, "Clear orf! We don't want any bloody gypsies here!"

"I ain't cum to sell yer nothin'. I just want a werd with yer an' its important, so yer betta open yer door an' listen!"

After keeping her for a while, Polly opened the door and as she began to glare she yelled out, "What yer want to talk to me about? And you better make it quick, I'm too busy to listen to the likes of you people with casting spells and curses!"

"Well yer betta listen or summat is goin' ter 'appen to yer one of these days!"

"I don't know what you're blabbering about. Who's sent you here?"

"Nobody's sent me, an' I don't want any lies. I've cum about yer niece Rose. I've cum ter ......"

"What about her? Anyway what business is it of yours?"

"I'm makin' it my business, so now you'll listen to wot I 'ave ter say. The other day I 'appened ter see Rosie by the stream. She looked lonely, frightened and 'ungry, so I took 'er to me caravan an' give 'er a feed."

"Well where is she now?"

"She's 'appily playing with my daughter and the other children."

"Well you'd better send her back or else ....."

"Or else wot? I've seen bruises on that poor child wot would put you an' yer 'usband in prison!"

"Don't you dare threaten me!" she yelled out as she tried to close the door.

But the gypsy wedged the basket to stop her closing it as she called out, "I can see wot sort of woman yer are! But before I go you'll 'ear this! When Rosie knows I've bin 'ere, she'll be afraid ter cum back, so I'm askin' yer ter let 'er stay with me an' me daughter for a while until somethink betta is sorted out."

"Yer can keep the bloody bastard for good for all we care. Me and my husband were thinking about sending her to service or the workhouse anyway."

"Very well, then yer agree ter let 'er stay with me then?"

"You heard what I said, an' if yer want it in writing yer can have it! Now clear off!" she exclaimed as she slammed the door shut.

When she got back to the caravan and explained to Rosie where she had been and what she had said, Rosie began to weep. "I can't ever go back there now, 'cause I know she'll beat me more."

"No she won't, she's told me she don't want yer. Now yer can stop with me an' Martha as long as yer like."

Rosie Lee now had love and affection which she had never known. Other gypsies were kind too, soon she became to mix happily in the ways of the tribe. Soon she became one among them, travelling from town to town. Often she had feelings that her aunt would find her and bring her back, but as the weeks went by Rosie soon forgot her fears, when she heard that her aunt's cottage was empty and up for sale.

Rose often thought about those many years ago when Ruth had taught her the tricks of the trade, going from market to market buying bright coloured ribbons, bits of lace and assorted coloured beads. Also gathering wild heather and all kinds of roots and wild herbs for making soups and medicine which were believed to cure all kinds of ills. She also learned how to tell fortunes and read from the cards. She knew no other life and was happy to belong.

But it was a sad time when Ruth's daughter ran away with an elderly Gorgio man when she was fifteen. Although her mother grieved for her, she never forgave her. Rosie did her best to comfort her, but when Ruth became ill no gypsy concoction ever cured her. Rosie did her best to nurse her, she seldom left her side. Before Ruth died, she left a Will leaving the caravan and all she possessed to Rose.

But Rose was feeling lonely without the loving care Ruth had given her over the years. She saw several young gypsy girls marry their own clan and settle down, and when she was sixteen she often felt the need of a man's love and comfort. Although many of the young gypsy men tried to court her, she ignored them.

Often she regretted the day those many long years ago when she happened to meet a dark, handsome vagabond who had come to stay at the camp. Almost at once she fell in love. He told her his name was Jake Patrick and often he would make arrangements to meet her secretly in a nearby dark lane at night. She was often afraid some of the tribe would see them, so later she invited him to her caravan, where he often whispered sweet nothings in her ear. Foolishly she could never say no to his endearing charms. That same night they made love.

Several weeks later, when she told him she was carrying his child, he promised to make the marriage arrangements and would come again two days later. Rose never saw him again.

Although she still travelled with the tribe, many of the gypsies snubbed her. Therefore she began to be a bitter, lonely young woman, trusting no one. She kept herself to herself and when she gave birth to her son, she named him Rammon. Yet at times she wished he had never been born. If only he would settle down and marry the gypsy Rhoda, she knew she would feel contented.

She lit her pipe and after filling her lungs with the tobacco smoke, she placed the pipe back on the shelf and lay down on her narrow bed. Tomorrow she would have a good talk to her son and get something settled for her own peace of mind.

With these thoughts, Rose fell asleep, but next morning it was time for her to call him from the wagon, but he had already left. Now she had to wait until he returned.

*

As Rammon was strolling along the narrow lane deep in thought, he was surprised to see the farmer coming towards him. Rammon often did odd jobs for the farmer, but he was surprised to see him so early in the morning, for it was only just breaking dawn.

"Good morning, Rammon," the farmer greeted him. Farmer Jones had not called him "gypsy", not since the night they sat drinking together in the local inn, when Rammon had told him about his birth.

"Good morning, sir," Rammon replied as he raised his cap.

"I was on my way to see you and your ma."

Rammon began to look surprised. "What about, sir?"

"Well I know you all will be leaving to go to another town soon and I was wondering if your mother and you would stay on a bit longer to help me fix some fencing. I could get outside help from the village, but they want to send three chaps along. It means they would want to charge the earth, but I'm sure you and me could manage in less than the time they would take."

"I understand, sir. When do yer want me to start?"

"In a couple of days. That's if your mother agrees to stay."

"Leave her to me, sir. I'll soon persuade her," he replied as he winked.

"Perhaps you would like to come back with me and see what I want done," replied the farmer.

After he gave him instructions, he took him inside the farmhouse, where they had a drink of cider and his wife gave him some eggs and a small slab of butter to take to his ma.

On the way back he thought as he looked at the gifts, "This'll please her."

But as soon as she saw him return she cried out, "I wanta talk ter you, so yer betta cum inside."

"Yer better listen to me first," he exclaimed.

"Very well, go on," she replied impatiently as she sat down.

"I've just met Farmer Jones and his lovely wife and she's sent you these eggs and butter."

"Why should she send me eggs and butter? I don't believe yer."

"It's the truth, Ma, and if yer don't believe me, you'd better come back with me and ask her yourself."

"Wot did yer do fer 'er ter give 'em to yer?"

"I didn't give her nothing. It's what I'm going to do for the farmer. Now sit down and listen to the truth."

"Very well, let's 'ear it then," she replied impatiently as she flopped down in her chair.

"The farmer knows we are all moving to another town soon and he's asked me if you and me, Ma, would stay a bit longer as they want me to do a few jobs. He'll pay well, Ma, but if you don't want to stay, I will. Now think it over, I've got to let him have his answer tonight."

After she had calmed down she cried out, "But 'ow lung for?"

"He said two or three weeks, that's if the weather holds out."

"Alright then. Now yer betta go back an' tell 'im, an' don't ferget ter thank the good lady fer the eggs and butta."

"Oh by the way, Ma, she said yer not to mention the gifts to any of the gypsies. She said she don't want them or their brood coming begging."

"Stuck up then, is 'er?"

"No, Ma, but yer never know what she thinks about them gypsies. I'm off now, I won't be late," he added as he swung the two halves of the caravan door open and left.

As he walked down the narrow lane towards the farmhouse, he thought about his mother, hoping she would never find out about his visits to Jermyn Passage.

*

That same afternoon, as Esmee was scrubbing the front step, she heard the postman call out, "A package for you, Miss Esmee."

"A packet fer me? Who can it be from?" she replied.

"I don't know who it's from, but it's got your name on an' it ses on the stamp, "Aberdeen", so it must be from Scotland."

"Thank you," she replied as she wiped her hands on her apron and took the packet from him and went indoors.

As soon as she opened it, she saw a note inside. No address. "Dear Esmee," she read, "I have to stay another three months, but don't worry. I have made arrangements with the post office for you to draw your allowance each week. I hope you'll like this gift I have bought you for your birthday. I also pray that you have forgiven me. Take care of yourself till I come home. Love and best wishes, Uncle Simon."

Esmee couldn't believe her eyes when she eagerly looked inside the narrow red velvet box and saw what lay beneath tissue paper; a gold pendant and chain. She felt so excited, for she had never had anything like this, not even a row of glass beads.

As soon as she fastened it around her neck, she began to admire herself in the mirror, and when she took it off and saw what was engraved on the back, "To Esmee from Uncle Simon", she thought he must have been thinking about her to buy her such a wonderful present for her birthday too. She put it back in the box and after putting it in the drawer, she was so excited. But she wasn't going to wear it now until Jake came.

Although Esmee was living alone in her uncle's old house, she only had Jimmy to talk to. But Jimmy was only a tom cat. Her only visits were to the little antiquated shops in the village, where she walked twice a week to buy what was needed. She never made conversation and seldom spoke to anyone. She thought the people in the village were too old. Often she wished she could meet someone about her own age, even before Miss Maggie died.

She could have gone to the Mission and mixed with the local people there, but she didn't believe in God, not since her mother and father and her two little sisters and her Miss Maggie, whom she had loved, had died suddenly. But now that Rammon Lee had come into her life, she eagerly looked forward to his visits, when he would take her in his arms and kiss her ardently.

*

As soon as Rammon came that evening, he noticed at once Esmee was all excited.

"What's happened to my lovely sweetheart?" he asked as he took her in his arms and kissed her passionately.

As soon as she returned his kisses she cried out, "Sit down and close your eyes, and no peepin'."

As soon as she saw his eyes closed, she brought out the gift and as soon as she fastened it around her neck, she cried out excitedly, "You can open your eyes now."

As soon as he saw what she was wearing, he cried out, "Where have you got that from, dear?"

"Uncle Simon sent it for my birthday."

"But you're not sixteen till next week and I'll have a better surprise for you then."

"Tell me now, please."

"No, not yet my lovely. It's to be a wonderful time when it happens," he replied, crushing her to him.

Little did she know that this plausible rogue was going to seduce her that night.

As she threw her arms around his neck, she cried out, "Oh, Jake dear, I love you. I'll always love you, but it's such a long time now before we can get married."

"Oh darling Esmee, I love you too dear. I don't think I can wait until your uncle comes back. Let me make love to you now. Please, my darling."

"I want you too, but I'm afraid I might have a baby."

"I'll be careful, dearest. Anyway, we can get married before your uncle comes home."

As he held her closer and began kissing her eyes, mouth and neck, she began to weaken, and as he opened her blouse and kissed her breast she felt powerless. But she loved him, trusted him and believed him.

Soon he helped to undress her. Then after he had taken off his trousers, he lifted her up in his arms and as they lay on the mat in front of the fire, they made love.

As soon as their passion was spent, they began to get dressed. Then suddenly he looked up at the clock on the mantle shelf.

"Oh my God, it's nearly midnight. I'll have to hurry now."

"But why wan't you stay a bit longer?"

"Why do you ask when you know my ma waits up for me?"

"Well Jake, you never do stay long and I thought tonight you would have supper with me, and I'm lonely without you."

"So's my ma lonely Esmee. I'll see you tomorrow."

"But when are yer going to take me to meet her?"

"All in good time," he replied impatiently. "Just trust me."

"I do trust you, Jake, but I ....."

"I'll talk to her when I get back and I'll give you her answer tomorrow night. Now I must hurry."

"Don't be late. I'll cook you a nice supper like the one you say your ma always cooks for you."

"Yes, that'll be nice, dear," he replied as he took her in his arms again and kissed her goodnight.

*

The following day she got everything prepared, the rabbit and dumplings. She also bought a jar of cider, which he often told her he like a drop of at night.

Later that evening while the rabbit and dumplings were simmering on the fire, she laid the table with the best cloth and best dishes. She had already washed her lovely long fair hair and tied it back with a bow of pink ribbon to match her frock. She also wore her gold chain and pendant. She was now ready to serve it out as soon as he came. She was feeling on top of the world, knowing he would walk in and take her in his arms.

But the grandfather clock struck nine, then ten, then eleven. It was nearly midnight. When she knew he wasn't coming, she sat down and wept. Even the pot had boiled dry: the supper was wasted.

She locked the door and went to bed wondering and worrying if he had met with an accident, or was his mother ill again and couldn't be left.

But I know he will come tomorrow and explain. I know I'm foolish to worry. I know he loves me. With these thoughts she drifted off to sleep.

But he didn't arrive the next night and when he didn't come the second or the third night, she really began to worry. The following night she made up her mind to go to his caravan and find out what had happened. As soon as she began to put on her hat and coat he walked in. As soon as he went to take her in his arms and kiss her, she turned her face away.

"What was that for?" he asked.

"You know what it's for. I've been worried sick. Why didn't you keep your promise?"

"I couldn't, my love, I couldn't get away, love," he lied.

"Well if you hadn't come now, I was going to see your ma and find out why."

Suddenly he replied angrily, "Don't you dare go to see my ma, unless I take you!"

Esmee could see how annoyed he was and wondered if his mother was bed-ridden or mentally ill. She dare not ask him in case she upset him again. "He'll tell me in his own good time," she thought.

"But I was worried. I didn't know what to think."

"Well I'm here now. Now let's both sit down and listen to what I have to say."

As he sat down beside her on the couch and put his arm around her, he began to tell her what happened.

"While we've been living on the farmer's land I been doing odd jobs for him and the other day he asked me if I would stay and to do work for him."

"What farm's that?" she asked.

"It's about three miles from here. I'll take you one day," he lied again. He had no intention of taking her anywhere.

"I've got several weeks work putting up fences and laying a path. That's if we don't get more bad weather. And the wages are good. Anyway," he added, "I've been working late and I was dead tired, ready to drop. So I went straight to bed. I thought about you, love, and I missed you, so I made up me mind to come to see you and explain."

"Why didn't you send me a message? I would have understood."

"There was nobody I could send. All the gypsies have gone now. Now me ma and me are staying on till the job is finished. The farmer said he may take me on for good, so you can understand why I can only get to see you at least twice a week. Don't look so disappointed, my love. I can save a good part of my wages, so that we can get married."

"But that's a long way away."

"I know, but the time will soon fly by. Now let's have a drink of that cider and drink to the day when we can be together forever."

"But we've still got to wait for Uncle Simon," she replied.

"No dear, if that's going to be another four months I can't wait, so what do yer say we get married before he comes back? Now get two glasses and we'll drink."

"Two? Why two? I don't think I'd like it."

"It's not alcoholic. Just have a little drop to please me."

After a couple of sips she began to like the taste and after drinking two glasses it was now taking effect. He told her again how much he loved her, thrilling even at the touch of his hands. The cider was now taking effect.

They stood up facing each other, clinging to each other and smiling into each other's eyes. Hers with love and adoration, his with lust, and as he undid her blouse and kissed each breast, he cried out, "Oh, Esmee, my darling, I've missed you so very much. I could hardly sleep at nights." What a plausible liar he was, and he hadn't even told her his real name was Rammon.

As soon as he began undressing her, she didn't even resist. He lifted her naked body and carried her upstairs and lay her on the bed. Hurriedly he stripped himself. As soon he jumped in beside her, they began to make passionate love.

She knew she couldn't refuse him now, whatever he did. She became frantic with desire, knowing it was better than the first night he had entered her as she lay on the mat. All thoughts of her becoming pregnant had now vanished.

As he lay back exhausted, she saw him close his eyes. Soon he fell asleep. She had hoped he would take her in his arms again. As she covered the quilt over his naked body, she began to wonder if all men were like this when they had made love, but she had no experience of life or real love.

She lay awake for some time wondering and thinking and hoping she would now become pregnant. And when my uncle knows we love each other and wish to get married, I'll ask him if we can live here. If not, I'll live anywhere, anywhere and be happy with my Jake. With these fantasies she lay back and fell asleep.

It was one o'clock in the morning when he woke up and realised he hadn't meant to fall asleep or stay late. Now he knew he had to give some explanation to his ma. He crept silently out of bed and quickly dressed, hoping she wouldn't wake up until after he'd gone. Carrying his boots, silently he crept down the stairs. Finding a piece of paper and pencil he began to write a note. Creeping back upstairs, he left it on the pillow and left.

When she awoke she was disappointed he had gone without waking her, but when she read the note she understood why. "My darling Esmee," she read, "I didn't mean to fall asleep. I had to hurry, you understand why. I didn't want to wake you, you looked so lovely laying there. I won't forget to see you in three weeks time or sooner. Love and kisses, Jake.

A week later she was surprised to see him. He told her the farmer was waiting for some timber and he wouldn't be needed for a couple of days. But he didn't tell his mother. She thought he was still working and working late. She too foolishly believed him the lies he often told. Now he told Esmee he had more time to spend with her and make love. Those two days went quickly by when he had to leave her again.

One morning, as soon as she had fed Jimmy and let him out, she sat deep in thought. Three weeks was a long time before she saw him again. She was now feeling lonely, with too much time on her hands. She knew she had to find something else to do beside cleaning the house and other chores. She thought, maybe I could find a part time job in the village. But she couldn't make her mind up then what she intended to do. If only Uncle Simon was here we could get something settled, for she was feeling out of sorts.

Then one morning she felt sick and off her food. She knew the symptoms. She remembered her mother was always sick and off her food when she became pregnant. Yet she wasn't sure until she began to miss the date of her periods, but she knew she was never regular. Now this sickness and going off her food, she knew she must be pregnant. She thought to keep her secret a bit longer and tell him when he was in a cheerful mood, for she had noticed he could be very moody at times. Esmee had always been thrifty where money was concerned. Often she put to one side some of the housekeeping money for herself from the money her uncle provided. She also still had the money her kind Miss Maggie had left her before she died. She never caught the tram, she always walked to the village shops, which were two miles away.

One morning as she walked to the village to buy some wool to knit for the coming event, she noticed a young girl looking at some baby garments. Esmee had never seen her before. She was the first young girl she had seen since she came to live with her uncle and her Miss

Maggie. As soon as she bought what was needed, she went into the library next door and as she was looking for a book to read, she happened to see the same girl staring across the room at her.

"Are you alright?" the girl asked as she came across the room.

"Yes," Esmee replied pleasantly, "Why?"

"Only yer looked pale. I wondered, can I 'elp yer, 'cause I seed yer in the shop buyin' wool? Are yer 'avin' a babby then?" she added.

Esmee was beginning to like talking and answering questions with this cheerful, inquisitive, outspoken girl. "Why does it show?"

"Yes a bit. I'm 'avin' a babby too."

"I can see that," Esmee replied, smiling at the girl.

"I don't want it, not really. Yer see this chap I fell in love with was full of love and promises, but I daint know 'e was such a plausible liar, until I told him I was goin' to 'ave 'is babby. Then 'e done a bunk, but me mom's standin' by me. 'ave you got a mom?" she added.

"No, my mum died when I was twelve."

"O dear, I'm sorry. Are yer married?" she asked.

"No not yet. I will be soon."

"Does 'e know yer 'avin' 'is babby?"

"I haven't told him yet. I'm keeping it secret for a while."

"Well yer wanta tell 'im befower it's too late or 'e might change 'is mind, like the bloke I thought loved me. Wot did yer say yer name was?" she added.

"I didn't, but it's Esmerelda."

"That's a lovely name. Mine's plain Annie. I don't care wot the girls in our street call me now, an' they snub me, but they don't know what they've gotta cum to one day. I 'ope yer daint mind me chattering away to yer. My mom alwas ses I talk the leg orf an iron pot. P'raps we'll meet agen an' 'ave a cuppa tea with me an' me mom."

"I'd like that," replied Esmee.

"Well ta-ra fer now. See yer in 'ere next week?"

"Yes," Esmee replied. "I'll look forward to that."

On the way home Esmee began to wish she had met this chatterbox before, but she felt sorry she had been let down by her young man. She knew how she would feel if her lover did the same. She wouldn't be cheerful, but Esmee began to have her doubts now after that conversation she had with Annie. Yet she thought again he would never desert her. She loved him and he'd so many, many times said how much he loved and worshipped her.

The following week she walked to the village to meet her friend Annie. She waited in the library over an hour. Esmee was disappointed when she never came and wondered what has happened.

She went again the following week, but still no sign of her. If she had told her where she lived, she could have made enquiries, but she only knew her name was Annie. Maybe I shall meet her again one day. With these thoughts she walked back home, disappointed.

The following week it was time for her lover to call, when she would tell him she was pregnant.

As soon as he came he took her in his arms and as he crushed her to him she cried out, "Be careful, Jake darling, or you'll hurt our baby."

"What baby? Whose baby. What are you talking about?"

"Yours and mine," she replied, as she smiled up into his eyes. "I'm pregnant. Isn't it wonderful?" She didn't see the anger on his face until he pushed her away from him

"No!" he exclaimed. "It ain't bloody wonderful. How far have yer gone?" he added as he glared at her.

"Three months," she managed to say, as the tears ran down her face.

"Three bleeding months and you've only just thought of telling me! If I'd known you wanted to become pregnant, I wouldn't have touched yer!"

"I thought that's what we both wanted," she replied tearfully.

"No! I didn't want it this way!"

"If you didn't want it this way, why didn't you wear something?"

"What do you know about such things? It seems to me you're not so innocent you make out to be."

"I read it somewhere in a book, but it seems now you only wanted to use my body, and like a fool I believed you when you said you loved me."

"You wanted it as bad as me. You could have refused me."

"Well Jake, what are you going to do now? Whether you love me or not, you'll have to marry me," she replied. As she wiped her tears away she became angry. "I want an answer now!" She knew now he didn't really love her. He never had.

"I have to explain first to me ma. I know she'll be angry. She won't like it, but I'll tell her anyway and see what arrangements we can make."

"I don't care what your ma says. You've got to marry me now in any case. If you don't, I'll follow you to the end of the earth," she cried out as tears began to fall again.

"No use you crying. Just give me a couple of days to make some arrangements," the very plausible rogue replied.

"Very well, two days, and if I don't get your answer then, I'll make it my business to come to the caravan and see your ma myself."

"There's no need for that! I don't want her upset. Please trust me and wait."

She still loved and trusted him to come again and give her an answer, but what she didn't know was that the job with the farmer finished a week ago and he and his ma were already packed to be leaving soon to another town. If only her uncle was here or her Miss Maggie. She would have known what to have done, but her Miss Maggie was dead now.

She sat by the fire and began to weep, as she began to think of her Miss Maggie. She remembered the day Miss Maggie had had a stroke and could not speak, only to make those awful noises when she saw him put his arm around her. Esmee thought nothing of it at the time, but now she began to think, was Miss Maggie trying to warn her about him? Now her thoughts were taking shape. She would go this very night and front them both and hear what they had to say.

"O God, please help me. I can't face this disgrace alone," she cried out as she began to dress.

She washed her face and after combing her lovely long hair, she put it into two plaits. Then putting on her best shoes, blue velvet dress and her best coat and hat that Miss Maggie had bought, then fastening her gold locket around her neck, she fed Jimmy and after putting him outside, she locked the door. It was pouring with rain, but she didn't care if it was a snow blizzard or a hail storm.

As she walked across the field the rain began to ease off. As soon as she walked across the waste ground, she saw the light from the caravan.

When she got nearer, she noticed it was painted gold, green, red and yellow and on the side was the name, "Gypsy Rose Lee". She knew this must be the one. Suddenly she felt nervous and afraid, but she had come this far and knew it had to be done.

After hesitating a while, she made her mind up and picked up courage. As she knocked on the bottom half of the door, wondering what to expect, the top part flew open and when she saw this hard-faced, buxom woman lean her heavy breasts on the bottom half, she became nervous.

"Who's theea? I don't tell no fortunes at this time of night! Anyway, clear orf!"

She was about to close the door when Esmee asked, "Are you Jake's ma?"

"Jake. Who's Jake?"

"He is your son, isn't he?"

"No, I ain't got a son named Jake! Now clear orf!"

"But he told me his name was Jake."

She began to think his ma was denying she had a son. Well I've come to see Jake and I'm not leaving here till I see him."

"If yer cum ter see 'im you'll 'ave a lung wait. He left me nearly forty six years ago."

"But I'm looking for your son. He told me his name was Jake Lee. I'm three months pregnant and he promised to marry me."

As soon as Esmee tried to explain how he came to visit her and worked for the farmer, Rose began to realise who she meant.

"Just yer wait 'ere," she cried out as she bounced down the wooden steps. As soon as she made her way to the wagon she called out, "Rammon! Rammon! Yer betta wake up an' cum out 'ere. There's a wench 'ere ses you've put her in the family way."

Esmee had never seen him drunk or so dishevelled. When he saw her standing there with the light from the caravan shining on her, he seemed to sober up.

"Wot do you want?" he cried out.

"I've come to see your mother and you to see what you're going to do about marrying me!"

"'e carn't marry yer! 'e's already engaged ter marry the gypsy Rhoda, so goo 'ome an' blame it on some other silly bastard!"

"I'm not leaving here till he comes with me! If he don't, I'll follow you both wherever you do and have him arrested!"

"Don't yer dare threaten us you, you, you -"

"Leave her to me, Ma. Go inside while I talk to her."

Esmee still stood there weeping and hearing them both quarrelling.

"Don't yer order me about you foolish bastard! I never thought I'd see this day that you'd tern out like that drunken rogue of a father! Anyway, yer betta get rid of 'er befower I get me whip out to yer both!" she yelled out angrily as she went inside.

Esmee became scared now of what she might do, so she ran away. When she got out of breath, she stopped to lean against a tree trunk. Soon she began to sob. "O God, what's to become of me?" she cried out.

When Rammon caught up with yer, she pushed him away.

"Esmee, darling, let me take you home," he pleaded.

"Don't you darling me, you, you, you lying, conceited bastard!" she cried out angrily. "You won't hear the last of this, Rammon Lee, or whatever yer call yerself, because I'm going to follow you and your ma wherever you go and I'll tell your gypsy Rhoda, whoever she is, what you're like and what you've done to me! She won't want to marry then!"

Suddenly he lost his temper. "Shut up! Shut up!" he cried out, as he slapped her face hard. But she didn't let him get away with that. She kicked and clawed his face until she fetched blood. Suddenly he struck her so hard she fell backwards against the tree trunk and there she lay.

"Esmee, Esmee," he began to cry out, "I didn't mean to hit you. I'm sorry." But when she didn't answer and saw the blood coming from the back of her head, he began to panic and ran.

He almost fell inside the caravan. Suddenly he cried out, "Ma! Ma! I think I've killed her!"

"Wot yer talkin' about? Is this mower of yer lies?"

"No, Ma. I hit her and she fell and hit her head on a tree trunk."

"Are yer sure she's dead?"

"Yes, Ma. Her head was pouring with blood."

"Oh my God, wot we goin' ter do now?" she cried out as she crossed herself.

"I don't know, Ma, but I'm scared. Let's move now. Tonight."

"No! We carn't leave 'er theea. Somebody'll be sure ter find 'er an' know it's us. Yer betta cum with me."

"Where yer going, Ma?"

"Don't ask questions! Ye've done enough damage. Gimme me shawl an' follow me."

When they got to the place, he pointed out where Esmee was still laying. As soon as the old woman bent down and saw the blood, she began to feel her pulse. 'er ain't dead, thank the Lord. She's unconscious. We carn't leave 'er 'ere to die. Yer betta carry 'er an' lay 'er down in the wagon."

"Are you taking her with us, Ma?"

"No, yer bleedin' stupid bastard! An' wipe that blood off yer face!"

It was still dark and it was raining as they drove about three miles down a lonely road.

"Yer betta get an' look in the wagon. I don't want 'er ter come to yet."

He was afraid to look at her. He could still see her face was swollen where he had struck her, but she was still unconscious.

"Now," she said, "a few yards done this lane to the left you'll see a big, old building. It's called the werkus. I want yer to carry 'er theea an' lay 'er on the steps, then quickly pull the bell in the wall an' run fer yer life. Now 'urry yerself before the dawn cums up. I wait fer yer 'ere."

She felt heavy in his arms as he carried her in his arms, but he managed to lay her on the wet steps and pull the rusty bell. He felt no pity or shame.

As soon as he ran back to his mother she cried out, "Now let this be a lesson to yer an' I 'ope you'll be able to live with it the rest of yer life!" she added as they drove away.

THE WORKHOUSE - PART TWO

Molly Green was one of the workhouse lackies. She was forty years of age and looked older than her years. She had a sallow complexion and her grey, wiry hair was always cropped to her ears. Her little turned up nose and flat face made her look rather ugly when she grinned. She also wore her long, grey uniform longer than any of the other inmates, to hide her club foot, which was encased inside a wooden boot, which made her drag one foot behind the other. Although she was thin, she was very strong. She also had a vile temper and often punished. Some of the women often said she was off her rocky, but some were kind when she helped them with their chores. But Molly Green was not so simple as she looked.

One of her punishments was when whipped she was put into a dark, dismal narrow room in the corridor near the big gates, where she had to answer the bell day or night. Often some of the inmates would smuggle a well used love book for her to read when she found time to lay on her narrow mattress.

Molly couldn't understand some of the words. She hadn't had much schooling, but she knew what some of the words meant. Yet she would skip through it and often giggle at the naughty bits of the story.

It was such a night as this when Molly heard sounds like someone moaning. Quickly she hid her book beneath the mattress and limped as quickly as she could along the dark, dismal corridor and listened behind the door. She wondered at first that someone had left a baby on the steps outside the doors. This was no surprise for Molly to find a baby or a young woman seeking shelter. When she realised this was no baby cry, she managed to open the door wide.

As soon as she saw a young girl laying there with her face all swollen, she did her best to drag her inside and close the door from the cold winds and rain.

As Molly got her underneath the gas light she stared down at her as she cried out, "O my God, you poor wench, ye've cum ter yer last 'ome w'en yer cum 'ere."

But there was no answer, only a faint moaning.

Molly hobbled as quick as she could to the Master's office. Although it was everyone's duty to knock before being asked to enter, she didn't wait. She almost fell inside the office, where she received another shock. She saw the Master with the matron up against the wall, where she had her clothes up to her waist. When Molly saw what they were doing, she began to giggle out loud.

Quickly the Master pulled away when he heard and saw who it was. She knew they both looked angry and red-faced when they saw they had been caught in the act.

Suddenly, Molly cried out, "There's a young girl lyin' in the corridor," she managed to say between giggles.

"Well don't stand there staring! Go and get help!" he replied as he turned away to button his flies up. "And then you come straight back here!" he added.

"I better go and help," replied the red-faced matron.

"You'll do no such thing! You will stay here till I come back. And you, wench," he added, "go to the boiler house at once and tell big Tom he's wanted here at once, and if you speak to anyone on the way, I shall thrash the life out of you."

"Yes, sir," she managed to say, smiling at her thoughts of what she'd seen.

As Molly tried to hurry she saw big Tom across the cobbled yard. When she got near to him she cried out, "Cum quick, Tom, there's a young wench lyin' in the corridor an' I think 'er's dyin'."

"Wot yer talkin' about? Bugger orf befower I throw a lump of 'ot coal at yer!"

"But Tom. I'm tellin' the truth. The Master's sent me ter fetch yer."

"If you're gettin' me on, I'll put yer bleedin' head in the furnice!"

Suddenly she began to weep, "I ain't Tom. Please cum quick or we shall both be in trouble."

"Alright, wipe yer eyes, wench. You carry on an' I'll catch yer up, when I've put another shovel of coke on."

In the meantime the Master and the matron were discussing what was to be done about Molly seeing what they were doing.

"Oh Peter, it'll be all over the building if she tells them what we've been doing here," she cried out with tears.

"Leave the wench to me, Mary love. She won't say a word when I threaten what I shall do to her."

"You want me to leave the room while you talk to her?"

"No Mary, I want you to stay here and hear what I've got to say. Now sit down, there's nothing to worry about."

As soon as big Tom Jenks saw the young woman, he noticed at once the blood on her hair and face. "Go an' tell the Master, Molly, at once!" he exclaimed.

"I've already told 'im. 'e knows an' I aint gooin' in theea again. Goo in an' tell 'im yerself."

"Wot's the matter with yer, wench?"

"You'll laugh yer 'ead orf when I tells yer wot I saw 'em both doin' in that office."

Before she could say another word they looked up to see the Master making his way towards them.

As soon as he gazed down at Esmee he said, "Tom, you better carry her over to the infirmary and fetch the doctor. I'll come later. And you, wench, you come with me!"

"You cold, bloody hard bastard, yer must have a heart of stone!" How often Tom had loved to have said this to his face, but big Tom knew where his best place was: in the boiler house, where he could keep warm and bake a few roast potatoes on the shovel and smoke his clay pipe to his heart's content without anyone knowing. Big Tom put her over his shoulder and made his way to the infirmary.

There were only six beds in this small ward. Two were already occupied with two old ladies. As soon as they saw Tom, the one old woman cried out, "Who is she, Tom?"

"I don't know. 'er was lyin' outside in the rain w'en Molly found 'er."

As he lay her down on the hard bed, the other woman asked what her name was.

"I don't know. Yer betta ask the doctor!" he snapped.

"Keep yer bleedin' 'air on, big Tom! I only asked!"

As soon as the doctor came to examine her, he called the nurse to get her stripped. As he began to examine her, the doctor cried out, "Who is this young woman?"

"I don't know, doctor. I only know Big Tom said she was found in the workhouse corridor.

"Now who have we here, nurse?" the doctor asked as soon as he saw Esmee.

"I don't know, doctor, until she's come to, but Big Tom brought her in. He said Molly Green found her lying outside on the steps."

"Molly? Isn't that the woman with the club foot?"

"Yes, I believe she is," she replied.

"Very well, you had better get her stripped so I can examine her."

After examining her all over, he replied, "Well I don't see any bones broken, but she is pregnant," he replied. "Now, nurse, I want you to bathe that cut in the back of her head," he added. "And when she comes to, give her these two tablets and stay with her. I'll be back again shortly."

As soon as the nurse bathed the wound, she slipped a brown calico gown over her head, when Esmee came to.

As soon as she opened her eyes and tried to sit up, she looked around that almost bare, cold ward. "Where is this place and why am I here?" she cried out.

"It's the workhouse infirmary, but I don't know why you're here," Nurse replied kindly.

"Don't leave me, please," Esmee replied.

"Now take these two tablets and when you've rested, you'll be able to tell me who you are and what your name is?"

But before Nurse Stephens had finished speaking, Esmee closed her eyes to fall asleep.

*

As soon as the Master dragged Molly back into the office, he pushed her roughly on to the chair. As he glared at her, he cried out, "Now wench, I want you to listen very carefully to what I have to say. Do you understand?"

"Yes, sir."

"If I hear a word of gossip from you or anyone about what you saw in here, I'll thrash you within an inch of your life. You understand what I mean?"

"Yes, sir," Molly replied. "I won't breathe a word to a soul." But Molly was still smiling to herself as she thought about what they had both done, as she looked across at matron.

"Now the matron and I have decided to give you a few privileges, so if there's anything you need or want, within reason, just come and ask me or matron."

"Thank you, sir. Thank you, Mary."

"And you must still call her matron. Now you may go, and on your way, go across to the infirmary and tell Nurse Stephens I'll be along shortly."

"Yes, sir," she replied as she bowed and grinned as she opened the door.

As soon as she left the room, the matron put her arms around him and as she kissed him she said, "Peter, I've never liked that old woman. I don't trust her."

"Well don't let her see it now. Don't worry your sweet self, Mary. She'll obey me, but be careful, don't be too hard on her now. Now you'd better leave."

As she walked towards the door, she began to giggle as he pinched her bottom.

Molly knew now she could ask for anything within reason. She knew how to keep a secret, yet she wasn't going to ask too many privileges. She knew how far to go. She didn't want to spoil a good thing.

*

Molly and the inmates loved this elderly Nurse Stephens. She always had a kind word and a smile for everyone. As soon as Molly arrived in the ward and saw the nurse writing at the desk, she gave her the Master's message.

"Thank you, Molly. Is that all?"

"Yes," she replied, "'as the girl woke up yet, nurse?" she added.

"Yes, only once, but she's dozed off again."

"Can I just 'ave a peep?"

"Yes, but you must not make a noise."

"She's a nice looker, aint she? Must be a maid from the big 'ouse nearby."

"What makes you think that?"

"Well she was wearin' lovely clothes when I found 'er lying out theea in the rain an' a gold locket round 'er neck, an' I'd love them shoes she was wearing. Any'ow," she added, "I wouldn't be able ter wear 'em with my club foot."

"has the other nurse or matron looked at it lately? When did you have the boot changed?" she added.

"O I don't know an' some days it 'urts summat awful."

"You better let me have a look at it then," Nurse replied. She was shocked when she saw the sores. "You better come and see me first thing in the morning!"

I carn't Nurse, I 'ave ter scrub the corridor."

"Never mind that! They will have to get someone else. I want to see you get that boot changed! In the meantime go and see Matron and tell her what I've said."

"She won't bother. I've showed 'er the sores before an' she ses she'll get someone ter treat 'em but she never does. I don't like 'er, Nurse, an' I know she don't like me."

"I know how you must feel, but I can't go over her head, much as I'd like to. I'm over-worked, now that two more nurses have left. I too will be leaving at the end of the month, but I'll look into your troubles and get your sores treated and a new boot."

"O don't leave us, Nurse. We all love yer, but where will yer go? Goin' to another infirmary?"

"No, dear, I'm retiring to make way for a younger nurse. Now you must go now before the Master comes and don't forget I want to see you early in the morning, also to get you a larger casing for that foot."

"Thank you, Nurse," Molly replied, as tears filled her eyes. Everyone Molly was friendly with would be upset too, when she told them that their favourite nurse was leaving.

Molly was on the verge of telling her what she had seen in the office between Matron and the Master, but she held her tongue until the time was ripe.

As soon as she left the room the Master came into the ward, followed by the Matron.

"Well, Nurse, how is the patient?" she cried out sharply.

"I believe she's coming round now."

"has she spoken yet to say who she is or what her name is?"

"No, she only kept mumbling about a Miss Maggie."

"Did she wear a wedding ring when she was brought in?"

"No, sir, only the pendant which she's still wearing."

"Has she any other jewellery in her purse?"

"No, sir, only six half sovereigns and a few pennies and farthings."

He unfastened the chain from around her neck. He saw the inscription on the back of the pendant: "To Esmee from Uncle Simon."

"There is nothing to go on by this, but I'll take them along, Nurse, until she can tell us. I'll be back shortly."

"As soon as he left, he entered the office, put the purse and the pendant in the safe.

Half an hour later, Esmee began to open her eyes. As soon as she sat up she called out, "Nurse, can I have a drink of water?"

"Yes, dear. I see you've got a bit more colour in your cheeks." She added.

"Now," the Matron asked as she stood by the bed, "perhaps you can tell me how you got here?"

"I don't know, and that's the truth," Esmee replied. "She was beginning to dislike this hard-faced woman. She made up her mind there and then she would never tell her how she quarrelled and fought that night with Ramon.

"What happened before you got here?"

"All I can remember was hitting my head on a tree trunk. I don't remember anything after that."

"But you must know who brought you here!"

"I keep telling you, I don't know and that's the truth!" she exclaimed, as tears ran down her cheeks.

"No need for tears!" she snapped.

The nurse standing near would have liked to have taken hold of the matron and slapped her face hard, but she knew it was not her duty to interfere.

"Are you married? You know you are pregnant?" she added.

"No, I'm not married an' I do know I'm pregnant!"

"What's your name? I suppose you remember that!" she exclaimed.

"Esmee."

"Esmee what?"

"Esmee Rabone. Why all these questions? Am I in some kind of prison?" she added.

"No, you are in the workhouse infirmary and we want you now to tell us where you lived."

But Esmee was afraid to say. She knew she couldn't give her uncle's address. He would probably be on his way home now and if he should find out the whole truth, she knew he would turn her out. Anyway, she knew she couldn't go back there. Just as she was about to say something, the doctor entered.

After he felt her pulse and took her temperature, he told Matron she must rest and if she wished to question her again, it would have to wait until later.

As Matron left the room, she was furious. She never liked anyone giving her orders.

As the nurse took off the dressing, he was pleased it had healed up and said to leave the dressing off.

"I notice the girl is very flushed. Has Matron disturbed her again?"

"Well, doctor, you know her methods. How she asks questions."

"Yes," he replied, "Between you and me, I think she's a frustrated old maid, maybe been crossed in love," he added as they both smiled.

"By the way, doctor, I saw Molly's leg this morning and that case she's wearing is much too tight. She's also got sores where the casing has rubbed the flesh. I've told her to come to me for treatment. I've noticed her limping very badly lately, but I believe it's a larger casing she needs," she added.

"How long has it been changed?"

"I don't know. She don't know either, when I asked her."

"Well I think it's about time then that the casing was got rid of then! I'll see to it straightaway and get her a well padded boot, and if Matron upsets my patient again, just give me a call. You know there's an elderly nurse coming to take your place from the other block?" he added. "I also hear she's a tartar. She'll be a match for Matron," he smiled. "But I'm sorry you're leaving us at the end of the month. I was hoping you would stay a bit longer. I shall miss you, Margaret, and so will the inmates."

"I shall miss you too, William. I'll not be far away."

"Where did you say you were going to live?"

"I didn't," she replied, as she smiled up at him. "I'm going to live with my friend Elisabeth. She's got a cottage in Broadstairs. She is married and has two young children, whom she wants me to be nursemaid to."

"Well I hope you'll be very happy, Meg. I'll see you again in the morning and if my patient's temperature goes up, just give me a ring."

While the nurse had been talking, the two elderly women in the opposite beds were sitting up, trying to listen to their conversation. Little did anything seem to miss their eyes or ears.

As soon as the doctor and Nurse Stephens left the room Aggie leaned over the side of her bed to whisper to her friend. "Wot yer think, Alice, that poor wench lyin' theea. I wonder who 'er can be? An' in the family way an' all. An' did yer see them nice clothes she was wearin' wen Big Tom carried 'er in?"

"Yes," Alice replied. "I wonder who she can be? I bet she could come from one of them big posh 'ouses where the big knobs live an' 'er's bin took advantage of, like me."

"You was never in one of them big 'ouses, yer liar," Alice replied, as she gave her friend a gentle push.

"Well me mother was," Aggie replied.

"Yer doin' yer romancin' agen," Alice cried out.

"That's all we can do in this bloody foresaken 'ole," Aggie replied. "Now listen, Alice, to wot I gotta say an' wot I heard the doctor say. Now lean over closer."

"Well you afta speak up, yer know I'm a bit deaf."

"Don't kid me, Alice Fielding! You aint so deaf as yer mek out! Now listen!"

As they both leaned over across the edge of the bed, Aggie whispered in her ear, "Well I 'eard the doctor say we're gooin' ter 'ave another nurse from the other block an' the doctor said she's a real tartar, an' 'e said she'll be a match for the Matron. Now we'll see plenty of trouble and bleedin' firewerks," Alice replied, grinning.

"Yes, an' that's the truth, Alice, an' I'd luv ter see the day wen that Matron's took down a peg or two, the bleedin' old battleaxe! Want a pinch of me snuff?" Aggie asked.

"Where did yer get it from, Aggie?"

"Ah, that's tellin', she replied, as she put her finger to her nose. As Alice helped herself to a large pinch between her thumb and two fingers, Aggie cried out, "I dain't tell yer ter tek the bleedin' lot!"

"Well yer betta 'ide it afower the nurse sees it."

"She knows, but it wouldn't mek any difference if 'er dain't."

*

Molly loved Big Tom Jenks. She knew everyone called him Big Tom, but she always addressed him as Tom, or my Tom, to the inmates. Molly really loved this middle-aged, rugged, kindly stoker. He knew she loved him, but his feelings towards Molly were just friendly, but often he would tease her.

She was now happy and excited to show Tom her new boots, as she hurried across the cold, wet cobbled yard. He hadn't seen her enter the boiler house and as he stood stripped to the waist, she began to admire his every movement. As he placed some potatoes on the shovel and put them in the fire to bake, she thought, if only he'd just let me stroke 'is back or take me in 'is arms an' kiss me, just once. Just as she gave a big sigh, Tom turned around and saw her.

"Hello, Molly. I aint seen yer for two weeks and I wanted to tell you how sorry I was the way I spoke to yer the other night. Anyway, what brings you here in the middle of the day? Aint yer supposed to be working in the laundry?"

"No, Tom. I got a betta job now an' more freedom. Any'ow, aint yer noticed any difference about me?"

"No, Molly, unless yer having a baby," he teased.

"Don't be bloody daft, Tom! Not at my age. Who would want an ugly old woman like me?"

"You aint ugly and you aint old. How old are yer now?"

"Over forty, Tom."

"Well it's not too late," he replied, as he smiled and winked his eye.

"I'm waiting fer you, Tom," she replied, as she smiled back at him.

"You'll have ter wait a long time for me, Molly dear. I just want ter be as I am," he replied.

"'ow hold are yer now, Tom?" she asked.

"Nearly seventy," he replied. "Now tell me what's different about you," he added.

"Well I've 'ad this operation on me right foot an' now I'm wearin' proper boots. Only the right one is well padded. Look," she added, as she began to demonstrate up and down the yard. "See, I only 'ave a bit of a limp now."

"That's wonderful, Molly. They should have operated on that foot years ago."

"I think they would 'ave done, if I aint bin runnin' away. But I never did get far, did I Tom?"

"That's all in the past now, Molly, and yer want ter try and forget it. Now sit down on that crate while I turn me spuds over," he added.

As she sat down and watched him she cried out, "Tom, can yer keep a secret?"

"Yes, I believe so," he replied, as he placed the shovel back into the furnace fire. "I'll be with you in a minute," he added.

As soon as he filled his clay pipe and lit it, he came and sat down beside her. "Now come on, Molly, let's hear this secret. I can see you're trying to tell me."

"Well," she began, trying to demonstrate with her hands, "yer know that young girl we 'elped ter drag in the corridor, well 'er name's Esmee Rabone. W'en I first found 'er before you cum, I ran ter the office ter tell the Master. I daint stop ter knock, I barged in an' seen 'em both doin' it against the wall." Suddenly she began to giggle.

"Doing what? And stop giggling."

"Yer know," she replied, as she pointed to Tom's flies. "Mekin' mothers an' fathers."

"Who with?" Tom asked, still smiling.

"The Matron. An' I 'eard 'im call 'er 'Mary darling'."

"What him and the Matron? It's a wonder he could find it underneath that pot belly of his."

"But 'e did, Tom, an' I saw it."

After they both laughed out loud, he asked her if anyone else knew.

"No, but after yer carried Esmee ter the infirmary, 'e dragged me in 'is office. I was scared bloody stiff in case 'e was ready ter beat me an' lock me in that punishment room, but yer know wot 'e said, Tom?"

Tom was still smiling as he replied, "No, go on."

"'e said if I daint breathe a werd ter anybody wot I'd seen, 'e said 'e'd find me a light job an' few privileges. Now I've 'ad me foot treated an' I can walk in the grounds two or three times a day without any questions asked. So yer see, I 'ave ter keep this secret."

"But why did yer tell me, Molly?"

"Well I 'ad ter tell somebody an' I know yer won't say anythink."

"Very well, but see that yer don't tell anyone else. Now," he added, "you better go. I've got to chop some logs and stoke up ready for the night stoker to come on."

"I wish I could werk 'ere with yer, Tom, w'ere it's nice an' warm," she replied, smiling up at him.

"I couldn't imagine you stripping yourself down to yer waist," he teased.

"I'd do anythink fer you, Tom, 'cause I love yer."

"Now, now, Molly, no more of that talk. I love you too, but only as a friend. Now you better go, but you can always come and have a chat and a warm, and don't forget to take a couple of taters with yer."

"Thanks, Tom, but you aint angry with me, are yer?"

"No, Molly, but you mustn't say such things, and keep what you feel and hear to yourself. I know how you feel," he added.

"Alright, am I forgiven? If I am, will yer just give me one little kiss before I go?"

As soon as he saw the tears he replied, "Very well, but you must not tell anyone or they might misunderstand."

As he bent down to kiss her cheek, she couldn't resist throwing her arms about his neck and kissing him on the lips. As soon as he pushed her gently away and as he hurried through the door, he playfully slapped her bottom.

Molly hurried back to her room, thinking only now of Tom. But she knew he would never return her love. But she had her dreams and often pictured him sitting in his armchair smoking his clay pipe, and herself curled up at his feet with her head resting on his knee, beside a cosy fireside.

She knew Tom was married. He had often talked to her about his wife, who was an invalid, and his two sons, who were now married with a family in Canada. They didn't visit often, but always sent them money. Tom was not an inmate in the workhouse. He was employed as a stoker, therefore he could come and go when he pleased. He also had a neighbour who came to look after Elsa, his wife. Also a daily help, when he was on different shifts. But Tom's life for years had been the same routine. After work he would come home and after washing himself down, he would go in the next room to kiss his wife and take her a meal that he would cook, or the neighbour had cooked for them both. After, he would go to the local for his usual pint and a chat or a game of dominoes. But Tom never stayed late. He would bring Elsa a bottle of stout and curl up by the fire to read his paper and smoke his pipe. To some men this would seem a very humdrum sort of life, but Tom was contented to be as he was, caring for his wife whom he loved dearly.

Often one of the men at the local would ask Tom to join their fishing team on his Saturday or Sunday afternoons off. But Tom was quite content to stay at home and read all the gossip pages to his wife from the "News of the World".

Tom was also happy when he came home one evening to hear Elsa say that the doctor had paid his last visit, and that she was now able to get up for a few hours each day, but to keep taking her medicine. Elsa too was happy, to know she would soon be able to help her husband around the house and to help with the cooking. He had often talked to Elsa about Molly and the stories she once told him about her life before she was taken to the workhouse, and how she managed to escape for several weeks.

"Well when you get your health back, I'd like yer to meet Molly. She's a cheerful soul," he said.

"How long 'as she been there, Tom?" she asked.

"Since she was ten. Now she's about forty two or three. I'm not sure."

"The poor soul, to be locked away in a place like that," replied Elsa.

"Oh she's not locked away. Not in the asylum. She has a little freedom."

"But couldn't she leave now, after all them years?"

"I don't believe she wants to leave now. She's made some friends and often says it's the only home she'll ever have."

Tom couldn't tell her about what Molly had seen going on between the Master and the Matron. Maybe, he thought, when it was convenient, but until then his lips were sealed.

*

Esmee was now sitting up in bed. She always looked forward to seeing Molly. Some afternoons Molly would come and talk and tell her bits of the love story she'd read from her tuppenny novel, and bring her a bit of chocolate she managed to buy when she was sent to the general store. Molly didn't eat them herself. She said they made her old teeth ache. When she asked Nurse Stephens if she would like one, the nurse knew she was not allowed to take anything offered to them by the inmates. As soon as she saw Esmee and Molly enjoying them she called out, "I'll have one, Molly. Why not? I'll be leaving in a few days time anyway."

"But who's gooin' ter tell?" she asked, as Nurse took the chocolate.

As soon as Nurse looked across the room and nodded towards the two old women in the opposite beds, Molly whispered, "O, them two snuffy old key 'ole Kates."

Esmee and Nurse Stephens often smiled at Molly's witticism.

*

Three days before Nurse Stephens was leaving, the doctor and the Sister came to see how Esmee was progressing. They knew that she was always cheerful when Molly visited. As the doctor took her temperature, he said she was now well enough to be moved.

But Esmee still wouldn't tell anyone who she really was, nor where she had lived. The only lie she told was that she had been in service and one of the boys had got her into trouble. Yet she didn't know who had brought her to this Godforsaken place.

"But if I go from here, where can I go back to? My uncle's house? He's perhaps on his way home by now anyway. Let him think I've run away. I've got nowhere else to go until my baby is born, then I'll search the whole countryside until I find that lying scoundrel Rammon Lee and his ma."

Molly was now getting worried, thinking about where her young friend would be moved to. She knew she couldn't ask the doctor or the Sister. After they had both left the ward, Molly spoke to the nurse. "Where do yer think they'll move her to, Nurse?" Molly asked.

"I don't know for sure, Molly. It maybe she will be moved to the cookhouse or the laundry."

"O' no, Nurse, it'd kill 'er! She's too kind and gentle ter werk amongst that rough lot. They'll try an' bring 'er down to their own level w'en they start askin' oo she is an' where she cums from, an' she won't tell 'em, an' she'll die if she 'as ter sleep in that dormatry with 'em."

Molly Green was like a mother hen. Nurse remembered those many years ago, when Molly was not yet fifteen and gave birth to a baby boy. She almost broke her heart when the midwife took it away, not to see it again.

"It would only be for a few months, until she has the baby."

"I carn't see 'er lastin' that lung, Nurse, an' 'er bein' anaemic an' all. I think I'll ask the Master if she can sleep in my room. There is a spare bed," she added.

"I don't think that would be wise, Molly, to go over Matron's head."

"I wouldn't ask that old battle axe anyway," she replied.

As soon as she saw tears in her eyes, the nurse said, "I'll have a talk with the doctor and the sister, and I'll let you know what their answer will be in the morning. Now don't get upset, I can hear the tea bell," she added.

As soon as Molly left, she began to hope that she could give Molly some good news later. Luckily she happened to see the doctor coming down the corridor. As she walked towards him, she greeted him with the usual, "Good morning, doctor."

As there was no one near he replied, "Good morning, Margaret."

"Can you spare me a few moments, William?" she asked.

They both addressed each other by their Christian names, for they had been close friends for many years.

"You had better come in the office then," he replied.

As they both sat down facing each other, he asked what was the trouble. He could see she looked concerned about something.

"It's about Esmee and Molly I come to see you about, William."

"Why? But I thought those two were very friendly."

"Oh yes they are William," she replied, smiling at the look on his face. "The trouble is mostly with Molly. She's beginning to worry where Esmee is to be moved to when she leaves the ward."

"I presume she will have to start work with the others."

"Molly is concerned about where her friend will be working. She's also worried about her sleeping in the dormitory with the other inmates, and so am I, William. She also tells me there's a spare bed in her room where she can keep an eye on her. As we both know, William, she is very anaemic. I know she's been a tonic to Esmee and Molly treats her like a mother hen."

"Very well, I'll have a word with Sister and put it through the other channels."

"Thank you, William," she replied as she kissed him.

After he returned her kiss he asked, "When will you be leaving us, Margaret?"

"In three days time," she replied, "but I shall see you again before I go," she added.

"I know I shall be looking forward to your letters and your visits. Now," he added, "If you will come back this afternoon, I may be able to sort something out."

"Thank you, William," she replied as she kissed him before she left. They had been close, intimate friends for several years and she had told him previously that she was leaving to be governess to her friend's two young children.

*

72

The workhouse was built in early King George IV's reign and she knew the routine of the old workhouse, where neglect, carelessness, strict discipline and cruelty applied to many of the inmates, young and old. She also knew the whole building should have been pulled down years ago, but she knew she couldn't do anything about what went on behind locked doors. Yet she always said when she retired she would "Let the cat out of the bag."

*

During the meantime, Molly sat on the side of Esmee's bed and told her about some of the running of the workhouse.

"You get on well with Nurse Stephens, don't you Molly?"

"Yes, an' she likes you too Esmee," she replied.

"Yes, she's very kind. The doctor too."

"O yes, I know the nurse since I cum 'ere. Let me see now," she replied as she began to think, "I cum 'ere w'en I was about five or six years old. That must be about forty years agoo. She was only a young nurse then. She looked after me w'en I 'ad me bloody beatin's after I run away, but I dain't get far with me club foot draggin' be'ind me. It's a long story, Esmee. I've never told the other women an' wenches 'ere, but one day w'en we're alone, I'd like ter tell yer about my life an' wot 'appened the second time I ran away. Anyway I've told yer wot these women are like and the young wenches in the dormatry."

"Yes, Molly, those two old women oppersite have told me and I'm scared if I have to sleep with them in that dormitory."

"Now listen 'ere," she replied as she whispered, "I don't want them two Key'ole Kates listenin'. I asked the nurse ter see if she can get yer a light job an' if yer can sleep in my room."

"That's kind of yer, Molly. I think I would like to still be with you."

"Well I'll let yer know the news in the morning, so pray and keep yer fingers crossed."

*

As soon as the nurse walked into the ward the following afternoon, Molly and Esmee knew at once by the smile on the nurse's face that she was pleased. Molly knew that the two "Keyhole Kates" were trying to see and listen to what the nurse had to say, so she drew the curtains around the bed and began to whisper.

"I have done the best I can for you both," she whispered, "and tomorrow Esmee will be sleeping in your room. Also she will be given a light job in the canteen, helping to make the teas and taking the trolley around the infirmary wards, until after the baby is born. Now, Molly," she added, "when I leave here, I don't want you to abuse these privileges or take advantages, or you will know the consequences."

After they thanked her and promised they would do as she asked, Nurse drew back the curtains. "Now, Molly," she added, "I want you to take a letter to Matron. There's no need for you to wait for answers, but if she's not in the office, just push it through the letterbox."

As Molly followed the nurse towards the desk, she whispered, "Now, Molly, as you know Esmee is very anaemic. She's also not very strong after her illness. I want you to see that she takes her medicine regularly, also to let the doctor know if she has a relapse. There's nothing more I can say or do. As you know, I shall be leaving in two day's time."

"Thank yer, Nurse. Yer've bin very kind and I'm very sorry you'll be leavin' us. We all are," she added, as tears filled her eyes.

"Now hurry along and take that letter to Matron," she replied.

But Molly didn't want to see the Matron. She didn't even knock, but dropped the letter in the box and hurried away.

The next morning Molly was up earlier than her usual time. She was happy now to know she wouldn't be alone at nights, sleeping in this dismal room. She began to sing as she brushed away the cobwebs from the corners of the ceilings, and spit and polished the dark green iron bedstead where Esmee was to sleep. She also cut out animal pictures from old magazines she had underneath her mattress and stuck them on the bare, damp walls to brighten up the room. After giving the old knotted floorboards an extra scrub, she sprinkled Keatings powder down between the gaps of the wainscoting to keep the cockroaches at bay. Now all she had to do was to wait for someone to come and tell her to help carry the flock mattress, pillow and blankets from the storeroom.

*

One night about three weeks later, Esmee asked Molly if she would like to hear about her life. Who she was and where she had been living and how she became pregnant.

"Yes," she replied, "but if yer wanta change yer mind, that's alright by me."

"No, I won't change my mind. I feel I'd like to tell you and you're the only one I can trust."

"Fire away then, Esmee," Molly answered as she smiled.

As soon as she sat on the side of Molly's bed, she began to relate parts of her life.

"I was only twelve years old, Molly, when my mother and father and my two little sisters died. We were very poor and when my Uncle Simon came and took me to his home, I was broken hearted to leave behind the kids I knew and played with in our yard, whom I had grown up with and attended school with.

My uncle had a housekeeper whose name was Maggie. I always called her Miss Maggie. She was very kind to me. She taught me to speak properly too, besides showing me how to cook. The day I was fifteen, she was making a cake for my birthday and as she was stirring in the fruit, she had a stroke, and when I ran to the phone box to call the doctor, I met this handsome gypsy. Foolishly I fell in love at first sight. Little did I know then what a plausible rogue he was.

As soon as the doctor had left, Miss Maggie was making funny noises. I didn't understand then that she was trying to warn me against him. Oh Molly, if only I could have understood her mumblings I wouldn't be here today.

He told me one day that he loved me and promised we would be wed when my uncle came back after his travels, and while he was away we made love several times. Then one night my uncle came into my room and tried to rape me, and when he put his tongue in my mouth, I bit it as hard as I could and spat the blood in his face, I shall never forget that terrible ugly look on his face as he tried to jump across the bed. But before he could reach me, I picked up the chamber pot and hit him across his head twice. As soon as I saw the blood run down his face, I ran out of the house.

There was nowhere I could run to, only to the gypsy caravan where he lived with his ma. When I told them I was pregnant and I had nowhere to hide, his ma said his name was Rammon, not Jake, as he had always led me to believe, and that he was soon to be married to a gypsy widow named Rhoda, who was also pregnant. I called him every name I could think of, but when she said she would get her whip out to me, I became afraid and ran.

I remember standing against an old tree trunk trying to get my breath back, when I saw he had followed me. He tried his plausible way to win me over, but I went mad. I kicked and clawed at his face, and when he struck me, I remember falling and hitting my head on the tree, but I don't remember any more, or who brought me here, until I found myself in this Godforsaken hole.

But I feel better now I have told you Molly, and as soon as I'm able to get away from here, I'll comb the countryside and every town and city until I find that bastard and his Gypsy Rose Lee, as he calls his ma. I'll also have them arrested for the thieves they are, for I remember too that night I was wearing my gold chain and locket and a purse with six gold half sovereigns and some loose change."

"They didn't tek them, Esmee. You 'ad 'em w'en yer cum in 'ere an' I saw the Master tek yer necklet an' yer purse."

"Why haven't they been given back to me then?"

"Maybe you'll get 'em back w'en yer leave 'ere, but I shouldn't 'ave told yer this, Esmee, an' I 'ope yer don't ask for 'em before yer leave, because 'e'll guess I've told yer an' I don't wanta be whipped agen an' put in that cold, dark punishment room."

"I won't, I promise. Anyway," she added, "they're no use to me while I'm here."

"It's time for yer medicine now, Esmee."

"I'll take it, but I don't think it's doing me much good. I feel so depressed when I have to go through the wards and see them all staring at me and whispering to each other."

"Do any of 'em ask yer any questions about it?"

"No, their looks are enough, especially the older women. I'll be glad when it's born. I don't want it, Molly," she added.

"But yer will. W'en old Tilly Bullivant puts it in yer arms, ye'll change yer mind."

"Not me, Molly and I mean that, because every time I look at it, it will remind me of that bastard who put it there, and when I've had it, I've made up my mind to escape from this hole."

"But w'ere will yer goo?"

"Perhaps into service for a short time."

"But they wunt 'ave yer with a babby in yer arms."

"I'm not taking it, I'm leaving it here."

"Yer wunt get far, Esmee, believe me. I've tried it three times, but you're a nice lookin' wench an' well spoken, p'raps yer'll be luckier than an ugly old cripple like me. Anyway, I'd like ter tell yer wot 'appened to me w'en I tried to escape, then it will give yer some idea wot yer up against. But not now, p'raps termorra. It's time fer lights out."

As Esmee walked across the room towards her bed, the lights began to dim, as she called out, "Good night, Molly."

"Good night, Esmee."

As Molly lay back she began to feel sad knowing that in a few months time she was going to dread the time when this young girl, who she had come to love and care for, was going to try what she had failed to do. Although she knew she would miss her, she prayed and hoped that when the time came Esee would be luckier than she was. She felt now that she must tell her the story of her life and those cruel, unhappy times forty years ago, when she was nearly six years old, and being dragged to this place by two men from the Board of Guardians.

She felt too sad now to read a chapter from her novel by the light from a piece of candle that she always had hidden underneath her mattress, and as her eyes filled with tears, she thought, this is my world, not some paperback romance.

*

A few nights later, after Esmee had taken her medicine, she was about to get ready for bed. Molly was already sitting up in bed when she called out, "Would yer like a ter 'ear me story before yer go ter sleep, an' before it's too late?"

"What you mean? Where are yer going?" Esmee exclaimed.

"Now're yet, but I've never told yer before, I get these awful pains in me back an' in me arms an' legs."

"Try a drop of medicine," Esmee replied.

"That wouldn't do me any good. It's pain killers I need. Wot Nurse Stephens always gave me, but she aint 'ere now an' I wouldn't ask that new Nurse Patrick. 'er's worse then that Matron. Anyway, they'd only put me in that ward with the older patients. Anyway I know yer wunt tell anybody wot I'm goin' ter tell yer, but it wunt matter oo knows w'en they carry me out of 'ere in a wooden box an' bury me somew'ere."

"Don't talk like that, Molly!" replied Esmee. "You're the only friend I've got here and I love you," she added as tears filled her eyes.

"I love you too, Esmee, so if you'd like ter bring that old chair an' sit beside me, I'll tell yer."

"Do yer feel well enough?" Esmee asked.

"Yes an' I think I'll feel betta w'en yer know, then you'll change yer mind about escapin'."

"I don't think so, Molly," she replied.

"Very well, but I want yer ter listen ter wot I 'ave to say. I don't remember me mam. Me gran told me she was a loose woman an' went off with different men, an' that she died givin' birth to me. Me gran lived in an' old bug infested cottage in Essex Street. It was overrun with cockroaches an' mice. Gran was a cripple too an' couldn't do much. I was nearly six years old. W'en she was eighty, she died, but before she died I couldn't walk, only crawl around the room until I was nearly five, an' w'en I tried ter stand I'd try pullin' meself up by grabbin' the leg of a chair, which alwas cum down on top of me. An' when I grabbed the table leg, all the crocks would land on top of me.

"I've never fergot them beatin's she give me. Often she would becum frustrated an' say she'd put me in a 'ome. Then one day she borrowed an old pram from one of the neighbours. 'ow she tried to push me alung un it, an' 'er being a cripple too, I'll never know. I remember being wheeled along to some 'ospital ter see if they could do somethink with me foot, but we was turned away, saying that there was nothink to be done. In desperation, Gran wheeled me ter the Salvation Army Mission to get 'elp from them.

They was very kind, Esmee. They gave us a bun an' a hot mug of cocoa and a few coppers the Captain give ter Gran. But Gran liked 'er drop of gin, if yer know wot I mean," she added as she smiled. "A few days later the Salvation Army sent their van an' I was driven to a cripples' 'orspital, w'ere I saw lots of crippled children of all ages, some bein' lernt ter walk.

Soon I was fitted with an iron casin', an' with the aid of a walkin' stick I was able to attend school. But children can be very cruel w'en they see you aint ser perfect as them an' often they would shout after me "'opperty kick! 'opperty kick, Molly carn't 'obble without 'er stick", an' they used ter call gran an' old witch an' throw stones at us. But I swore one day that I would 'ave me revenge.

A few days later I was able ter 'obble alung without me stick, w'en I saw two lads from the gang sitting on the edge of the kerbstone playin' Jack Stones. The dain't see me creepin' up be'ind 'em. As soon as I got near enough, I lifted me foot with its iron on an' kicked them as 'ard as I could in the middle of their backs. I began ter laugh w'en I saw them run away screamin'. They never called after me nor me gran again, an' w'en me gran died, she was buried by the parish an' buried in a pauper's grave.

I locked meself in that old 'ouse an' cried fer days, an' w'en the School Board man came, I still wouldn't go ter school, an' the only time I opened the door was w'en I 'ad ter goo across the yard to the closet.

"Then one day two men broke the door down. They sed they was from the Board of Guardians. I tried ter run up the stairs, but it was 'opeless tryin' ter drag me foot after me. I screamed and kicked an' as they dragged me along I 'eard the only woman that lived near say, "Poor little bugger, 'er's goin' to 'er last 'um"."

"But why couldn't someone take you into their homes?" Esmee asked.

"I wondered that at the time, Esmee, but who wanted a cripple? Anyway the all 'ad big families, and they was all on parish relief.

As soon as I arrived 'ere, I was put into an empty white-washed room w'ere I saw two elderly women in grey frocks covered by a thick calico apron. I was deloused an' taken into another room, w'ere they cut all me 'air off and pushed me into a bath of strong disinfectant and scrubbed all over with carbolic soap. After the one woman helped to dry me, she pushed a brown calico shift over me head ter wear. Then the other one brought me a dish of porridge with brimstone an' black treacle. I'd 'ad nothin' ter eat fer three days an' w'en I galloped it down, I was sick all over the shift.

"Back agen, I was flung back in the bath an' scrubbed all over agen an' after givin' me another shift, it was mower like a bell tent, an' w'en I cried, I was slapped several times across me face an' bare arse. They took me into another room w'ere they pushed me on to a flock mattress. "Stay theea!" I 'eard the one big buxom woman say, "Till I can see wot's ter do with yer!"

I must 'ave fell asleep. The next mornin' the same two women almost dragged me off the mattress. As soon as she slapped me face she shouted, "Dain't yer 'ear the bell?"

"No I dain't," I shouted back Suddenly she began ter laugh, "We've gotta right one 'ere, Liz, but she'll soon learn this ain't no 'ome from 'ome."

I 'eard 'er say, "Now 'ere's yer clothes yer gat ter wear an' 'urry yerself or yer porridge will be took away," she added.

The routine of the werkouse was up in the mornings with two other girls older than me. We had to be up at six o'clock, empty slop buckets an' clean out the dead ashes from the fire grates. Bein' the new girl, I 'ad all the dirty jobs, black leading the ranges, an' if it wasn't cleaned an' polished to perfection, these women that were called Mothers would throw ashes all over it an' yer 'afta start all over again.

"Then there was old knotted floorboards ter scrub on yer knees, an' the stone corridor. I remember one Mother kicked me bucket of suds over an' began to laugh as she said, "I'm sorry, but you'll 'ave ter start agen"."

"If she'd have done that to me, Molly, I would have picked up that bucket and pushed it over her head."

"Believe me, Esmee, I felt like doin' a lot of things ter that one. I even thought of liftin' me iron foot an' doin' the same to 'er as I did ter them kids, but I 'ad ter learn the 'ard way ter keep me mouth shut.

"When I was thirteen I was given a job in the cook'ouse w'ere I 'ad ter polish all the copper pots an' pans until they shone like gold, without a speck of dust or soot on 'em. But there was always a large iron cauldron that hung over the fire that was never cleaned an' seldom emptied. It contained som kind of stew. Often I used to see the cook scrape leftover food off the plates that the inmates couldn't eat. There was bones, bits of fat mutton an' even crusts of bread. God knows wot else went in that cauldron, but who was we ter complain. We 'ad ter eat it or starve.

One day I was moved to another small bedroom along the corridor, with an older girl called Lydia. There was something about 'er I didn't like. I didn't find out until one night she said she couldn't sleep she was cold, an' feelin' sorry for 'er, I pushed me bed against the wall ter mek room for 'er ter sleep with me. I was cold too. It was a very cold night. We snuggled up close together and after a while I must 'ave dozed off, w'en suddenly I felt 'er 'and strokin' me fanny.

Suddenly Esmee burst out laughing.

"It's no laughing matter, Esmee. I was really scared."

"What happened then?"

"If yer'll stop grinnin' I'll tell yer," Molly replied as she too began to smile. "Well I struck 'er across 'er face as 'ard as I could, then I lifted me club foot up an' kicked 'er out of me bed."

"That foot of yours comes in very handy at times," Esmee replied, smiling.

"Yes it sure does," she replied, "But w'en she landed on the floor she yelled, "Murder" at the top of her voice. When one of the Mothers cum runnin' in an' I told 'er wot 'ad 'appened, she wouldn't believe me. I was dragged out of me bed an' put in the punishment room fer three days."

"What happened to the girl Lydia?"

"I don't know, I never saw 'er agen. It was in that small punishment room that I noticed a small window open, just big enough fer me ter squeeze me body through. It was dark an' quiet, so I dragged the iron bedstead beneath it an' climbed up. Then I landed on the wet grass. As I 'urried across the grounds towards the iron gates, draggin' me foot be'ind me I dain't get very far, w'en I saw a light shinin' in me face. "So that's yer little game, is it?" I 'eard this man say. "Well yer better come back with me."

I was more scared now than before, I even wet meself. I began ter cry and plead that 'e'd let me goo, but he said it was more than 'is job was worth. He was a tall man, but I couldn't see 'is face in the dark. Now I was more frightened than before, I wet meself. I began to cry as I pleaded with 'im agen ter let me goo. When I managed ter tell 'im 'ow I tried to escape, 'e said 'e would try an' get me back agen before I was missed. As soon as 'e took me 'and an' led me towards that open winda, 'e bent down an' cupped 'is 'ands an' lifted me back up. As I got 'alfway inside, I 'eard 'im whisper "Good night" and' I was not ter try any more silly tricks as "too many 'ave tried an' failed"."

"He sounded a kind man, Molly."

"Yes, yer don't find many of them sort 'ere. Anyway, as soon as I landed inside, I flopped down on me flock mattress an' cried meself ter sleep.

"Two days later it was Sunday, w'en I was taken out ter goo ter church. Two by two us children marched dressed in similar frocks we wore week days, but our Sunday frocks were a lighter grey an' a white starched pinifores an' misfittin' straw 'ats. I dreaded gooin' inside that old church for everyone there knew why I 'ad bin punished, an' w'en the preacher began 'is sermon, with 'is 'ell fire an' brimstone, I see 'im look over the top of 'is specs an' stare at me. Do you know, Esmee, I felt if only that floor would open up fer me ter vanish.

Do yer believe there's an 'ell an' 'eaven, Esmee?" she added.

"I don't think so, Molly. Heaven and hell is what we make it. Anyway, Molly," she added, "I often wonder if there's a God, when so many good, kind people suffer for no fault of their own."

"That's wot I think too, Esmee. But next time I'll tell yer wot 'appened w'en I escaped fer over twelve months."

"Yes, Molly, but you must lie back now an' get some rest. We have to be up at six, but I'm pleased you've told me about yourself."

"You ain't 'eard 'arf of it, but I feel betta now I've told you. Goodnight then, Esmee," she added.

"Goodnight, Molly," she replied, as she leaned over and kissed her wrinkled skin.

As soon as she lay down on her mattress, she began to think about all Molly had told her with tears, but Esmee knew whatever more Molly had to tell her later, it would not deter her from making plans of escape when the baby was born. If only Molly had had two good feet she may have been more successful. But she was young, not yet sixteen, and could plan ahead.

*

A few days later Molly was not well; when she had to stay in bed, Esmee came whenever she could to cheer her up and talk about what went on during the day. But Esmee was worried to see her friend ill and began to think she was going to lose the only friend she had. But as the days went by, Molly got better and was able to continue her duties, and it was a few nights later that they sat alone in their room when Molly began to talk about the rest of her story.

"I was about your age, Esmee," she began, "when I went ter church with the other girls one Sunday evenin'. It was very dark and not bein' able to keep up with the others, I was always left be'ind. Lucky fer me no one saw me as I 'urried across the grounds an' found meself outside the iron gates. There was not a soul to be seen, everyone was in church, so I knew I wouldn't be missed until everybody returned back to the "homes". I must've gone miles. It was breakin' dawn, I was tired, cold an' 'ungry an' wished then I'd never attempted ter get away, but I 'ad got this far. W'en I saw a few yards down the lane an old farm'ouse, thinkin' they might give me a crust and a drink, I knocked on the door several times, but nobody answered. It was now beginnin' to get lighter, I 'ad ter hide somew're. As I looked around, I saw an old barn with two cows inside. I was too tired to walk any further, so I managed to squeeze meself inside an' there I lay on some old bags in the corner, hopin' nobody would see me.

"I must 'ave dozed off, w'en I 'eard a young girl called out, "Wot yer doin' theea an' who are yer?" I began ter weep, I couldn't even answer. W'en she pulled me up she cried out, "Yer from the werkus 'omes, ain't yer?" I just nodded. I was afraid now she would fetch the farmer an' tek me back. W'en she asked if I was 'ungry an' I told 'er, she said, "You wait 'ere then while I goo an' get yer somethink ter eat." W'en she came back agen with a large chunk of bread an' a jug of milk, I couldn't believe I'd met such a kind girl.

As soon as I 'ad me fill, she told me the farmer an' 'is son 'ad gone early ter market an' w'ere was I mekin' me way to. I told 'er I daint know, only that I 'ad ter get away. She told me then she too 'ad been in the 'omes but was farmed out. "I'm the milkmaid an' maid of all werk too, but it's better than being back in then 'omes."

Then she told me that Freddy would be comin' ter tek the cows out an' that I could 'ide in the loft. "Then yer'll 'afta be gone befower the farmer gets back." I climbed the ladder and soon fell asleep on the warm 'ay. I daint even 'ear Freddy cum ter lead the cows out. I must 'ave slept through the day. W'en I woke it was gettin' dusk, w'en I saw the girl climbin' the ladder. She brought me up a mug of tea and some more bread an' cheese an' one of 'er old coats, which she said would keep me warm. "Now w'en you've drunk it, I want yer ter goo before anybody sees yer, an' I'll get into trouble. Now try an' get as far away as yer can, but if yer goo down the lane until yer see a left turnin', goo along as far as yer can, w'ere you'll see a farmhouse. But don't say I've sent yer. If yer ask theea I know the farmer will 'elp yer." She wished me luck, but w'en eventually I arrived at the farm'ouse, a big buxom woman cum ter door. She didn't wait fer me to ask fer 'elp. She cried out, "Bugger off, I'm sick an' tired of answerin' me door ter beggars," an' slammed the door in me face.

"But I didn't give in. I kept walkin' draggin' me foot be'ind me, until late afternoon an' it was becoming dark, w'en I saw in the distance two broken down old cottages. I never dreamt anyone would be livin' in them, but win I cum ter the first one, I look through the dusty winda an' saw a lamp was lit on the table, but I seen no sign of life. In desperation I knocked on the door. Suddenly I 'ad the fright of me life win the door flew open an' a tall man stood almost fillin' the doorway. From the light of the parrifin lamp I could see 'e was very ugly. If 'is face 'ad been black, I would 'ave thought 'e was some kind of gorilla. 'is long, black matted 'air reached almost to 'is shoulders, an' 'is eyebrows almost covered 'is eyes an' 'air sproutin' from 'is nose an' ears. I felt like runnin' away, but I knew I couldn't move any further, but I 'ad ter trust 'im to 'elp me.

I noticed 'is voice was very gentle wen 'e told me ter cum in out of the rain, an' wen 'e asked me wot I was doin' 'ere, I tried to explain. He said, "Well you better come inside and sit down." 'e dusted an old chair for me an' as I sat down, he poked the fire from the rusty grate and as 'e went outside ter fill the iron kettle, I 'ad a good look around the room. It was filthy an' dust everywhere. There was fly papers an' cobwebs all 'angin' from the ceilin' an' the table was laden with dirty plates an' dishes. Everywhere I looked was covered in dust. I dreaded ter think wot the place would look like in the daylight. I felt like runnin' away agen, but w're could I goo? There was only one answer, I 'ad ter stay some place.

As I watched 'im clear a place on the table an' give me a piece of bread and brawn an' a mug of tea, then 'e asked me wot me name was an' w're I'd cum from. I told 'im the truth 'oping he'd take pity on me an' let me stay.

"Well Molly Green," 'e said, "W're do yer think you'll end up by runnin' away?"

I said, "I don't know, sir." 'e began ter smile wen I called 'im Sir an' that I was ter call 'im Jules.

As soon as 'e saw me gazing around the room 'e said, "You'll afta excuse the place, Molly, if yer want ter stay. Yer see me sister Eliza who lives in the other cottage at the end of the lane, don't cum ter clean any more an' I 'ave to goo out ter work. I've advertised several times, but nobody wants the job, but if yer like ter tek it on, I'll give yer free board an' lodgin's an' nobody will know w're you are." So I decided ter stay.

Later that night 'e told me that 'e'd been married, but 'is wife 'ad left 'im years ago with a son who was then four years old, an wen 'e was six 'e died with whoopin' cough, an' that if I liked ter clean 'is room out, that's w're I could sleep.

The next few weeks while 'e was away workin', I got rid of the cobwebs an' spiders, the silver fish an' the cockroaches, fly papers -"

"Wasn't you afraid of all of them?" Esmee asked.

"No," Molly replied, "my granny 'ad more than them we 'ad ter contend with. Anyway this was goin' ter be me 'ome for the twelve months," she added. "Later I made the place look an' smell fresher. I even found faded sheets an' blankets in an old wardrobe upstairs an' some lace curtains wot worn't needed. I 'ad a good old bonfire at the back of the cottage an' burn'd wot was not needed. Jules was pleased with the efforts, but 'e would never let me goo ter the village shops. 'e said it would be safer if no one saw me an' ask questions who I was. But I was 'appy, Esmee, an' content ter be 'is 'ousekeeper. 'e was the only friend I 'ad in the world an' 'e was so kind and considerate. 'e even bought me frocks and underclothes, includin' a calico shift. Wen I asked 'im 'ow 'e knew me size, he said the girl at the shop was my size.

"Then one day 'e cum 'ome, I dain't reconise 'im. 'e'd 'ad all 'is beard and Mustache shaved off an' 'is 'air cut. 'e also wore a new shirt an' corduroy trousers. 'e looked twenty years younger an' 'e warn't a bad lookin' bloke, in a rugged kind of way, now that 'e'd spruced 'imself up."

"How old was he?" Esmee asked.

"'e said 'e was fifty five but 'e looked much older, until 'e decided ter alter 'isself. That night as we sat down to our tripe an' onion supper, I couldn't tek me eyes off 'im an' I couldn't resist gooin' over to 'im an' say 'ow lovely 'e looked an' ter thank 'im fer all the kindness 'e had shown me. I remember I kissed 'is cheek wen 'e replied, "That's alright, my dear, an' thank yer for all the things you've done fer me." After supper 'e 'elped me wash the crocks an' put 'em back in the cupboard, an' wen it was time fer bed, I couldn't resist kissin' 'im agen. That time 'e returned me kiss an' then believe me, Esmee, I fell in love with 'im."

"But he was old enough to be your father," Esmee replied.

"I wouldn't know wot a father or a mother would be like, I never 'ad no one. Only me old granny an' she died before I was put in the werkus. Anyway, do yer wanta 'ear the rest?"

"Yes, Molly," Esmee replied, all ears.

"Well one night there was a terrible storm which must 'ave blew some slates off the roof an' wen I woke up, I saw the rain comin' through the ceilin'. Me an' the bedclothes was wringin' wet, even ter me shift. I crept down the stairs quietly, not ter wake Jules, 'opin' there was still a bit of fire left in the grate. I took me shift off an' dried meself on a towel, an' after wrappin' another towl round me, I lay down on the 'orse 'air sofa, were I dozed off. Next thing I knew, Jules was shakin' me. Wen I told 'im wot 'ad 'appened, 'e said I'd betta go an' get in 'is bed before I catch cold.

"Do yer know, Esmee, it was a lovely, wonderful feelin' wen 'e picked me up in 'is arms an' laid me gently down on 'is warm bed, an' wen 'e lay down beside me an' took me in 'is arms, I fell asleep.

It was not until we 'ad slept together fer several nights that we med luv, an' wen I found out a few weeks later I was gooin' ter 'ave 'is babby, I felt on top of the world, an' so did Jules. Often 'e'd bring 'ome some fancy tit-bits, also some wool an' needles ter knit the babby's clothes. Nothin' was too much trouble for this man I loved.

Then one day as I was 'angin' out the washin', I saw this elderly woman mekin' 'er way towards the cottage. I was afraid she'd see me, so I ran indoors. Wen she knocked, I opened it a little way, but befower I could say a werd, she almost knocked me over as she barged in. Wen she said she was Jules sister an' wen I told 'er Jules was away werkin', she cried out sarcastically, "So it's Jules now is it? An' I see yer bin busy by the look of the place. Anyway who are you an' wer yo cum from?"

I said, "That's my business, an' if yer wanta know yer betta ask yer brother wen 'e cums 'ome."

"I'll do that" she said an' bounced out of the room.

"I thought me luck was too good ter last, Esmee, an' if she found out I was from the 'omes, I'd soon be back agen, so wen Jules cum 'ome, I told 'im.

'e said, "It aint took 'er long ter find out. I suppose she wants the cleanin' job back, now that it's spic an' span, but I don't wanta see 'er, Molly. She's evil an' the cause of me wife leavin' me."

The followin' Saturday afternoon, just as Jules cum in with the groceries, 'is sister walked in. Wen 'e asked 'er wot she wanted, she said, "I've cum ter see wot's goin' on 'ere since I saw yer last."

"'e told 'er 'e'd found someone at last ter 'elp 'im an' that 'e loved me. Then she said, "'er's only a bit of a wench. Are yer thinkin' of marryin' 'er then?"

"Yes," he said, "if she'll 'ave me, but I aint ask 'er yet."

There was nothing I could say or do, only ter listen to their arguments. "But yer carn't!" she said. "You've still gotta wife somewhere."

She left me over twenty years ago an' might be dead fer all I care. And remember this, Eliza, you're the one that 'elped ter drive 'er away with yer wicked lies an' superstitions! Now get out of me 'ouse, befower I throw yer out!"

"I'm gooin'," she said, "but yer can rest assured, Jules, I'll mek it me business ter find out w'ere's 'ers cum from!"

"You do that, Eliza, an' see w't'll 'appen ter you! Now get out!"

I was scared now, thinkin' they would cum ter blows, but as she went through the door I 'eard her say, "I'm gooin', but neither of yer 'ave 'eard the larst of me!"

As soon as she banged the door after 'er, I sat down and wept, an' as Jules came towards me an' took me in 'is arms, I remember 'im saying, "Don't worry yer little 'ead, Molly. I love yer an' as soon as our babby is born I'll sell up an' we'll find somewhere else ter live wer nobody will find us."

"I daint see 'er agen until me babby was nearly due. But I 'ad a feelin', Esmee, that me good fortune an' 'appiness was not gooin' ter larst.

It was one cold, wet November afternoon wen I 'ad the news from 'is sister Eliza that Jules 'ad died of a 'eart attack while at werk. I can still see that wicked woman's face leerin' at me as I broke down an' wept, an' wen I told 'er I wouldn't be able ter manage, an' if she would 'elp me, I was shocked wen she said that was nothin' she could do an' that I would 'ave ter goo back to the werkus. That 'ard, bitter woman must 'ave found out wer I 'ad cum from.

After the funeral she told me she'd sold the cottage an' I was ter clear out at the end of the week. I packed wot few clothes I possessed an' started me long journey. The bottom of me world 'ad fallen out wen I lost the only man I ever loved and believe me, Esmee, if I 'adn't bin carryin' his babby, I would 'ave killed meself, but with the thought that I would 'ave Jules' child ter luv, I began me tracks towards the werk'ouse, wer I knew it was the only place who would tek me in.

Before I got 'alfway me pains started, but eventually after tekin' several rests, I manage ter get ter them bloody 'eavy doors. Just as I was about ter ring the bell, a young nurse came out. As soon as she saw I was 'avin' me labour pains, she 'urried me inside. I didn't 'avta say who I was, they already recognised me wen I'd run away before.

I was put straight into the labour ward an' two days after me son was born. But wot was most 'eart-breakin' of all, they took 'im away, Esmee, an' I never say 'im agen, an' wen I asked ter see 'im, I was told 'e was dead. I yelled and screamed an' dain't believe 'em, an' wen I tried ter get out of bed, they 'eld me down an' injected a needle in me, an' wen I woke up a few 'ours later, I found thay 'ad bound up me breasts ter sway the milk away.

It was several weeks later that I was able to tek up me duties as a lackey agen. Now I've learnt me lesson not ter run away agen, so now, Esmee, this is me only 'ome until they carry me out in a wooden box an' bury me some place.

Now you've 'eard me story, Esmee, I 'ope yer tek a warnin' from me, because yer wunt get far before they catch up with yer."

"Well, Molly, I'm still going to try, with or without my baby, when it's time. Anyway, as soon as I've had it, I'll find a way to fool them and I don't intend ter be buried from here. I'm not sixteen yet and I still have my plans ready.

Molly had grown very fond of Esmee. She dreaded the day when she would try to escape, but Molly knew she would help her, whatever happened. But she wondered if she would get far. She knew Esmee was anaemic, also not strong to carry out the heavy duties allotted to her. Yet Molly would help her when no one was about, and when she complained to Nurse Patrick, she was told the exercise would help when she was in labour.

Often Molly wished the kind Nurse Stephens hadn't left. She knew she would have understood, but this young, hard-faced nurse never listened to any complaints. Therefore Molly knew Esmee had to suffer inwardly or given harder tasks.

Many nights before Esmee's confinement, she listened to her moaning and watched her restlessness. She often wished she could help. Often she prayed that Esmee's baby would be born soon. Having given birth to her own baby, she knew she was suffering. But little did Molly know then what was to happen a week later.

Esmee told her about the sharp, shooting pains. She knew Molly would hurry and fetch the nurse. Yet it was always the same impatient answer or harder tasks.

Two weeks later the final day came. At six thirty the fourth of November; Esmee was on her knees scrubbing the stone floor of the labour ward, when she screamed and fell as she rolled over the iron bucket. As soon as Molly heard her screams, she ran to help. As she tried to pick Esmee up, she saw beneath her a pool of blood. She ran for the nurse.

Esmee was still screaming and clutching her stomach as the nurse lifted her up and almost threw her on the bed. The old midwife was fetched, as Molly watched from the other side of the room Esmee giving birth. She couldn't understand why she was screaming with pain, when she heard the old midwife cry out, "Oh my God, there's another one there!" Esmee gave birth to twins, a boy and a girl, but after the midwife began to clean her, she told the nurse to fetch the doctor at once. During the night Esmee died.

Molly grieved for the loss of her young friend, whom she often blamed for the women in charge for giving her those heavy jobs, when they knew she was not even strong enough to carry one heavy galvanised bucket, let alone two.

The next day the Master and the Matron sent for Molly to be in his office at ten o'clock.

As soon as she knocked and entered, she was told to sit down at once. As they both sat facing each other on the other side of the desk, she was surprised to hear that hard-faced, cruel Matron say, "The Master and I are both very sorry that you have lost your friend."

"She'd still be 'ere if that Nurse Patrick 'ad reported Esmee's pains months before!" she cried out angrily, as tears filled her eyes.

"It was God's wish," the Master replied. "Now she is at rest in heaven."

"I don't believe there's a God or even an 'ell an' 'eaven! Yer mek yer own 'eaven an 'ell on this earth!" she yelled out.

"We're not here to talk about these things at the moment," he replied as he glared at her. "I want you to tell me your friend's name and address and where she came from before she came here. Also any relatives she told you of."

"She would never tell me," Matron exclaimed.

But Molly was not going to tell them. She had promised Esmee never to tell anyone, therefore she was not going to break that trust.

"I only know she told me 'er name was Esmerelda Rabone. She never told me anything else," she lied.

"But you two were very close," Matron replied. "She must have told you something!"

"I've told yer both that's all I know!" she lied again. "An' that poor girl would be 'ere alive terday if you 'adn't givin the orders fer 'er ter do them 'eavy, dirty jobs!" she added.

"But why didn't she complain or come to me? I could have helped," the Master replied.

"Complain! Can yer see any of us complainin' to 'er?" Molly cried out. "Where would it get us? Only in the punishment block fer wot yer call disobedience!" she added, as the tears ran down her cheeks.

"Don't be insolent or we will both take away your privileges," Matron exclaimed.

"That's more than yer dare do," Molly replied.

"This is getting us nowhere, Matron," the Master replied. "We will have to see the Governors and make further enquiries, otherwise she will have to be buried by parish rules. Now, Molly," he added, "you may go!"

As she went towards the door she turned and leered at them both. She knew they wouldn't punish her for speaking out, she still held their secret, also Esmee's gold locket and the purse with the six gold half sovereigns, which they had hidden away some place, and while she held this secret, she knew they would not take her privileges away, neither would they punish her.

Two days later she went across the yard to the boiler house to tell Tom what had been happening. She was surprised to see an old man stoking up the fire and a young lad about nine riddling ashes and burnt out coke. As soon as she asked where Tom was, the old man said he had retired over a week ago. The shock of losing the only two friends she ever had was too much for her to bear.

Each night she would cry herself to sleep, after looking across at the bare bed where Esmee had slept. She refused to eat and do her daily chores. As soon as Matron saw she was ill, she sent for the doctor. The doctor said there was only one remedy; she would have to be moved to another part of the building, where she would not be alone to grieve.

Later Molly was transferred to the children's block, where she was made one of the "Mothers". She liked the new job and soon settled down, but she knew she must not get too fond of the children in her care. She also knew when they grew older they were farmed out; some to Australia and Canada, or put into service.

Often she wondered what had become of Esmee's twins; if they had been fostered or had died. But she knew there was no way of finding out. Therefore, Molly Green settled down contentedly for the next twenty years.

PART THREE

James Waldron was the vicar of the local church where his wife Elizabeth and eldest daughter Ada attended, but their youngest daughter Tilly was often disobedient. If she could get away from attending, she would do so.

Their father was a God-fearing man who believed the bamboo cane was the only punishment. His wife and daughter Ada lived in fear of him, but Tilly often mocked him when he did his religious outcries. When he found out, he'd tie her to the iron bedstead and beat her unmercifully. She never forgot the times when her mother and sister stood by to watch, yet did nothing to stop him. Therefore she grew up to dislike her mother and sister and to hate her father.

As she grew older she began to rebel and often she flirted with the local lads. When her father found out, she was beaten again, but she was getting hardened to his beating and religious outcries.

One day she packed a few things she needed in a bag and ran away form home and stayed with an old school friend. Two days later she made up her mind to go back home, but as soon as she opened the door, her father was waiting for her.

As she tried to get past him, he grabbed her arm as he yelled, "Get up them stairs to your room at once! I'll deal with you later you! You! You harlot!" he stammered as his colour was rising. Suddenly her sister cried out, "Father, can't you listen and hear what she has to say and forgive her?"

"No! No! Never!" he yelled. "If God is a forgiver of evil, I cannot forgive evil. She's a wanton!"

"But father," Ada pleaded, "you haven't asked her yet why she ran away or where she's been."

"She's been out all night! That's enough for me!" he exclaimed, as he stormed up into the bedroom.

Tilly vowed this time that she would suffer her punishment in silence. She wouldn't give her father the satisfaction of crying out loud, which she had done before. She vowed to suffer the pain from his beatings in silence.

At each stroke of the bamboo cane, her body winded as the tears she shed soaked the pillow that lay beneath her face.

Her mother and sister had heard it all before when they had stood at the foot of the stairs, weeping and afraid. But after the fifth stroke they looked at each other. They couldn't understand the silence. No yelling from upstairs nor no sound from Tilly.

"You'd better go up, Mom, and see what's happening," Ada whispered.

"I can't!" her mother replied. "If I do he'll turn on me!"

"Well one of us will have to go, Mother. Perhaps it's better then if I go." Ada crept quietly up the attic stairs. As soon as she tip-toed into the room, she saw her sister sitting on the side of the bed, grinning down at her father, as he knelt on the floor. His hands were spread wide and his eyes looked wild, as he stared up at the ceiling as he cried out, "Oh Father, forgive our wanton child who is in our midst this day and forgive her for all the sins she has committed."

"Tilly," her sister whispered, "let's go downstairs. He won't miss you while he's in prayer."

"Prayers! You call 'em prayers?" Tilly cried out. "He's nothing but a sanctimonious old hypocrite. He don't know his God from his devil."

Suddenly her mother cried out as Tilly came downstairs, "You just remember that's your father you're speaking of!"

"And don't I know it!" she replied bitterly. "I know too that you're both afraid of him, and maybe you hate him almost as much as I do. Yet it puzzles me sometimes why you both don't stand up to him! Anyway, this is the last time he's ever going ter beat me again. I'm leaving here tonight and don't tell him to try ter find me, because I never want ter see him ever agen, and whatever happens I won't be coming back."

As Ada followed her into the room, seeing her eyes red and swollen, she whispered, "I'm sorry, Tilly, you're leaving. I shall miss you and so will Mom."

"I shall miss you too, Ada," she replied, as she began packing her clothes.

"But where are you going to live? If you tell me, I'll come and visit you."

"And let him know? That bleeding hypocrite."

"I wouldn't tell him, believe me, and please don't swear," she replied.

"He's enough to make a saint swear. Anyway, I don't know where I'll be living yet. I've managed to save a few pounds, so I'll be able to find lodgings somewhere. When I do, I'll send yer a letter care of the post office."

"I shall miss you, Tilly. Can't you forgive him and stay?"

"Forgive him?" she replied. "You must be out of your mind, Ada. He has never forgiven me since some hypocrite from his congregation told him about seeing me arm in arm with a feller, coming out of the dancehall."

"I know, but if you didn't mimic him and answer him back, life would be a bit easier for us all."

"No, Ada! They both treat me like a wicked child. I'm nearly eighteen and I need some space to sort myself out and so do you!"

"You know, Tilly, I must stay. I am the eldest and it's my duty to stay until such times they won't need me."

As she carried her suitcase outside, both sisters threw their arms around each other and wept as they said their goodbyes.

"You can say goodbye to Mother for me, I don't want her preaching the gospel to me again," Tilly replied as she turned to wave at her sister Ada.

*

Tilly Waldron knew where she was heading for: to meet her secret lover at the Boar's Head public house. The past weeks with him had been times of love and laughter.

Dennis Rabone was different from any other man she had flirted with. He was tall, dark skinned and handsome, with thick, black wavy hair and laughing brown eyes. But Tilly didn't know there was a deep side to his character. He had told her he was a bachelor and lived with his twin sister in a house that he had rented for her, and where he was now taking her to stay. He had also promised to marry her, but little did she know he was already married. As soon as she saw him she was in his arms.

"Hello darling," he said as he hugged her tightly. "I've been waiting for over half an hour. I was beginning to think you'd changed your mind."

"I'm sorry I was late, Dennis, but I had the usual quarrels at home." She had told him about her father's religious ravings, but never about the beatings he gave her, or why.

"You're here now, darling. We'd better go inside before it starts to rain." As they entered they saw the bar was almost crowded with laughter and song.

"It must be a celebration of some sort," Tilly cried out.

"It won't be long, darling," he managed to call out above the din, "for us to celebrate our wedding day."

As she smiled up at him she replied, "I hope so soon, Dennis. But I hope no one sees me in here who knows my parents."

"What if they do?" he exclaimed. "You're not thinking of changing your mind, are you?"

"No, Dennis, but -"

"Never mind the buts, you're here now!" he replied sharply.

She sat down at a wooden topped iron-legged table opposite the "Out Door Dept." where she could see anyone who came in who may recognise her.

Dennis brought her usual gin and tonic and his pint of mild and bitter. They were laughing and hugging each other when she suddenly looked over his shoulder.

"Oh my God, no!" she cried out, as she saw the two elderly spinsters that attended her father's church. "Come on, Dennis, let's get out of here."

"You'll stay put! Are you afraid to be seen with me?" he replied when she told him who they were. "Anyway, let 'em gossip."

But Tilly knew they had seen her. She could almost see the fires of Hell blazing from their eyes. But Tilly was adamant. "Well, I'm going!" she cried out.

As Dennis and Tilly began to leave, they heard one of the sisters cry out, "Did you see what I saw, Margaret? That brazen hussy Tilly Waldron."

"Yes, Florence, I surely did, and hugging and kissing each other," her sister replied.

"Do you know, Margaret, that's the fourth different man I've seen her with and I wonder if her saintly parents know how she flaunts herself?"

"She aint up to no good, I'm sure of that!" replied Margaret.

"Just you wait till I tell the vicar and his good lady wife on Sunday," her sister replied as she tut-tutted and shook her head from side to side.

As soon as the two old busy-bodies were out of sight, Dennis pulled Tilly towards him, and as he hugged her tight he cried out loud enough for them to hear, "Just forget 'em, darling. But I can just imagine them two lying awake tonight in their frilly caps and calico nightgowns, sipping their gin and rehearsing what they're going to say to your father and mother and sister."

"I was thinking the same, Dennis," Tilly replied as she began to smile at her thoughts.

On the way to his sister's home they both began to hurry from the rain.

*

Dennis Rabone was a womaniser like his gypsy father before him, and his job was a travelling salesman. When he came back from Canada he was twenty two years old, and when he came back to England he rented a small cottage in a village in Warwickshire, where he met a pretty young country girl and settled down. But after a few months of married bliss he began to stay out late at nights, sometimes until the early hours, often lying and telling Maud that it was his job driving a lorry. As soon as Maud gave birth to their son, she noticed he seldom came near her or to look at his child. After the boy was six months old, she threatened to leave him and go back to live with her parents, but Dennis didn't want that to happen.

He thought if he could find out where or if his twin sister was still living, he would make it his business to see her, and if he could persuade her to come and live with him and his wife and baby, she would be company for his wife while he was travelling.

The only information was from the workhouse. After some enquiries and identification of who he was, he was told she was in service at Apple Tree Farm, a couple of miles from where he was living.

He didn't even know what she would look like. As soon as he arrived at the farm and knocked on the cottage door, Emma answered the door. As soon as she saw him standing there, she knew at once who this tall, dark, handsome man was. She couldn't mistake the likeness to herself, with is dark, wavy hair and big brown eyes and dimpled chin.

Suddenly her eyes filled with tears as he said, "You're Emma, my twin, aren't you?" he added, holding her hands.

"Yes," she managed to reply through tears.

"I often prayed that one day we would meet, Emma," he lied, "and now my prayers have been answered. Can you take a walk for a few minutes? I have something to ask you."

"Well," she replied, "it is my afternoon off, but I seldom go out much. There's nowhere really I'd like to go to, and I've seen all the places I want to see."

"Well, would yer mind asking them inside if you can come out for a little while."

"That won't be necessary, Dennis. They have all gone to the Goose Fair."

As they walked hand in hand and feeling happy to meet again after so many years of parting, Emma saw the fallen tree trunk, where they sat down. As soon as he hugged and kissed her cheek, the tears ran down her face. Soon, as he dried her tears, he asked her if she would come and live with him and his wife and baby. He also explained that she would have a good home and be company for his wife while he was travelling.

After thinking over what he had said, she told him she'd be pleased to leave this place, as she had never been happy. As soon as Emma served her notice, he came in his car to fetch her.

All went smoothly along for a few weeks, when Emma and Maud began to quarrel about Dennis's late hours, and sometimes in the early hours, and Maud going out and leaving the baby for her sister in law to look after, while she was also coming back all hours.

As soon as Emma told her she was a bad mother, Maud cried out angrily, "Can you expect anything else! I never wanted this babby and his father never takes any notice of him, or me now, and I know he's got another woman he stays with on his travels! Well let me tell you this, Emma, I'm fed up with his lies and deceitful ways! I'm seriously thinking of leaving him and go back and live with my parents. I've told them everything."

"What about the babby? You can't leave him with me, surely?"

"Oh, don't fret yourself!" she snapped. "I shall take him with me, no fear of leaving him here."

"Does my brother know?"

"Oh yes, he knows alright! So there's no use for you to tell him."

"I think that's your business whether you've told him or not, but I hope you know what you're doing Maud. But," she added, "although I was not happy in service, I often wish now I'd never given it up. Although I didn't like it, at least I knew where I stood."

There were more quarrels when Maud found out that they had both lied about their birth to an unmarried girl in the workhouse. A few days later Maud packed a few belongings, and after telling Emma she would send for them later, she picked up her baby and walked out of the house.

As soon as Dennis knew where she had gone, he made it his business to fetch her back. But it was not as easy as he thought. His father-in-law was a large, robust man who could not be trifled with.

"Well! And what have you come for?" Arthur Gregory cried out as he opened the door and saw who was standing there.

"I've come for my wife," he replied rather sheepishly.

"Well you better come in then," he snapped.

As soon as they walked in the front parlour, he called out up the stairs, "Maud! You'd better come down here! Your husband's asking for you."

"I don't want to see him, Dad. Never! And I mean it, never!" she called down.

"You heard what she ses," her father replied. "And I believe you should be downright ashamed of yourself, the way you have treated my daughter!"

"Whatever she's told you, is all a pack of lies."

"I believe my daughter and so does her mother, and you've heard what she ses, so now I think you had better leave!"

"I'm not leaving here without her or my son!"

"You've got a bloody nerve, Dennis Rabone, wanting him after leaving them to go off with other women!" he exclaimed.

"I've not been with no other woman! It's all in her mind."

"Don't lie to me! You've been seen and we can prove it. Now you'd better go before I tell you some more home truths!" he replied angrily.

"I'm going, but if she thinks she can get even a penny out of me, she's got another think coming!"

Suddenly his father-in-law lost his temper, as he yelled, "Get out, you gypsy's bastard, before I throw out!"

Dennis knew it was useless to argue, so he left with his tail between his legs.

*

It was a dark, cold, wet night and as the rain came pouring down, Tilly held on to Dennis's hand as they ran down the lane towards her lover's home.

As soon as he led her through the cottage door, he noticed the angry look on his sister's face as she stood with her back to the fire.

"This is Tilly Waldron, Emma," he cried out, before she could say a word. "Tilly's the girl I'm going to marry one day."

Emma glared at him and was about to say something, when she saw him give her a warning glance as he stared back at her. Emma knew at once there was not time yet to question or argue with him.

Tilly noticed at once there was something wrong between them, but whatever it was she was not interested. She thought it was their business to sort matters out between them.

"Good evening, Emma," was all Tilly could say, hoping she would reply and welcome her, but Emma did not reply. She just stared right through her and frowned. Tilly noticed too how like her brother she was with her big brown eyes and black wavy hair, which was brushed back off her broad forehead. Tilly thought she looked more like a gypsy with her dark skin.

At last his sister found her tongue. "You'd betta take yer wet hat and coat off if yer staying!" she snapped.

Suddenly her brother spoke volumes with his eyes, as he replied. "Now, now, Emma, no need to speak that sharp. I'll speak to you later."

"Very well, you'd better take her case up. That's if she's staying," she replied more calmly, "and show her the room."

As they both walked up the stairs, Emma slammed the stairs door behind them.

Tilly noticed the bedroom was scantily furnished, but clean, and as Dennis put the suitcase down beside the bed, he took her in his arms and kissed her, but he could see she looked upset.

"Don't let my sister worry you, darling," he said in his plausible manner as he kissed her again.

"But why did she bang the door after us? I don't think she likes me, Dennis."

"Yes she will, when she gets to know you."

"Is she always like that?"

"How do you mean?"

"The way she snaps."

"No not really, but I told you what a funny mick she is at times, but her bark's worse than her bite. Just try and ignore her. You'll like her in time and she'll like you."

"But at least she could have been a bit more sociable."

"She's not always like that, Tilly darling. She was just angry tonight because I didn't come home earlier, as promised," he lied. "Now let me see that lovely smile," he added, as he gazed into her eyes. "That's better. Now I'll leave you to unpack while I go down and bring you a cup of tea. Is there anything else you want?"

"No, Dennis. Just a few biscuits with the tea."

"I won't be long, sweetheart," he replied, as he hurried down the lino stairs.

As soon as he entered the kitchen and saw his sister sitting at the table eating her supper, he quickly pulled her out of the chair, and as they stood facing each other, he glared hard as he whispered, "I'm warning you, Emma, don't you dare drive her away or I'll stop your allowance. Then you'll end up in service again or back in the workhouse."

"That'll never happen and you know it! All I ask is you treat this one differently, not like the other one, and does she know you're a married man with a wife and son?" she replied.

"No, I'll tell her later."

"Alright, but if she does find out, it won't be from me. Here's the biscuits and tea. You'd better take 'em up." she snapped.

As he went to go back upstairs, he turned around to glare at her again, as he whispered under his breath, "Remember what I've said, Emma, and don't bang the door after me!"

But she did.

After a few weeks living together, Emma became more friendly and was also glad of Tilly's company, and sometimes Tilly would talk about her mother and sister, also her religious, cruel father. But Emma was wary when Tilly asked if she had any relatives living. She would reply that her and her twin brothers were orphans and if she wanted to know more, she was to ask Dennis.

Tilly never brought up the question again.

Yet Emma often felt she would like to confide in her and tell her what sort of man her brother was, and why he could never marry her, but she was too scared. She still remembered the night he came home and beat her, when he found out his wife had left him. She prayed at nights hoping that Tilly would find out some other way before it was too late, but while she lived here she would try to make her welcome.

One night, several weeks later, as they sat facing each other, reading a novel, Tilly placed her book on her lap as she looked at Emma she wondered if she should tell her she was pregnant.

"Emma," she began to say, "I wonder when we're going to the banns up?"

Emma didn't know how to answer, but when she asked if she had asked him, she replied, "Yes, several times, but he keeps saying that he's trying to find a house that will suit us. But I don't care, I love him and I'd be happy living in one room, as long as we're together."

"But why the hurry? Aren't you content to live here for a while until he makes his mind up?"

"Yes, Emma but he still keeps making excuses about his job that's not paying enough. And now I'm pregnant," she said, as she burst out crying.

"Oh my God," Emma cried out. "Have you told him?"

"No, not yet."

"Well I think you had better tell him when he comes home, and hear what he has to say. How far have yer gone?"

"About three months," she replied, as the tears began to fall.

If only she could have found the courage to tell her he was already married, with a wife and baby son. At least it would be one less trouble off her mind.

"Dry your eyes, Tilly, while I go in the kitchen, while I make us both a cup of tea. Then I'll sit up with yer until he comes home. Then you can tell him while I'm here and hear what he has to say."

It was two o'clock in the morning before they both retired to their beds, thinking he was still travelling. Sometimes it was three or four days before he would park the lorry outside the house, and always had an excuse that he'd been up to Scotland with the firm.

It was during the following week, while he was away, that a very attractive young woman knocked on the door. As soon as Emma opened it and saw who it was, she tried to close the door, but Maud pushed her way inside the room.

"Where is he?" she cried out, as she glared at Emma.

"He's not here," she cried out nervously.

As soon as Tilly heard voices, she called out from the kitchen, "Who's that you're talking to, Emma?"

"It's alright Tilly, it's someone for me."

"Who's Tilly?" Maud cried out. "One of his fancy women?"

Please go, Maud. I'm not feeling well. If you call tomorrow, Dennis will be here," she managed to say as she tried to edge her through the open door. But Maud stood her ground.

As soon as Tilly came into the room, Maud cried out, "Who are you?"

"If you want to know, I'm engaged to be married to Dennis, Emma's brother."

Suddenly Maud burst out laughing. She couldn't stop until she yelled out, "Yer carn't marry him, you bloody fool!"

"And why can't I?"

"I'm his wife and we've got a son, eight months old."

"I don't believe you."

"If yer want to know more, ask Emma or that bastard, Dennis!" she yelled out angrily. "And tell him from me when you see him, I'm going to divorce him."

As soon as she bounced out of the house, Tilly felt sick. She couldn't believe what she had heard and as she sat down on the sofa, she wept. Emma came into the room and said, "I'm sorry, Tilly. I should have told you."

"You're sorry! What about me? Why didn't you tell me when I first came here and began sleeping with him? I feel sick thinking about it and now I'm carrying his bastard. I'm just a whore," she replied bitterly.

"Don't say that. You're not."

"It's the truth. So no more lies I want to hear from you or your twin bastard. I'm leaving now!"

"I know I'm to blame, Tilly. I should have told you he was married the first night he brought you here. Won't you stay to see what he's going to do when you tell him?"

"No! I don't want to see him ever again. You've both lied and deceived me!" she yelled out.

"Well, before you go, will you just listen to what I have to say?"

"You can say whatever you like, but it won't make any difference. My mind is made up. I'm leaving, but I'll listen if it will ease your conscience."

"I was told that my mother was raped by a gypsy when she was only fifteen, and we were born in the workhouse. We never knew what love or affection was. Only to be pushed from one place to another. And when I was twelve, I was taken into service and Dennis was sent to work on a farm in Canada. I didn't see him again until he came to the farm where I was working, to ask me if I would make my home with him and his wife and baby. I was happy to live here for a while, until one night and several nights later, I heard them always quarrelling. Then when he came home in the early hours, I told him his wife had left him. He blamed me and beat me and I've been afraid of him ever since. Although I was never happy in service, I often wished I'd never let him persuade me to live with them. But," she added, "I'm leaving him too."

Tilly looked surprised. "Where are you going to then?" she asked.

"I've already been to see this farmer and his wife where I was in service, and they told me I could come back any time."

"I think that's the best thing you can do, before he comes home and finds us both missing, because I'm leaving today. I've got to sort my own life out now."

"You will forgive me for all the trouble I've caused?" Emma asked.

"Yes," she replied, "but I blame myself really, Emma, for not seeing through him before now. But there's an old saying that "Love is blind"," she added.

"But where will you go?"

"I don't know, but anywhere far enough away from him," she replied bitterly.

Tilly went upstairs and packed her few belongings, and as she came downstairs again to wish Emma goodbye, they flung their arms around each other and wept.

"I shall miss you, Tilly."

"I believe I shall miss you too, Emma."

"I still can't forgive myself."

"Perhaps I'm as much to blame for trusting him."

But Emma had forgotten to tell Tilly to write to her. She had also forgotten to give her address and that she too was already packed to leave that same afternoon.

As they embraced again with tears and said their goodbyes, Tilly left carrying her suitcase and a parcel of food Emma had made for her journey into the unknown.

*

Tilly Waldron trudged along in a trance, not knowing where she was heading for. Only that she had to get away as far as possible. She trudged for miles carrying her heavy burden inside her. When she came to a park, as she sat down on a bench she began to eat the sandwiches, she felt her feet were swelling. She knew she couldn't walk any further. Suddenly, she broke down and wept, as she began to think of her parents, but she knew it was too late to go back to ask for their forgiveness. They would turn her away from the door when they saw she was with child. As soon as she began to dry her eyes, she looked up to see a middle-aged woman bending over her. Tilly noticed she was pregnant too.

"Can I 'elp yer?" the woman asked.

Little did Tilly know that this kind woman was to become a friend and neighbour.

"Thank you kindly," Tilly replied. "I'm looking for lodgings."

"P'raps I can 'elp. What's yer name?"

"Tilly Waldron, Mrs," she added, "a widow."

"I'm Sally Carter. Can I call yer Tilly?"

"Yes, yes," Tilly replied, as she nodded her head.

Tilly knew she had lied, but she didn't want anyone to know she was single.

"You can call me Sally or Sal, as all me neighbours call me."

Tilly at once began to like this middle-aged woman with a pleasant smile and was sorry she had lied to her.

"I can p'raps put yer up on me sofa for a couple of nights. I aint got much room, just living in a back 'ouse with me 'usband and two young sons, but I know they won't mind. I'm always teking strange dogs and cats in. No offence, I didn't mean what it sounded like," she answered as she began to smile. "Where you from?" she added.

Tilly was afraid to tell her the truth, so she had to lie, hoping she wouldn't be found out. She felt ashamed, but she had to lie.

"I'm a widow. I've been living with my husband's people, but now they have a large family, it's over crowded and I'm looking for lodgings."

"Come ter think of it, Tilly, there's an empty 'ouse in our yard what's ter let, so if you'd like ter come and 'ave a cuppa tea while I pop round the corner and see the landlord. 'ave yer any money? Because if 'e let's you 'ave it, 'e'll want a week in advance."

"Yes," Tilly replied, "I have a few pounds in my purse."

"Now don't worry, I'll do me best," she replied and off she went.

Sally Carter was a kind, homely woman, always ready to help anyone. As soon as her two young lads came home from school and saw a strange young woman sitting supping tea, the eldest boy cried out, "Who are you and where's me mom?"

"She's just gone to see the landlord about the empty 'ouse across the yard. She won't be long."

As soon as Sally entered the derelict office where her landlord came when he collected rents, he was surprised to see her.

"What's to bring you here for, Mrs Carter?"

She could see he had on his top hat and coat, ready to leave.

"I won't keep you a minute, landlord, but I want to know if number seven across the yard is still fer rent."

"Why? Do you want to rent it?"

"No, landlord, it's for a friend. She's a widow."

"Any children?"

"No, she's a widow, but she's expecting one."

"Well I was just about to leave, but I can spare you a few minutes, so you better bring her along."

As soon as Sally hurried back to her home, she told her two lads to get their own tea for once, or wait until she came back.

"But where yer going, Mum?" the eldest boy, Jack, asked.

"We're going ter look at Annie's old 'ouse fer Mrs Waldron."

"What house?" Freddy asked. "Not that buggy old house where Annie Do Dar used to live?" Jack exclaimed.

"Yes, and don't let me 'ear yer call 'er Annie Do Dar! You remember, my lads, she's a poor old woman that's lost 'er mind."

As they walked across the cobbled yard Sally said, "I think yer better look at it before yer make up yer mind."

As soon as they reached number seven, Tilly peeped through the dusty, grimy window. She was disappointed to see everything inside was covered with dust and dirt. An old wooden table, two old, broken chairs, and a cracked mirror hung down from the peeling, plastered wall, and a rusty fire grate piled up with ashes and burnt out old boots. On the floor were patches of well-worn brown lino, and in a small alcove was a shallow brown earthenware sink, but no tap or running water. The water tap was in the centre of the yard, opposite the dry wooden closets, muskins and washhouses.

"How long has it been empty, Sally?"

"About three or four years I should say."

"But why hasn't it been taken before?"

"I don't think anybody wants it. But once it's 'ad everything thrown out and a bit of elbow grease, between us it'll look better, until yer find something better. So you'll 'ave ter make up yer mind, Tilly, before the old miser changes 'is mind."

"Thanks, Sal. Let's go and see how much he'll charge."

As soon as they entered the tiny room he called his office, Tilly noticed at once he was a Jew; with his sallow skin and goatee beard. Also she saw he wore a little black skull cap. His eyes too were black as he stared at her as they entered.

"Sit yerselves down then," he cried out rather abruptly.

As soon as they sat, Tilly noticed he had a habit of rubbing his hands together, which was making her nervous.

"Well, I hear you're interested in number seven."

"Yes, Mister - er, er."

"My name's Abraham Wolfe, or landlord if you're interested, and Mrs Carter tells me you've been looking at the house."

"Yes," she replied.

"Mrs Carter tells me you're a widow and expecting a child."

"Yes, that's correct."

"Well if you're interested, the rent will be six shillings a week. Two weeks in advance."

"Why?" Sally piped up. "That's 'alf a crown more than any of us are paying and it's only got one bedroom and it's in a terrible state. Wants some repairs down to it as well."

"Take it or leave it!" he snapped.

Suddenly tears filled Tilly's eyes as she whispered to Sally, "I'd better take it before he changes his mind."

As soon as he saw the tears, he said he would find someone to do the repairs, when Sally piped up again.

"Me 'usband and me two lads will willingly do what's needed. Cheaper than sending somebody in a month's time. My friend's desperate and wants ter get settled before her babby's is born, and me and Tilly could give it a good clean out," she added.

After he stopped to think and rub his hands together again, he replied, "Well, I think you'd better send Mr Carter to see me at ten o'clock in the morning. Now," he added, as he looked across at Tilly, "I want your name and two weeks rent in advance."

As she paid over the twelve shillings, he gave her the rent book and a key.

As they were both ready to leave he said, "Mrs Waldron, you won't find a better neighbour than Mrs Carter, but I can't say that for my other tenants. And don't forget to tell your husband to look at what repairs want doing and tell him I want them done cheaply."

"No fear of that, landlord. You'll 'ave three men doing the price of one while the lads are on school holiday."

"Very well. Good day," he replied.

As soon as they left Tilly said, "Do you know, Sal, I thought for a minute he was going to refuse me."

"I thought so too, but 'e knows my Fred saves 'im pounds when it comes to the neighbours wanting odd jobs done. 'e always obliges and never charges 'em. But the landlord aint a bad bloke after all, if that Sarah Whalley daint run to 'im to tell 'im tales. Anyway," she added, "I'll give yer a line up later about me neighbours. Now come and 'ave a cuppa with me an' a bite to eat, while I get me 'usband's supper."

It was long before her husband and the two boys walked in. "Hello, Sal," he greeted as he kissed her. "I 'ear you've 'ad a busy day."

"News soon gets around." she replied, "Anyway, this is to be our new neighbour." Sally replied as she introduced Tilly to Fred. "Now let's all sit up ter the table and eat, then I've got a lot ter tell yer."

After they had eaten and Fred and the boys heard all the details, Fred asked Tilly for the key. As soon as she gave it to him, he smiled and said, "Come on you two lads, nothing like the present." Just then Tilly went to help Sally in the kitchen.

Jack was eager to go, but Ted was nervous. He'd heard that the old woman the lads called Annie Do Dar often haunted the old house where she had died. "I aint going," he cried out.

"You'll do as yer told or I'll put me strap around yer," his father cried out as he glared at him.

"Come on," Jack said, "We might find some hidden treasure."

After some persuasion from his elder brother, he agreed to go. While Fred was making the list, he explained the smaller jobs he wanted the boys to do later.

It wasn't long before Fred locked the door after him and as they got indoors they saw their mother was making a bed up on the settee in the front room, and while Tilly was helping in the kitchen, Ted cried out, "Mom, that old 'ouse is filthy and there's bugs. We could smell 'em."

"Be quiet you or I'll shut yer up in there," his dad cried out. "Now, go out and play the pair of yer, I want ter talk to yer mum."

"I've made the list, Sal, but everything 'as ter be thrown out an' burnt. Then it'll 'ave ter be fumigated, an' lots of plastering an' painting and whitewashing the walls. He should be satisfied with what I charge him. Anyway I shall make meself a bit of profit what with me tools an' that 'alf a bag of cement an' lime, sulphur an' whitening I got left from me other jobs, still down the cellar. But 'e aint ter know that. I've worked it out cheap, so now let's 'ope 'e'll agree, an' when its fumigated, I'll start straight away. Anyway, 'ave yer decided where she's ter sleep?" he added.

"I've told 'er I'm makin' a bed up on the settee fer the time being. She's 'ad an 'ard life, Fred, but I'll tell yer about that later," she added.

"She seems a nice person, Sal, an' I can see you like 'er too. Now I'm going ter fumigate that place tonight."

"Nothing like the present," she mimicked, as they began to laugh.

After bringing up the sulphur and an old bucket, he got his two young sons to knock holes in the side. Soon he made his way across the yard to fill up the cracks and holes. Even the chimney was stuffed with old rags, and as he lit the sulphur after standing the bucket on a couple of bricks, he hurried out, locked the door behind him and left it to burn all night.

Next morning, after seeing the landlord, he came back half an hour later. Seeing Sally doing her washing in the communal brewhouse, he asked where Tilly was.

"She's gone to fetch a few groceries while I get on with me washing. Anyway, 'ow did yer get on?"

"A piece of cake," he replied, smiling. "I stuck a few extra bob on the list and when I told 'im what everything would cost, he looked quite satisfied."

"Yer daint tell 'im you already 'ad 'em, did yer?"

"I worn't that bloody daft, Sal. I've done enough cheap jobs for that old skinflint."

There was only one woman who complained: Sarah Whalley who lived in the top end of the yard. She made it her business, like a bobby on his beat, to tell the landlord about the smell. But she didn't seem to get any satisfaction.

*

While Fred was trying to get the house ready, Sally thought it was now the best time to put Tilly in the picture about her neighbours.

They both enjoyed going to secondhand shops for furniture and other things she needed for the house. When all was ordered and delivered, curtains switched by neighbours to nose what the van was bringing, when Mrs Brown brought a pot of tea over just for an excuse to have a nose and a gossip. But Tilly thanked her and said it was very kind of her. As Tilly lit the fire, Sally asked, "'ave yer got enough money ter tide yer over fer yer confinement, Tilly? I know it's been an expensive time for yer, an' there's still your babby to provide for, so if yer need 'elp, don't be afraid to ask."

"But you aint got much yourself, with a family to bring up, but thanks, I'll remember, although you've done a lot for me already, and I thank you, Sal, for saving me from ending up in the workhouse."

"Now, now, no more tears. Oh and before I forget," she added, "don't buy any coal off the wagon. I swear we don't get a proper 'undred weight. The lads will always fetch what yer want from the coal yard around the corner. Now I'll leave yer to settle an' I'll pop round agen ternight."

"Thanks Sal," she replied.

As soon as the two lads came home from school, their mother gave them their instruction. "Now you two, I want yer ter call on Mrs Waldron to see if she wants errands."

Tilly often wished she had told Sally the truth about herself, but she knew she had many miles from her home town and as long as everyone thought she was a widow and was called Mrs Waldron, she felt safe.

PART FOUR

Two months later Sally gave birth to a lovely baby daughter. She had wished she would have a girl. Now she was overjoyed and so was her husband Fred, and the two lads. Later the baby was christened Helen Sarah Carter.

Tilly gave her friend all the help she could until she was well enough to carry on her daily tasks.

Two months went by when Sally noticed her friend was having pains. As soon as she saw how quickly they were coming, she cried out, "Why aint yer sent somebody over ter tell me before now?"

"But I only thought it was belly ache. I thought it was too many plums I'd eaten.

"What plums?" Sally cried out.

When I went shopping I saw these green egg plums. I fancied a few, so bought meself a pound and I ate 'em all."

Suddenly Sally began to laugh, as Tilly began to have another sharp pain. "That aint no bloody plums, Tilly. It's yer babby pushin' its way out, tellin' yer 'e wants ter see its Momma. Now you sit down while I 'urry fer the midwife. 'ow long 'ave yer bin 'avin yer pains?"

"In the night," Tilly replied, as she began to wince again. "But they're coming more often now," she added.

"Now I won't be five minutes. Yer won't 'ave it yet. I'm goin' ter fetch the midwife."

Sally came back to tell her Mrs Grove would be about ten minutes. While Sally was sorting over the baby's clothes that she had given her and putting a kettle and saucepan on the fire to boil, she asked Tilly if she would like a boy or a girl.

"I don't care what it is, Sal! I'm not looking forward to it, whatever it is! I wish I had never become like this!"

"Well Tilly," she replied, trying to cheer her up, "You've 'ad the sweets, now you must 'ave the pains, and don't talk like that! You'll love the babby when yer see it, just like I did when I 'ad my first."

After another twinge, she replied, "I don't like ter say this to you, but I aint looking forward to it, whatever it is! I have no husband and the babby will have no father, and I'm still young. I've seen no life yet!"

"All the more reason ter love yer babby when it comes, an' when you settle down again, you'll find a nice feller what'll love and care for you and your child, an' be a good stepfather too, as the years come and go."

"But I don't want another feller, Sal!" she cried out.

"But why not? You're young and attractive an' you'll think differently when it's all over. I know you're feeling depressed. Every woman feels depressed at times like these. I know you'll feel better when yer 'old the babby in yer arms. Now let's 'ave no more of this silly talk, I can see the midwife comin' across the yard."

The following morning she gave birth to a healthy baby girl. Tilly had a hard confinement. Although, after everything was cleared away, Sally handed the baby over to its mother to be fed, she noticed that she didn't look at the baby while it sucked at her breast and smile down at it, like any other woman, but turned her head away.

She never knew what Tilly was thinking, therefore Sally asked no more questions or gave any lectures. She only hoped everything would sort itself out in the near future.

When the baby was a month old, Tilly christened her Elizabeth, after her mother, but later called her Lizzie. But her mother never really loved her child.

As she grew up, Tilly could see the likeness of Dennis, with the same black wavy hair and big brown eyes and dimples.

But Elizabeth was a pretty child. Also was Helen Carter, who had fair hair, blue eyes and sharp features like her brothers. She was well loved by her dad and her two brothers, Jack and Ted, who often called her Nellie. Her mother adored her for being her only daughter that she had often wanted. The two children grew up together and were life long friends.

Sally didn't want any more children. She was happy now with the family she had already got, but when her daughter Nellie was six years old, Sally knew she was pregnant again. When she told her husband he would have to give her a bit more money, Fred flew into a rage.

"Good God, woman!" he exclaimed. "I aint got no extra ter give! I'm workin' all the bloody hours that God sends, an' I give yer all I can out of me poor wages."

"Well you'll 'avta draw yer 'orns in an' drink less."

"That's me only bit of pleasure I get. You thank yer lucky stars you aint got a man who comes 'ome drunk every night, like some blokes in the yard, an' beat up their womenfolk fer naggin'."

"I aint naggin', Fred, but it teks me all me time now ter mek ends meet and this babby's on the way, I don't know 'ow I'm goin' ter cope."

"Mrs O'Leary seems ter copy an' 'ers got ten of 'em."

"Don't dare ter mention that woman's name ter me. Anyway they lives on parish relief, but I'd sooner tek in washin' agen sooner than ask them fer 'elp."

"Well," he replied after some thought, "I'll see me gaffer an' ask 'im if I can do a few extra hours overtime. But don't bank on it, Sal," he added as he stormed out of the house.

A few days later Sally applied for out-work at the button factory near her home, where she began to card hooks and eyes and linen buttons. Often the boys helped, so did Nellie, also Lizzie while her mother was working as a barmaid at the local Rose and Crown.

The day Lizzie was five years of age, her mother took her into the scullery, where she hurriedly helped to wash and dress her on her birthday morning, and as she stood and looked her over, she said, "Pity I can't get yer a better frock and a pair of boots to fit yer better. But never mind," she added as she began to comb her lovely wavy hair, "yer won't always be in rags and boots with bits of cardboard inside. You'll soon be havin' the Daily Mail issue when yer a little older."

"I wish we was rich, Momma, instead of waitin' fer them an' that rag an' bone man."

"No good yer wishin'," she snapped. "But maybe one day. Now come on or we'll be late. We've got a long way ter go an' me feet ache standing all hours in that bloody pub."

But all this went on deaf ears, for Lizzie was not looking forward to meeting other children, and her friend Nellie Carter.

The old Victorian school was almost dilapidated. It was in the centre of a narrow lane amidst several quaint tumble down cottages. As soon as they arrived at the oak door, her mother impatiently hung on to the rusty bell, almost tugging it from the wall, when suddenly, near their feet, a wooden trap door flew open and an old bald headed man popped his head up.

"Who's that, Mom?" Lizzie cried out with fright.

"'e's the caretaker that looks after the furnice fire to heat the pipes in the school."

"Yower late with that wench, I don't think they'll let yer in, it's fifteen minutes past nine. You'll 'afta cum back at two o'clock."

"Well I aint comin' back at no two o'clock, 'cause I still goin' ter ring till they do come!" she exclaimed.

"Please yerself, missus," he replied as he disappeared below.

Tilly was just about to hang on the rusty bell again, when it fell at her feet. Suddenly the door was flung open and there stood the school master with a cane in his hand.

"Well," he asked, as he eyed them both up and down, "what is it you want?"

"I've brought my daughter Lizzie ter be registered."

"I'm afraid you'll have to come back in the morning before nine o'clock. The infants are all in the middle of lessons."

"I carn't come agen, sir. I've got ter go back ter work or I'll get the push."

"Well you'd better wait inside while I see what the governess says."

While they both stood waiting, they both took stock of the long, narrow, dark painted brick corridor. The top half was painted dark green, the bottom half dark brown. High up on the wall was an iron gas bracket showing a naked flame. Along the whole of the corridor was a long wooden platform about a foot from the ground, where warm iron pipes lay beneath.

As soon as Tilly heard footsteps coming along the corridor, she whispered, "Pull yer bloody stockings up an' wipe yer nose."

As soon as Lizzie wiped her nose on the back of her hand, the governess came up to them. Lizzie noticed at once, and so did her mother, that this woman was middle-aged. She was also a large buxom woman, very stern and austere.

Suddenly she cried out, "You cannot bring that child here today. It's late and the infants are in the middle of their lessons."

"But I've come to register my daughter."

"I'm well aware of that, but you should have been here before nine o'clock," she replied sharply.

"Well I aint teking her back now I come this far!"

The governess, seeing Lizzie's tears, ragged clothes and bare toes peeping from her old boots, she took second thoughts. "Very well, you had better come into the office out of the cold. Follow me," she added. The office was warm, but almost bare of furniture. Just a roll-up desk, a well worn leather chair, also shelves around the walls, which were full of old dusty books and ledgers. Around the wainscoating ran the hot water pipes. There was no fireplace nor carpet on the floor, only bare boards that smelt strongly of disinfectant.

As Lizzie and her mother walked across to the other side of the room their heavy, shabby boots seemed to echo.

As they stood and waited while the governess reached down a ledger, and as she flopped her huge body in the chair, she asked, "Have you any other children attending the school, Mrs -"

"Mrs Waldron me name is, but no I aint, I've only got this one an' it aint likely I'll be 'aving any mower! Yer see it's like this, I'm -"

"I don't wish to hear what you don't want!" she replied hastily. "I'm only interested in your child and her name and age," she added.

"She was five terday an' her name's Elizabeth, after me mother, but I always call her Lizzie."

"Surname?"

"It's Waldron."

While questions were still being asked, Lizzie paid no attention. She had already taken off her old boots to warm her feet on the water pipes. Suddenly her mother yelled, "Put yer boots back on an' tek 'em off the pipes afor yer get chilblains."

Ignoring Tilly Waldron's remarks, she asked "Have you brought the child's birth certificate with you?"

"Yes, Mam," she replied. "Can Lizzie go in the corridor while yer read it?"

"Yes."

As soon as the governess read it, she cried out, "The poor child!"

Tilly knew what she meant as she cried out, "It's me what's ter suffer fer me mistakes! But let me tell you this! She aint the only pebble on the beach in this school!" she cried out angrily.

"Does the child know?"

"No, an' I aint goin' ter tell her neither."

"Well," replied the governess, "she won't know from me, but she will surely find out when she leaves school at fourteen and begins to work. She'll have to show her certificate then."

"Well we'll come to that hurdle when it comes. Now do I leave her here?"

"Yes, you may, after I've had your address, then I'll take her along to sit with the other infants."

"Thank you, mam. Now may I have the certificate back?"

"Yes, but I should put it away somewhere safe until you find the best time to explain. But if you'll be advised by me, don't leave it too late!"

As soon as Lizzie's mother walked across for her daughter, she told her the governess was taking her to the classroom. She pecked Lizzie's cheek and told her to do as she was told and to be a good girl.

"Yes, Mom," was her reply.

As soon as the governess saw Tilly, she cried out sharply, "Now Waldron, follow me quietly to meet your teacher Miss Haddow."

As Lizzie looked around the classroom she saw the infants drawing on a piece of slate with a slate pencil the words, CAT, SAT, MAT from the blackboard.

When the governess whispered to the head mistress that Lizzie was illegitimate, she said, "Oh well we have several here in the upper classes, so I don't think one more will make that difference," replied that hard faced elderly spinster as she threw her head back and tut-tutted haughtily.

"Remember, Miss Haddow, they are all God's children, whether they are born out of wedlock or not! They are to be treated the same as others!" With those sharp words she left the room.

"Come here, Waldron!" she cried out. Then scraping her scalp and looking between her two plaits with staring eyes and the pencil for nits or lice, she was satisfied not to complain.

Lizzie was then given a slate and lead pencil and told to sit in the back row and to copy the letters on the blackboard. With the help of the little girl she sat next to, she was able to manage. But now and again Lizzie kept looking around the room for her little friend Nellie Carter. But Nellie had seen her first. When Lizzie saw her she was about to call out to her, but Nellie opened her eyes wide and warned her by putting her finger to her lips.

Lizzie sat down, she understood as she began lesson one.

Miss Haddow was very strict, but not too unkind, but rules were rules she knew would not be broken. She often felt sorry for some of the poorer children in her class; the ragged clothes they wore which barely covered their nakedness. But as soon as they were six years old and moved up into the next standard, they were sorted out for the Daily Mail issue. The girls were supplied with leather boots or clogs, thick navy blue stockings, thick fleecy lined navy bloomers, a liberty bodice, a gymslip and a navy blue jersey.

The boys had almost the same, except they had a combination instead of bloomers, and britches that came past their knees. Each had a distinguishing mark. Should anyone try to pawn or sell any article, they would be prosecuted.

Lizzie and Nellie enjoyed being at school and being in each class together, and three times a week the glass partitions that separated the classes were pushed back by two strong older boys, for drilling and exercises, and two afternoons the girls were taught to knit and darn.

Ten thirty each morning was playtime for twenty minutes. The iron bell would ring, the children standing to attention like silent soldiers. They dare not move, murmur or fidget until the master led them out to the playground, otherwise they would lose their recreation or feel the bamboo cane on their legs.

There were two playgrounds. The boys had to march in single file like an army, down several steps to their playground below. The girls' was in the upper one, where they ate their meagre sandwich they called their lunch, and play Tic Tac or Ring-a-ring-a-Roses. Some would be lucky to own a skipping rope. Boys and girls were never allowed to mix. After play all were marched back to their classrooms. These were only a few of the strict rules to be carried out by the Master and the Vicar and the Headmistress.

*

Often when Lizzie came home from school she'd find her mother was still doing her part time job at the local pub. Her friend Nellie knew her mother neglected her and often she took her across the yard to her home, where Mrs Carter would have a pot of stewed mutton and vegetables or whatever she managed to buy to eke out her husband's wages. But the children never grumbled. They knew if they did refuse to eat what was put in front of them, it was taken away and placed in front of them for the next meal, until they were glad to eat. But they always relished grey peas and bacon days and pancakes with black treacle.

Nellie's two older brothers would come home straight from school. Sometimes they would wait for their sister and Lizzie and walk home together. They liked to tease Lizzie, but one day Jack went a bit too far and teased her about her squint.

"Do any of the lads think yer giving 'em the glad eye, Lizzie?"

"What yer mean?" she asked.

"When yer squint at 'em."

Suddenly she walked away with tears in her eyes, when all at once his sister kicked his shin. As he cried out Nellie shouted, "She carn't help her looks! 'ave yer ever stopped ter look at yerself? Yer own eyes aint no oil paintin', our Jack. Nor you, our Ted!"

"I aint said nothing," he replied.

"I'm sorry, Sis," Jack said as he was rubbing his leg. "I daint mean fer her ter tek it the wrong way."

"You've hurt her feelings and I'm telling me Mom when I get home."

"Please yerself," he replied as the two brothers walked on.

Nellie ran up the hill to catch up with Lizzie and as they walked towards their home she said, "Don't cry Lizzie. Jack said he was sorry. I'm sure he daint mean it, but I'm still going to tell Mom," she replied.

"I know I aint pretty like you, Nellie, but me Mom ses I'll have ter go ter the school clinic soon. Then when me eye is fixed, I won't be wearing these ugly glasses." After wiping her eyes she replied, "Don't tell yer Mom, Nellie. I don't want Jack to get a walloping. If he's sorry, p'raps he won't tease me agen."

"Alright, but you tell me if he does or anybody else."

As soon as the lads walked into the room, their mother knew at once there was something wrong. "Now what's he bin up to?" she cried out to Ted.

"Nothing, Mom," Ted replied.

"I don't want no lies, so come on, out with it, the pair of yer!"

"T'aint me, Mom, it's our Jack. He's bin - "

Ted got no further, as Jack pushed him away. I don't want you ter tell Mom, I'll tell her meself. I was only teasing Lizzie about her eye and I'm sorry, Mom."

"You wicked boy!" she cried out. "It aint her fault if the measles left her eyes weak."

"I said I was sorry. I won't tease her again."

"See's as yer don't or you'll have not only me to answer to, but yer dad. Now where is she?"

Suddenly Ted piped up, "Here she is with Nellie, coming down the yard."

As soon as they both walked into the room, Nellie couldn't wait to tell her mother. She just blurted out, "Mom, mom, yer know what our Jack's said?"

Before she could say another word, her mother replied, "Yer brother has told me. Now it's up to him to say he's sorry, and if I hear any more nasty remarks about anybody else, you'll be getting yer dad's strap around yer."

After Jack had put his arm around her shoulder and apologised, his mother asked if her mother was at home.

"No," Lizzie replied. "She left a note on the table to say she would be home later."

"Very well, I understand. Now sit yerself down at the table and you, Jack, reach me down another dish fer Lizzie."

Lizzie was always pleased to have a meal with the Carter family, no matter what the pot contained. Lizzie often wished her Mom was like Mrs Carter; always kind and helpful to neighbours' children, which were many in and around Stanley Place.

Her husband Fred had a steady job working at the brewery in Cape Hill and brought his wages home regularly. He was also allowed free beer whilst working, but he loved his weekends when he could go in the local pub and drink with his mates. Some Saturday afternoons he would take the lads to a football match. Villa Park was their favourite team, which the lads celebrated with their dad when they won.

Some Saturday mornings when their dad was working extra hours, they would walk the long journey to Smethwick and watch their dad lifting heavy wooden barrels up from a wooden trap door that opened up on to the street, then lift them on to the brewer's dray which were led by two Shire horses.

Fred never chastised his children. He left that to their mother. Often she would say, "Yer never here Fred when I need yer and when they start their pranks."

His reply would often be, "Don't get yerself all worked up, Sal love. I was a young lad once meself. Let 'em go their own way, they'll find out their mistakes when they're older, like me."

"I hope they'll never be like you, Fred Carter! Always coming home complaining about pains in yer belly after a night on the beer. Bloody "lunatic soup" I call it," she would say.

"I need it," he would reply. I work bloody hard, I bring me wages home an' I've never neglected me kids or beat yer."

"It'd be God help you if yer ever started that!"

Some nights they would argue while the children were asleep, but their quarrels were soon forgotten.

With all his faults Sally still loved her man.

When Nellie was six years old, her mother gave birth to another baby. Sally had never wanted to become pregnant again. She didn't want this child she was carrying, but the day the midwife lay the baby daughter in her arms, she loved her and as happy to see her sucking at her breast.

"Do you know," she said to the midwife, "I daint want this other babby, but now she's here she'll always be loved, but I'm going ter make this me last."

"They all say that, Sal," she replied smiling.

"I really mean it."

"Well thank the Lord you've got over it an' you've got a bonny daughter."

Sally really meant what she said.

As she sat up feeding the baby, she began to think about the past years when she gave birth to twelve children. Now only her two sons and Nellie survived. Now she hoped she would rear this pretty child.

A month later Sally noticed the baby was losing weight. Thinking there was not enough nourishment in her breasts, she began to feed her on boiled crusts of bread and Nestle's milk. The following week she had her christened Faith, hoping and praying she would gain weight.

She began to worry too about her husband, who often came home from work with pains in his chest. But Fred didn't believe in doctors. "Bleedin' quacks," he'd say. "What do they know how yer feel?" But when Sal reminded him it was the lunatic soup he was drinking, he'd reply, "I bloody well need it. It keeps me going when I 'afta work all hours. So don't keep on, woman. You'd have something to moan about if I beat yer like some of the husbands do around here."

"And it would be God help yer if yer start that."

Some nights they would argue after the children had gone to bed, but their quarrels were soon forgotten. With all his faults, she loved him.

Fred soon got well again and little Faith began to gain weight and the Carters lives began to get back to normal: taking in extra washing and worrying about how everything was going to end in the future for her young family.

Sally Carter was forty years of age and still an attractive woman, but the years of poverty sometimes took their toll. But she was a good mother and she often went without a proper meal herself, to feed her family. She knew her husband would never change his ways, no matter how she complained. Yet in her kind hearted way, she wondered why she still loved him.

Her young daughter, Nellie, who was now six years old, often helped her mother in the communal brewhouse, and often would help to mind and nurse her little sister while her mother stood in the pawnshop queues.

Sarah Walley was one of the neighbours who was well known to be an old maid. She lived at the top end of Stanley Close, where she had a large square open space outside her front door, where some children found time to play when she was not at home.

Often the children in the yard would watch in the alleyway, waiting for her to leave. As soon as they saw her turn the key in the lock and hurry down the back entry, they would come from their hiding place, knowing she wouldn't be back until later in the evening. Therefore they never missed an opportunity to play in her wide open space.

It was well known in the Close that she was the oldest tenant, but none of the neighbours liked her. Although she had no family or relations, people wondered why she never liked children and kept herself apart from the neighbours' gossip. Yet she always knew what went on around her.

Also she saw many quarrels, fights, drunken men and moonlight flits through the curtains. She also made it her business to inform the landlord of what was going on. Also she was known sometimes to take in a gentleman lodger, but the neighbours could never understand why they never stayed more than a few weeks.

Sarah had never lived anywhere else; only at number sixteen, where she was born, and when her parents died she had the rent book changed into her name, and occupied the house and all its contents at an extra rent of six shillings and sixpence.

Many of the neighbours envied her the larger house with an extra attic, and she knew this. That's why she kept herself to herself.

She was also a large woman with ample breasts which hung down to her waistline, and her old well worn frock, almost dragged along the floor, which covered a pair of men's size twelve heavy boots.

Her deep-set eyes were like two black shiny buttons and her crooked features seemed to peer at anyone whom she happened to meet. Her nose was almost flat against her face and her discoloured teeth protruded over her bottom lip. Her hair was her best feature, which was always done up in a bun on top of her head, with an ornamented comb. The neighbours never knew her age, but guessed she was about nearing fifty.

Sarah Whalley also had a bad temper if things didn't go her way. But she kept her home clean and tidy and was always seen cleaning and polishing her windows and swilling down the wide pathway that led up to the step of the house. Often too she would be seen on her hands and knees scrubbing the step.

Neighbours envied her wide open space, where they could have hung a washing line across for their washing, also where their children could play and kept a close eye on.

It was a bright sunny spring morning when young Nellie Carter ran across the yard to wish her school friend a happy birthday and to give her a birthday card, which she had saved her pennies to buy. As she knocked on the open doorway she called out, "Are yer in, Lizzie?"

Suddenly her mother replied angrily, "Yes she is in, an' 'er aint cumin' out yet. She's gotta 'elp me clean up befower 'er aunt cums!"

As soon as Lizzie heard her friend's voice, she ran to the door. "I'll be out soon, Nellie," she managed to say, when her mother dragged her back into the room by her hair and kicked the door shut.

Nellie knew about Mrs Waldron's bad temper from experience, so she slipped the birthday card beneath the door and walked away. She knew she would see her friend later that same day.

There was not much joy for children or parents in these close communities. Very seldom love or affection either.

As soon as Mrs Waldron left the house to do her part time job at the "Bull's Head", Lizzie saw her chance and ran across the yard to her friend's house.

As soon as she knocked on the door, Nellie's mother called out pleasantly, "Come in, Lizzie. Nellie won't be long. She's only gone on an errand for the old lady next door. I 'ear it's yer birthday," she added. "I aint got a card for yer, but 'ere's a threepenny bit to buy yerself a few sweets."

Lizzie thanked her and as she kissed her cheek she thought, I wish my Mom was like her.

"'ow old are yer now, Lizzie?" Mrs Carter asked.

"I'm nine terday an' thank yer agin for the threepenny bit."

"That's alright, luv. Pity I carn't give yer sommat else. Anyway, 'ere's Nellie comin' down the yard."

As soon as the two girls met, they flung their arms around each other. "Happy birthday Lizzie. Did yer get me birthday card I pushed under yer door?" Nellie cried out in one breath.

"Yes thank yer, Nellie. Me mom put it on the mantle shelf with hers an' one from your brother Jack and there's one too from me Auntie Ada," she added.

"Did yer get any presents?"

"No, but your Mom was kind. She gave me a silver threepenny bit. But I expect me Auntie Ada will bring me summat wen she cums. I'm nine terday, Nellie, but I wish I was fourteen, so I could werk in a factory an' buy meself some nice clothes, instead of these old rags I wear."

"Never mind, Lizzie. I'm only three months older than you and wen we leave school we'll both go ter werk tergether. Any'ow," she added, "I've managed ter buy yer a few liquorice allsorts."

After thanking her friend, they both sat on the step and shared them. As soon as they were all eaten, Nellie whispered, "Lizzie, I've got a piece of square wood an' a piece of chalk in me pocket ter play 'op scotch with."

"Where did yer get the chalk from? School?"

"No, I broke a piece of me Mom's ball of w'ghtin' wot she does the step with."

"But wun't she miss it?"

"I don't think so, Lizzie. Any'ow, she don't know 'ow much I use wen it's my job ter do the winda ledge."

"Cum on then, Nellie, it'll be betta than a piece of slate wot falls off the roof."

The two girls, knowing that Sarah Whalley was out on Mondays, both decided to use her wide open path to chalk the beds and play hopscotch. They also knew she went out most days and came back in the evenings, so there and then they decided to chalk the beds.

As soon as they were ready to hop and jump, Nellie said Lizzie could go first.

As she began to call out, "One, two, button your shoe. Three, four, knock on the door. Five, six, pick up the sticks," Lizzie got no further. The girls were shocked to see the door of number sixteen flung open wide and saw the old maid glaring down at them.

Suddenly she called out, "I'll give yer bleedin' sticks!" she yelled. "Clear 'orf an' chalk by yer own dowers afower I chuck a bucket of water over yer."

They didn't want telling twice, but before they fled Lizzie stuck her tongue out. Just as they ran into the next alleyway, they collided with Lizzie's mother.

"Now wotcha two buggers bin up to?" she cried out as she held them both fast.

Before either of them could answer, Sarah Whalley came bouncing down the yard. All the neighbours too came to stand on their doorsteps when they heard Mrs Waldron's loud voice, waiting to hear and see what all the shouting was.

As soon as the old maid saw Mrs Waldron, they faced each other like a couple of mad bulls. Red in their faces and hands on their hips, they began to glare at each other as the old maid bawled out, "them two varmints 'ave bin chalkin' by my door agen, an' the next time I catch 'em they'll get a bucket of water over 'em an' it wunt be clean water either!"

"Oh yes?" Mrs Waldron replied, pushing her face close up to her. "I'd like ter see yer try! Two can play at that game," she added.

"Well, I'm bloody well warnin' yer, an' anybody else's kids I catch chalkin' by my dower agen, I'll be tellin' the landlord about it and the other nuisances."

By now all the neighbours were standing on their doorsteps with arms folded, waiting for further results or blows. For there were often fights and hair being pulled out when neighbours lost their tempers.

Yet whatever happened, Tilly Waldron would have the last word, as she turned and shouted for the neighbours' ears too. "You can tell the bleedin' landlord wot ever yer bleedin' well like! An' let me tell yer this, in case some of yer in the yard don't know, I pay my rent regular every wick, not like some I could mention. Now chew on that!" she added.

Before Lizzie's mother could say anymore, several guilty neighbours went in and closed their door.

No more was said until Lizzie's mother almost dragged them both indoors. Slamming the door shut with her foot, she left Sarah Whalley talking to herself.

As soon as they entered the room, Lizzie cried out, "I'm sorry, Mom. We thought 'er was out an' there was now'ere else we could play hopscotch an' we was gooin' ter swill it away, worn't we, Nellie?" she cried out as she turned to Nellie for support. But Nellie was too scared of the look on Mrs Waldron's face to answer. She just nodded her head several times.

"Well wot's the matter with the recreation grounds? Plenty of room theea fer yer ter play 'opscotch! Any'ow if I do find out yer chalkin' by anybody else's dower, you'll get a right beltin'!" Turning to Nellie she shouted, "An' you can bugger orf, Nellie Carter, 'er aint cummin' out agen terday. She's gotta 'elp me tidy up a bit afower 'er Aunt Ada cums."

"Can I 'elp?" Nellie asked.

"No yer carn't! I want no slap dash, so yer betta goo an' see if yer mom needs yer."

As soon as Nellie tried to tell her mother what had happened, her mother replied, "I 'eard all about it, so in future keep away from Sarah's dower, otherwise there might be more trouble."

The girls never liked playing in the recreational ground. It was always full of rough lads of all ages and during the school holidays young gangs gathered there. Often the girls were chased and called dirty names. They also asked them if they still wore their "passion killers". (These were flannel, fleecy lined, navy blue bloomers, supplied each year by the "Daily Mail Fund", with jerseys, combinations and boots to the poorer boys and girls).

The girls knew if they told their mothers what the boys called them there would be more fights between neighbours. But if you had brothers or sisters, they would fight the battles for you. Many would return with a black eye or a thick lip.

Lizzie and Nellie and many young girls alike were used to cat-calls, therefore they found it best to keep away from them and their sick paternal jokes. Yet in later years they learnt how to gang up on their enemies.

Lizzie began to help her mother to tidy the living room and get things ship-shape before her Aunt Ada came to visit. Yet there wasn't much to clear away in this shabby living room. Beneath the window stood an old horsehair sofa which was shredding and hidden by well worn cushions. A square wooden table in the middle of the room, where two backless chairs stood beside the black leaded fire grate, and on the hearth lay a hand pegged rug which covered broken quarries and well worn lino. There were no pictures on these whitewashed walls; just a few cut-out pictures of coloured animals Lizzie had stuck on. The other oddments were a few cracked vases on the mantle shelf that held paper flowers, bills and pawn tickets.

It wasn't long before they heard a knock on the door.

"See who that is, Lizzie," her mother whispered.

As soon as she rushed to open the door, she cried out, "It's me Auntie Ada, Mom."

"Well, call 'er in then!" her mother snapped.

As soon as she saw her niece she kissed her cheek and wished her a happy birthday. Lizzie was happy to see her aunt, who always gave her a present and spoke very nicely. Not like her mother.

As soon as she got inside the living room, she cried out, "I don't know what all the noise was about, our Tilly, but I could hear you half way down the street."

"It's them kids in the yard an' this one 'ere," she replied, staring at her daughter, "chalking in from of that Sarah Whalley's dower."

Tilly knew at once there was going to be an argument, so she sent her daughter out to play, as she didn't want her to overhear whatever she said.

"You can come back when I call you, Lizzie. I'll then have a nice surprise for you," her aunt called out.

"OK, Auntie," she called back as she ran across the yard to see her friend Nellie.

"I can't understand why you can't dress her a bit more comfortable," her aunt cried out. "And that frock she's wearing is the same one she wore months ago! And them boots she's got on with her toes peeping out!"

"Are yer finished?" Tilly exclaimed. "Because if you have, hear this! I aint earning enough ter clothe or keep her in boot leather, when she's always climbing walls or hop scotching, and you don't help me much."

"You should thank yer lucky stars I help you at all, but no doubt you spend it in the pub where you work."

"What's it got ter do with you! Anyway, she's my child and I'll bring her up the best way I can!"

"You call this yer best? Look at yourself, Mom and Dad would turn in their grave if they knew how you've turned out, God rest their souls," she added.

"Let me tell you something, Miss High and Mighty," Tilly replied, hands on her hips. "If my mother had stood by me when I told her I was pregnant, I might never have come to this hole! But no, she cast me out and disowned me."

"Could you blame her, when she knew you was going about with that Sally Handcocks? A really right name for that prostitute," she added.

"Anyway, it's water under the bridge, so don't let's have any more arguments," Tilly replied, as she saw Lizzie coming back across the square.

"Very well, Tilly. But remember this, when Lizzie is fourteen and starts to work, she'll know then she's illegitimate."

"But how? Only you and I know an' she won't find out from me."

"She'll find out sure enough when she has to show her birth certificate before they employ her in a factory."

"We'll come to that when the time comes," Tilly replied.

As soon as Lizzie came through the door, her mother said, "Put the kettle on, Lizzie, and make yer aunt a cuppa."

As soon as Ada and her sister sat down on the backless chairs, Lizzie began to pour out the tea, when she said, "Thank you, Auntie Ada, for me birthday card."

"That's alright, love, but I haven't bought you a present. But seeing the boots yer wearing, I've decided to buy you a new pair."

Suddenly her mother piped up, "That's kind of you Ada, but I don't know what size she takes."

"What do you mean, you don't know her size?" Ada cried out, almost spilling the tea in her lap.

"Well I aint got money enough ter buy her new ones, so she has to do with what she's got until the Daily Mail issue."

"And when's that?"

"Once a year," Tilly replied.

Ada was now beginning to get angry, but thought it would be best to leave before she lost her temper again. Turning to her niece she said, "Lizzie, I want you to put on yer coat and come with me to the market, where I'll buy you a new pair of boots for your birthday."

"Can I have a brown pair, Auntie, like my friend Nellie's got?" she cried out excitedly.

Suddenly her mother piped up, "Beggars can't be choosers! You'll have what yer aunt thinks best!"

"If it's brown she wants, then brown she'll have!" her sister snapped back.

As soon as Lizzie put on her shabby black coat and pushed her iron framed spectacles further along her nose, Ada took hold of her hand.

As soon as they went out she said, "How long have you been wearing those, Lizzie?"

"I think about four years. My teacher saw I couldn't see to read properly, so I had to have me eyes tested at the school clinic. They're ugly, aint they, Auntie? But I have ter wear 'em because without them I've got a squint. Do you think I'm ugly, Auntie?" she added, as she looked up into her face.

"No, love, no. What makes you think such a thing?"

"Sometimes Mrs O'Leary's kids in our school say I am and call me Cross Eyes and Squinty Liz."

"Does your mom know?"

"Yes. But when I tell her, she goes across to her house and they row and fight, so I don't tell her now."

Ada dreaded to think what would happen if they found out Lizzie was a bastard.

"Yer know, Auntie, all the O'Leary kids 'ave got bugs and fleas and they're always being sent home from school with nits, but I don't dare call after them, because there's seven of 'em."

"They'll soon get tired of calling you names when someone else comes along. They're only jealous because you are prettier that them. You've a nice clear skin and two lovely dimples, and your teeth are perfect when you smile, so see that you brush them regularly."

"I do, Auntie. I got a toothbrush they gave me at the clinic and Nellie's mom gave me a threepenny bit for me birthday an' I bought a tin of carbolic powder, instead of cleaning them with soot."

"Now come along little chatterbox," her aunt replied, smiling down at her.

As Ada held her hand again, she noticed people passing by looking down their noses at Lizzie's bare toes that peeped out from her boots. Ada hoped that no one she knew would stop to speak to her, for Lizzie was now looking tired and lagging behind. As they neared the park gates, Ada thought it would be best if she left her niece here for a while. "Lizzie," she whispered, "I want you to go in the park and rest on one of the benches while I bring you back an ice cream, and take yer boots off and put them in this paper bag." As Ada hurried away carrying the old boots, she called out, "I won't be long."

It seemed ages as Lizzie waited for her aunt to return. She began to recall the time her mother left her on that very same bench and promised to return but never came. She then had to find her own way home. She began to wonder if her aunt was ashamed to be seen with her and why she hadn't taken her along with her. She also sensed the people passing by were staring at her stockinged feet. Yet she knew it was nothing unusual to see many girls and boys wearing hardly nothing at all.

"If she don't come soon," she cried out, "I'll put me boots on and go back home." But Lizzie had forgotten that her aunt had taken them with her. She was cold, tired and hungry and the bench seat was hard to her bottom. She began to cry, but decided she would wait a bit longer, when soon she lay down on the bench and fell asleep.

*

Ada went from one shop to another, trying to make the salesman understand. When an assistant came to help, she said, "I want to buy a pair of boots for a girl of ten years old."

"But what size, madam?" he replied, smiling across the counter at her.

"I don't know," she replied.

"Well if you don't know, madam, I can't help you."

Ada was getting angry and felt ashamed to take the old boots from the bag while customers were watching and listening. She hurriedly walked out and seeing no customers in the next shop, she entered.

As soon as she saw the salesman, she hurried towards him, took out the boots from the bag and cried out, "I want a pair of boots this size, but they will have to be about two inches larger, so the toes don't peep out."

"I'm sorry, ma'm," he replied. "If you take them, we can't change them. I think it would be best if whoever they're for is to bring them along and be fitted properly," he added.

Ada was wishing now she had brought her niece along. She knew she couldn't disappoint Lizzie so she hurried to fetch her.

By this time it was nearly five o'clock and it was getting dark, when Lizzie was suddenly awakened by the park-keeper's stick.

"Wot yer doin' sleepin' down theea?" he cried out.

"I'm waitin' fer me aunt," she cried out as she sat up.

"Well yer carn't wait 'ere! I'm waitin' to lock the gates, now bugger orf befower I put this stick across yer arse!"

Tears began to flow as he pushed her outside the wrought iron gates. Just as she was crossing the street, she saw her aunt running towards her. As she put her arms around her, she cried out, "I'm sorry Lizzie, not to get you an ice cream, but I've been busy trying to buy your boots."

Lizzie seeing her old boots in the bag, looked sad and disappointed.

"Daint yer get me any then, Auntie?" she cried out.

"I didn't know yer size, Lizzie, so if you'll slip yer old ones back on, we'll go back to another shop, but we'll have to hurry before they close."

Lizzie couldn't get them on quickly enough, and was pleased to know here aunt hadn't forgotten her promise after all.

They hurried back to the shop and waited until everyone was served, then they walked inside. Ada sat her down on a stool and quickly unlaced Lizzie's boots and hid them underneath the stool.

As soon as she was fitted with a new pair of boots, she began to get excited, running up and down the store. The salesman and Ada began to smile when she cried out, "Aint they lovely, Auntie, an' 'ark 'ow they squeak."

"Yes," replied her aunt. "Now come along, it's getting late and your mom will begin to wonder where we've got to."

After paying for the boots they hurried from the shop, both tired and hungry. But as soon as they had gone a few yards, she heard the salesman call out, "You'll 'ave ter take these old boots away. We don't want them!"

As Ada turned around and saw people gazing at her as he waved the boots in the air, she lost her temper and cried out, "Neither do we! Yer now what to do with them, keep 'em for the fifth of November."

Lizzie was so proud of the first new boots she had ever had, she'd also forgotten now about wanting brown ones, or an ice cream.

As soon as Ada took her home, the first greeting her mother yelled out was, "Where yer bin?"

"We had to wait while other customers were served," Ada replied.

"I thought you'd took 'er 'ome with yer," she snapped.

"I would like to many times and clothe and feed her properly."

Lizzie knew there was going to be a heated argument whenever the sisters met. She didn't like to hear them, so she asked if she could go out and show Nellie and her mom her new boots.

"Yes, an' don't cum back in till I'm ready ter call yer," she snapped.

As soon as the door was closed Tilly cried out, "Pity you aint got a couple of kids of yer own, then p'raps you'd 'ave feelin' fer others!" her sister replied unkindly.

"It's not for the want of trying, but since George came back from France gassed and wounded, he's not the man he was. But I love him and I wouldn't change him now for any man."

"Wot yer mean by that?" she replied, glaring at her sister.

"I'd rather not go into the sordid details, but I hope that one day you will met someone who'll make a good stepfather for Lizzie."

"I've had an' learnt me lesson with men, so don't try ter run my life for me!"

"'as she ever asked who and where her father is?"

"I told 'er 'e was killed in an accident. Anyway, I couldn't tell 'er the truth. I've told yer before, I don't know who 'e was."

As Ada began to shake her head, she replied sadly, "I hope she never does find out the life you once led."

"She won't unless you tell 'er, then God 'elp yer!" she replied angrily.

"She won't want to be told, she'll find out herself when she has to produce her birth certificate when she's fourteen."

"I'll come to that wen it happens," she replied.

"Very well, Tilly, there's nothing more I can say, so I'll say goodnight, and tell Lizzie I'll see her again in another month's time."

Tilly asked if she'd like to stop and have a cup of tea.

"No thanks," she replied, "I'd better be getting home."

"Please yerself, Ada, an' thank yer fer Lizzie's birthday present."

"That's alright, but if I find out you try to pawn these, there'll be sparks flying," she replied as she closed the door behind her.

Lizzie was proud of her boots and when she went to school she often put on extra pressure to make them squeak louder.

But her mother was not so happy when Lizzie's teacher told her would be no boots for her daughter that year, but she was due for Daily Mail clothes only.

*

Sally packed her husband's lunch ready for him to take to work, when he said, "Sal, I don't think I'll go in terday."

As she turned to ask him why, she cried out, "My God, Fred, yer look as white as a sheet. Is it yer stomach agen?"

"No love," he managed to say. "It's this pain in me chest."

"I think yer better go back ter bed and I'll send for the doctor."

"I don't want no bloody doctor! I've told yer before!" he snapped. "Anyway, I'll go back ter bed and lie down awhile."

"Very well. It might be that you've caught the 'flu. Now get back and get into bed and keep warm."

"Will yer tell Paddy next door ter tell 'em at the brewery I'll be in termorra."

As soon as she had fed the baby, she went and told his workmate. Paddy told her he was sorry and that he'd been complaining about his chest several times, but would take the message.

After she went upstairs and took a hot water bottle up, he said his feet were cold, so she hurried downstairs again and wrapped the hot oven plate in a piece of flannel and put it on his feet.

"I'll be back and bring yer a hot drink and a couple of Beecham's pills when I've got the kids off ter school."

As soon as they came downstairs, she gave them their porridge and told them to be as quiet as they could, that she had a headache. She never liked lying to the children, but she didn't want them to know their dad was in bed.

As soon as they'd eaten their porridge, they kissed their Mom's cheek and left.

Sal made some gruel, but when she took it up, her husband was fast asleep.

Several times during the day she went to attend to his needs and asked if he would like to get up for a while. When he came downstairs, Sally could see he was restless, and when she asked him if there was anything she could do, he replied, "I think I'll go fer a walk, Sal."

"Will yer be alright, Fred? Do yer want me ter come with yer?"

"No love, I might slip in the pub and have a drink."

"Well don't get having too much, if yer want ter go back ter werk termorra!" she called out as he went out.

Fred went back to work next morning with his neighbour Paddy and everything was back to normal. Then a few days later, she noticed little Faith wasn't eating her food again. She took her to the doctor's. When he examined her, he gave Sally a bottle of Parishes Food and told her to bring her back in a week's time. When she asked what was wrong, he replied, "Just teething troubles." But she knew it wasn't teething troubles: the baby was losing weight.

When she got home, she sat down and wept, "Oh God," she cried out loud, as the tears ran down her cheeks. "Am I to lose this one who never asked to come on this earth? Please answer me or give me a sign to tell me she'll live."

When she took the baby to the doctor's again, he said there was nothing more he could do, only that she was to be given her medicine and with love and care she would improve.

After a few days little Faith seemed to look better and began to eat. Instead of now watching over her, her mother was able to leave her asleep in the basket while she went across the yard to do the washing, but several times she was anxious to go and see if she was still asleep. A week later when she was sharing her washday with Mrs Willis, she heard Mrs O'Leary call out, "Yes, she's in the brew'ouse doin' 'er washin'."

Two more neighbours came to see what all the commotion was about, when Mrs Talbut and Mrs Freer fled across the yard and called out, "Sal! Sal! Cum quick! There's a copper wants yer! I don't know wot 'e wants, but we daint tell 'im anythink!

"O my God," she cried out, "I wonder if it's trouble with me lads?" Quickly she threw off her wet hessian apron and with soapy arms and hands she rushed across the yard and called the officer inside. After wiping her wet hands down her shabby frock, she picked up the baby and flopped down into the armchair. "Wot's the trouble, officer? Is it me lads? Or Nellie?" she cried out as she stared at him.

"Is your name Sally Carter?" he asked.

"Yes, that's me name, but what's happened?"

"Now calm yourself, Ma," he replied, as he could see she was shaking all over. "I'm sorry to tell you that your husband has collapsed on his way to work. We would wish you to go to Dudley Road Hospital as soon as possible."

Sally was in tears. She couldn't believe what she was hearing. "Are yer sure it's me husband, officer? He aint dead is he?"

"No," he replied, "but we would like you to get there as soon as possible."

"I must give me babby some titty first," and as she bared her full breast and pushed the nipple into the baby's mouth, the officer gave a pleasant smile, put on his helmet and left.

As soon as the baby was fed she called outside to one of her neighbours, "Maggie, will yer look after me babby? I've gotta go to the hospital. Me husband's been took there."

"Course I will, Sal. Now 'urry yerself an' I 'ope yer find 'im betta when yer get theea."

"'ave yer got any money fer yer tram fare?" Mrs Ellis called out.

"No, I was wanting ter get me washing dry ready for the pawn shop."

"Well 'ere's a tanner," the other neighbour said, "It'll get yer theea an' back, an' a cuppa tea."

"Thanks, Aggie, yer a good neighbour," she managed to say.

As Sally kissed the baby and thanked the neighbours, she drew her well worn shawl around her shoulders and hurried for the tram.

The kind neighbours finished Sally's washing and hung it out to dry.

As soon as she arrived at the hospital, she was told her husband had passed away. She was now a widow of forty one years old, her only bread winner gone, and now four hungry children to feed and clothe. There was only the Welfare Relief she could turn to, or send the children to a home.

Neighbours did their best to help, but everybody in and around that area were almost in the same boat. Kind neighbours went knocking at door to door where the Carters were well known, collecting a few coppers for wreaths.

Mrs Ellis was surprised when they knocked on Sarah Whalley's door and she handed them two shillings, and her man lodger gave them five. Many people found it hard to write their names on the collecting sheet, therefore they put a cross.

When the total was counted, it came to seven pounds, two shillings. That same evening Lizzie's mother collected an extra two pounds three shillings from customers and the landlord of the "Rose and Crown".

Next morning Tilly decided to go to the florist's for a wreath. As soon as she walked inside the door she asked to see Nora. When she came she said, "Nora, we've collected a few pounds, me and the neighbours, and we've all decided to give Sal the money, so could yer be so kind as to make up a nice wreath? I know Tilly and me will be ever so grateful."

"That's alright, Tilly, I'll make it up fer nothing and I'll send me husband around with it."

"Thanks, Nora. I'm sure she'll be thanking you herself after it's all over."

After the funeral Sally put a message in the newspaper shop window, thanking them for all their flowers, wreaths and money.

Several weeks went by and she tried to settle down to the old routine and took in extra washing to eke out the family budget.

One afternoon, while Tilly was getting dolled up ready to go to the "Rose and Crown" she noticed Sally was trying to hand out a heavy grey blanket to dry. Tilly went out across the yard and took it off her.

"Leave that ter me!" she cried out, "yer look done in. You go and put the kettle on while I finish hanging yer washing out."

"Thanks, Tilly, I could do with a break," Tilly replied to her friend. She knew taking in too much washing was getting her down at times. Until one day her luck seemed to change. Lizzie came to tell her there was a part time job at the "Rose and Crown".

"Me? A barmaid? I don't know the first thing about pulling a pint."

"It's alright Sal, there's nothing to it. I've spoken to the Missus. She said she'll show you the ropes and I shall be there, so if yer interested you're ter go and see her tonight."

"But I've only got this black frock I stand up in, an' who's going ter look after me babby?"

"Surely Nellie's old enough ter mind her till yer get back? Now if you'll mek up yer mind, I'll lend yer a couple of frocks I know will fit yer, so if yer come back with me after the lads have gone ter bed, I'll do yer hair and mek yer presentable."

As soon as the lads had settled down to sleep in their attic bed, Sally explained to her young daughter about the job.

"I think it will be better, Momma, than all this wet washing around the room when it rains, and I'll look after me little sister."

After giving the baby the breast and laying her down in the basket, she kissed her and said, "If she wakes or she's any trouble or restless, come and fetch me."

After hugging and kissing Nellie, she hurried across to her friend's house to get fixed up. But it was a nine days wonder when the neighbours saw Sally in a red and white check frock. "Fancy that," they was heard to say, "an' 'er husband still warm in 'is grave."

"And 'er werkin' in that pub with that widda, Tilly Waldron," Mrs O'Leary cried out.

"An' 'er in that frock wen 'er should be in black fer at least six months," Mrs Freer replied.

But it was as well that Sally or Tilly never heard their gossiping.

She got along well with Mrs Allen and her husband, George, owners of the pub, and she was told to call them Rose and Bill. She felt at home there, knowing some of the customers who lived near, also George Freer, Jack Tarply and Pat O'Leary, also Sarah Whalley's new lodger, who sometimes saw her to her door after closing time. All went well for about two weeks.

One night Sally came home to find Nellie crying, with the baby on her lap. Fearing the worst, she took the baby from her, when she cried out, "What's the matter with her?"

"She's been asleep ever since you left and I aint bin able ter feed 'er."

"Don't cry love. She's alright. She'll wake up shortly when her's hungry."

Sally knew in her heart this was not teething trouble. She wrapped the baby up warm and caught the last tram to Dudley Road Hospital, where she was told the baby had a wasting disease. There was nothing to be done but to take her back home.

Next morning the baby died.

They had all loved that frail little baby and couldn't understand why God had taken her.

Everybody in the yard paid their condolences, but life had to go on. After the funeral tongues began to wag again, gossiping at each other's doors.

But Sally did not care any more. She did her duties to her two lads and Nellie during the day, and after the lads had gone up to bed, Nellie stayed up until her mother came home.

She was a good help and so was Lizzie who came each night to help tidy and dust and play Snakes and Ladders. Some nights the lads would creep downstairs and play also.

But Lizzie was not allowed to stay out later than nine o'clock. At five to, she would run across the yard and be in bed asleep before her mother came home, otherwise she knew her mother would beat her.

Sally had never beaten her children. She always believed the last of her tongue was enough.

Nellie was now nine years old. Ted was twelve and Jack was thirteen. Nellie and Lizzie liked their new girls' school in Spencer Street, also their teacher, Miss Frost. The boys still stayed at the boys' school. They both got along well with their headmaster, but Ted always felt nervous when the vicar came to call.

*

The vicar was a large, well built man with rugged features. It was well known in the district that he had been a heavyweight boxer in his early days. He also had a broken, crooked nose to prove it. It was also known he didn't like girls. It was always, "And how are my boys this morning?" Although many of the lads didn't like him, they knew they dare not show it.

When the girls reached the age of about eight or nine years old, they were transferred to a girls' school where they were able to leave at fourteen. These girls had already been well disciplined at the mixed school, which helped them with their further education.

One day during the summer, Nellie was told to go to Baines's bread shop for a loaf of bread. "But why carn't I go to the Co-op, Mom? It's a penny cheaper there."

"You'll do as yer told. Anyway the bread's always stale from there, nor they never give yer a mek weight."

"That's why it's a penny cheaper," she replied.

"Never you mind how cheap it is, I want a new loaf from Baines's."

As soon as Nellie arrived at the bread shop and saw the vicar coming, she hid behind the door. Mr Ellis was already talking to Mr Baines when the vicar entered, but no one saw or knew Nellie was there listening, when she heard the vicar say, "I've called to see you both about the roof. You know, Mr Baines, I have already explained that the roof will be paid out of church funds. I'll call and see you again, my good man. Are you coming my way, George?" he added.

"No, sir, I've got an errand ter do fer me missus."

"Very well, I'll call and give you instructions what's to be done."

As soon as they left the baker went into the other room, when Nellie knew it was safe now to ring the bell on the counter and ask for a loaf. As he weighed it, she saw it didn't weigh quite two pounds, so he made it up with an extra piece of bread, which was called the "make weight".

As soon as Nellie got home with her loaf, she told her mother she'd seen the vicar in the bread shop and what she'd heard.

"He's p'raps going ter have the roof mended."

"But why's that? Baines's are closing down."

"How do you know?"

"I saw the notice in the window."

"That's news ter me, Nellie. I'll find out why."

Sally gave the children their tea and when they finished she left them to play Tiddly Winks while she went across to see the Ellises.

When she knocked on the door and told to come in, Sally didn't expect to see Mr Ellis there, smoking his pipe and reading the "Buff". Suddenly she said, "I'm sorry, I didn't know yer husband was in."

"Don't mind me," he answered, smiling as he added, "I'm only the bloke who lives 'ere."

"Stop yer silly twaddle an' let's 'ear wot she's come for," she replied.

"I aint come ter borra anything, but I wanted ter know if yer knew Baines's bread shop was closing down."

"How do you know, Sal?"

"My Nellie heard the vicar and you talking about putting on a new roof over the stable."

"Yes we know, daint we George? It's a big stable an' there's a lot ter be done, so the vicar asked George ter 'elp."

"But it's been like that fer years. Why are they leaving?"

"You bloody women," he cried out, as he threw the racing paper down. "Yer wants know the end of a bull's bloody arse! Anyway yer may as well know, the whole street'll know soon enough. Baines 'as sold up, the 'orse an' cart 'ave already bin sold, an' the vicar 'as bin given the stable. 'e's thinking of opening it as a kind of boxin' club, ter teach the lads ter box instead of fightin' in the bloody street. Does that satisfy yer?"

"That's a good idea," Sally replied. "Thanks for telling me. It was only the other day when I seen the vicar in the street banging two lads heads together fer fighting."

Two weeks later the roof was on, the wet straw and manure were cleaned away. The builder's yard nearby sent sand for the floor, also thick ropes were donated for the good cause and a collection was given from everyone for boxing gloves.

*

Sally Carter was still an attractive woman. She loved her job as a barmaid, but her young daughter and the two lads didn't like her working in the pub and coming home late at night. But Nellie said as long as their mother was happy, they shouldn't interfere. But the lads and their sister stayed up until their mother came home.

It was during this period that Jack noticed his brother was playing truant. One day he caught him hiding in the brewhouse.

"What yer 'idin' away from, when yer see the vicar come to the 'ouse?"

"That's 'is excuse, Jack. It aint Mom 'e cums ter see. It's me."

"You? Why you?"

"I don't like the way 'e grins at me an' when I see 'im comin' I'm scared."

"But why?"

"I don't like the way 'e strokes me 'air an' pats me face. Once 'e put 'is arm around me waist an' squeezed me an' asked me if I would like ter join the choir. When I said no, that I couldn't sing, he said, "Oh yes you can, I've heard you. Anyway, I want you to come into the vestry when the others have gone and I'll teach you." An' when 'e left 'e turned around and smiled that lopsided grin 'e 'as."

"You're imagining it," Jack replied, smiling.

"I don't imagine it! An' I'm not the only one 'e singles out after class!"

"You've got some queer notions, our Ted."

"No I aint! 'e's the queer one!"

His brother could see he was upset so he tried to change the subject. "Did yer know 'e's opening a boxing club and he's going ter teach me ter box with gloves on, and he wants me ter help him ter teach other lads."

"Watch 'e don't fondle you then!" Ted replied.

"He won't dare ter try it on me, or else 'e'll get what for. Anyway, yer better not tell Mom. Yer know how upset she gets, and if he tries anything else, you come and tell me."

*

Jack liked sparring with the vicar, but when it came time for him to box with tougher lads than himself, he thought more of his handsome features. When he caught a bleeding nose and a black eye, he told the vicar to find another punching bag.

"You've got to be tough, my boy, if you want to get on in this world. Anyway," he added, "how's your brother Ted? Can't you persuade him to come along?"

It was on the end of Jack's tongue to mention why Ted disliked him, but he thought not.

"I don't think it would wise, vicar. You see Ted's leaving school in a few days' time, and I spoke to my boss and we'll be coming home from work together."

Their mother was feeling more contented now that the lads were earning and brought their wages home. But Nellie felt lonely that her two brothers had found friends outside their home. She didn't see much of her mother now she was working at the "Rose and Crown". Sometimes her friend Lizzie came and stayed with her when Tilly wasn't home. But the lads didn't like their mother working as a barmaid. They thought there was no need now they were earning.

Then one night as they sat eating rabbit and bacon stew that Nellie had cooked, Jack looked across the table at his mom and as he lay down his knife and fork, he said, "Mom, we don't like you working in that pub and coming home late at night."

"But what's brought this up all of a sudden?" she cried out.

"Well we didn't mind when you was part time, you was always here. Now yer working full -"

"So you've been discussing this between yer!" she exclaimed.

"Yes, Mom," Ted replied. "But now we don't see much of yer and we're in bed when yer get back home."

"Well Nellie's quite capable of cooking and looking after yer needs."

"That's not the same, Mom, and Nellie don't cook like you."

"I do me best, Jack and you Ted, but I'd rather Mom be here ter do fer us!"

"You too Nellie! You've been discussing this between yer! Now you listen ter me. I like me job, I've never neglected yer, and I think the three of yer are being unfair, and I think you're a bit mean to begrudge my bit of pleasure. But remember this, the three of yer! If I was out all hours and neglected yer like Lizzie's mother does, you'd have something to grumble at! Now finish yer supper. I don't want to hear another word."

"But Mom, couldn't you go back part time?" Jack replied.

"What yer want me to do? Give up the job altergether and tek in washing and carding hooks and eyes and buttons agen?"

"No, Mom, but -"

"No more buts, and don't think because yer father's not here anymore, God rest his soul," she added, "you can tell me what to do!"

"But we're only thinking of you, Mom. It's about time you stayed at home and took things easy. You know we all love you," Jack added.

"I know that. I love you too and you, Ted, and Nellie. Now I don't want any more disagreements. This is our first and I want it to be the last! But I'll promise you this, in another few weeks, when I've saved enough for what I need, I'll give in me notice. Now off ter bed you two, and Nellie," she added, "you can help me with the dirty crocks."

No more was said until several weeks later.

Sally Carter enjoyed life working at the local. The customers, knowing Sally and Tilly were two widows, they were often treated to a drink or tips and a tease. Although Tilly would lead them on and sometimes make a date, Sally always refused. She loved her home and family not to go gallivanting after hours with someone she didn't even know.

Often Lizzie would come and stay with Nellie until it was time to be in bed before her mom came home, as she was often fast asleep. Yet her mother was always downstairs first, getting their breakfast ready in time for Lizzie to be ready for school.

She often wondered why her mother was always late coming home, but she knew she dare not ask a second time. There was always lies and once she beat her when she told her mother how neighbours were gossiping.

Sally knew that her friend Tilly was dating different men and knew what she was doing was all wrong, but she knew it was none of her business to interfere. Tilly was a widow, like herself, and could do as she pleased. Although at times Sally gave her some good advice, she ignored it.

Sally's only thought was Tilly's daughter, whom she loved like her own and where Lizzie spent more time in her home with her friend Nellie and her two brothers, Jack and Ted.

Sally Carter was content with her own life, her home and her young family, who were now growing up, to bother herself about another man. Although she was still an attractive woman and had many propose marriage to her, but always refused. But human nature has its twists.

One bitterly cold night there was a storm threatening with thunder and lightning. Many of the customers had already left the pub earlier before the rain began to beat down. Only three of the locals stayed, who only lived a few yards away.

Sally was helping in the bar, as it was Tilly's night off, and as Sally's three neighbours pulled up their stools nearer the iron piped stove, a short, stocky stranger almost fell inside the door from the wind and rain.

George Ellis, Paddy O'Leary and Pat Freer stopped talking, to stare at this handsome stranger as he made his way to the counter and ordered a double whisky.

As soon as Sally brought him a glass, she said, "Would you like me to take yer hat an' coat to dry?"

"That's very kind of yer, Missus."

"Sally's me name," she replied, smiling.

"Well thank yer kindly, Sally," he replied, as he took off his hat and coat. As she hung them up to dry, she cried out to her three neighbours, "Move over you chaps. Let the feller see the fire."

As Paddy drew up a stool for him, he asked, "Where yer from, stranger?"

"Me name's Ben Twigg an' I live with an aunt in Smethwick."

"That's a long way from 'ere," Pat replied.

"I missed me train an' I thought I'd walk, but then this damn storm came an' I lost me way. But I'll be on me way as soon as this rain gives over."

"Well," the landlord piped up, "yer wunt get theea ternight if this storm keeps up, but I can put yer up fer bed an' breakfast."

"Thank you, landlord. I think that will be best, until I can find out about me train."

He ordered another whisky and asked the three men to have a drink, Sally too. But Sally politely refused, but she was surprised when they asked for three whiskys, for they only ever drank beer. But the landlord was pleased to have a good customer.

While Paddy, George and Pat were busy talking to the landlord, the stranger whispered to Sally if it was alright to stay there for a night.

"Oh yes," Sally replied, "you have me word for that. An' he's a good landlord. Anyway," she added, "If he couldn't have put yer up, I'd have managed ter put yer up at my house. I wouldn't see a dog out on a night like this. Only me lads wouldn't be pleased, if yer know what I mean?" she added, as she smiled.

"Yes, I understand," he replied, returning her smile. "You're married then?" he added.

"I'm a widow," she replied, "with two young sons and a daughter, and I live across the street."

She wondered why she was telling this stranger about herself. But Sally only had the locals to talk to and it was nice, she thought, to see a stranger to talk to, instead of the usual everyday faces. She was beginning to like this dark haired man, with rather high cheek bones and smiling blue eyes and well built with broad shoulders and slim waist, and hoped he would call again when she knew he'd be gone the next morning.

As the rain eased off for a while, it was now time for Sally to leave. When he asked if she had far to go, before she could answer Paddy piped up, "It's alright, matey, she's our neighbour. We always see her to her door." Sally was a little disappointed. She would rather have let this feller see her across the street, so that she could talk and ask him about himself, but she knew she couldn't refuse her neighbour's offer, for one or the other always saw her to her door when it was closing time. But she hoped she would see him again before he left the next morning.

Sally wondered why she kept thinking about him. She didn't know him from Adam, but she knew she liked this stranger.

Next morning and she was up earlier than usual and, after seeing her two sons off for work and Nellie to school, she did her home chores and left soon after to go across to the Rose and Crown to do her duties.

Her two young lads had never liked their mother working as a barmaid. Often she had told them that it was only for a short time, until she could save enough money that was needed.

One morning as she was packing the lads' sandwiches for work, Jack brought up the subject again.

"Mom, now we're bringin' in a wage, there's no reason fer yer ter work at the local."

"I'll be giving it up as soon as Nellie starts ter work."

"Why? That'll be another eighteen months, Mom."

"I know. But remember this, both of yer! I don't neglect yer, do I?" she snapped.

"No, Mom, but you'll get a bad name, like Lizzie's mom."

"No fear of that, son. Now hurry or you'll be late for work. And you, Ted, yer better get a move on."

"Well, yer will promise us soon, won't yer Mom?" Ted replied.

"Yes, I promise. Now here's yer sandwiches," she replied as she kissed them both and waved to them from the doorway.

After doing her home duties, she was now ready to go to the local, hoping the stranger was still there.

*

As she entered, she looked around, a little disappointed seeing he was not about, when the landlord cried out, "Hello, Sal. You're early."

"Yes," she replied, "I wanted to get away early tonight. 'as he gone?" she added.

"Yer mean Ben? No, he's still having his breakfast in the kitchen. Now leave what yer doin' and listen ter me. Last night after you left he kept asking about you. He also said he'd like ter see yer agen some time. Now, Sal, he's got plenty of lolly and he seems a decent sort of bloke."

"Don't be daft Fred. Money aint everything. Anyway, he could be married."

"Well he told me his wife had been killed in a train accident three years ago. He has no family and lives with an old aunt."

"But why yer telling me all this? I only met him last night."

"Ah, but I could tell the way he looked at yer and you at him. Now if he asks yer ter see him agen and yer like him, there's no harm in seeing him agen, if he should call this way agen, is there, Sal?"

"I'll have to think about it," she replied.

"Remember, Sal, yer won't have yer family for long when they start spreading their wings and leave yer. I know from experience."

"I'll cross that bridge, Fred, when I come to it."

"Well the opportunity might be here, so don't leave it too late. Yer gettin' no younger, Sal, an' I'd like yer to have a decent bloke, not someone from around here, the sort that Tilly cottons on to," he added.

"Have yer finished, Fred, because I'd like to get on with me job."

"Very well, Sal, but think over what I've said. Me wife would say the same if she was here."

As soon as he left to go into the tap room, Ben Twigg came into the bar carrying his briefcase, ready to leave.

"Good morning, Sally," he cried out as soon as he saw her. "I'm glad to be able to see you before I leave, and to thank you for our little chat we had last night."

"That's alright, Ben. There's not too many strangers come this way. When they do, it's my job to be pleasant and welcome them, whether I like them or not," she replied, smiling.

"I'm really sorry. I would like to talk to you some more, but I have a train to catch. But before I go, I would like to see you again when I'm this way."

"Yes, I'd like that, Ben," she answered.

As they shook hands, he gently kissed her cheek, and as soon as he'd left, she hoped it wouldn't be too long again before he passed this way again.

*

It was now a few months later, when Jack and Ted were put back on full time, that their mother gave in her notice. She thought it was now about time to attend fully to her childrens' needs. She seldom gave another thought of ever seeing Ben again and tried to put him from her mind, but there were still odd times when she thought about him.

Although Sally loved her children dearly, she was missing the love and comfort of a man around the house. Since her husband had died, she had never thought of anyone else taking his place. But now she had mixed feelings about this friendly stranger, Ben Twigg.

Three days before Xmas, while she was putting up the Xmas trimmings, she heard a knock on the door. As soon as she opened it and saw who was there, she cried out, "Ben!"

"How are you, gal?" he smiled broadly, as he entered the room.

"I'm fine. It's lovely to see you again."

"I've brought you a little present. Just a box of chocolates."

"You shouldn't have, Ben. Anyway, thank you."

"I thought being it was Xmas time, we could go over to see the landlord and have a drink."

"I haven't been in there for months. Not since I gave me notice in."

"Yes, he told me. That's how I found out where you lived."

"Well if you wait a few minutes while I spruce meself up a bit," she replied.

"No need, Sal. You look lovely as you are."

Talk about flannel. He was a right real charmer.

As soon as they entered the Rose and Crown, Fred was pleased to see them. "P'raps you'd like ter go in the smoke room, where it's quieter there," Fred said knowingly that they wished to be alone and it was empty.

"I'd like a double whisky, Fred, and have one yourself. Would you like one, Sally?"

"Why not, it's a festive occasion. But I'll have mine topped up with water."

"After, would you like me to take you out for a meal?"

"I'm sorry, Ben, I'd love to, but I have to be home for when the lads come home from work. But you're welcome to come and eat with us."

"I think I'd like that, Sal. But there's no hurry yet, is there? I want to talk to you about myself. I hope you don't think I'm pushing, Sal, but ever since that first night I believe I fell in love with you, and I've thought of nothing else."

"But why have you left it all these months before coming back here again?"

"Well I gave my other job up and now I'm prospering."

"What doing?" she replied eagerly.

"I'm travelling, selling and buying household goods from door to door, taking orders."

"You mean like a pot man."

"Well, not quite".

"Well, she replied smiling you'll get more knockings than payments around this area".

"I've a car now well it's a converted van" he added "Where I'll be travelling to other districts with my wares, but now I'm looking for lodgings".

"But I thought you said you lived with an aunt?"

"Er- Er- died, but she lift me several pounds, but I expected to take over the cottage and furniture, I was shocked to hear it was rented furnished" he lied "I was hoping I could see more of you and your family, Sal".

"You're welcome to visit us anytime, but I've never taken another man into my home since my husband died three years ago, and my children, I know, wouldn't agree".

"I don't ask for any thing more than ter be a friend Sal, and to know you better. Will you have another drink before you go Sal?" he added.

"No thank you Ben, I have to hurry, I'll see you in here tomorrow as I want to tell my children about you first".

She was surprised when he kissed her on the cheek.

As she entered her kitchen to see how the pot of stew was coming along, she had a feeling she was going to like him. But Sally had a lot to learn from this charming plausible man.

As soon as her children had their supper Sally began to tell them about Ben, and how she came to meet him. Although Nellie and Ted where listening, Sally could see the frowns gathering on her eldest son's face.

"Stop staring at me! Like that Jack, he's only a friend, and I've already invited him here, so I want you ter behave yourself.

"I knew summat like this would 'appen, once you worked there!" Jack cried out as he sprang up from his chair. "But if I don't like him! He'll bloody well soon know it!"

"Well you just behave! That's all and don't think because you're me oldest you can say as you wish ter me!"

"Mom's right" Nellie piped up, she's always worked hard ter bring us up respectable, and now if she wants a man friend who are we ter say otherwise, yer gettin' too big for yer boots, Jack, since you and Ted started ter work!"

"You leave me out of this! Ted replied "I don't care one way or any other."

"Now! Now!" Sally exclaimed "I don't want to hear you quarrelling, but if it will satisfy you, I won't invite him here."

"Mom, you invite him" Nellie replied "And let's us see for ourselves if we like him or not."

"I'll do just that, I like him, but only as a friend, I didn't say I was going ter marry him! Anyway I've invited him to have Xmas dinner with us."

No more was said apart from a few sulks from Jack, who later said he also had invited two work mates for Xmas dinner too.

Xmas eve, the two lads went out and brought in a turkey, and while Sally and Nellie were helping each other to prepare it, the lads went out again to buy holly and mistletoe.

In the corner of the room opposite the black leaded range was a small Xmas tree already laden with gifts. While Sally and Nellie were frantically making sure everything was ready, the two lads went to meet their two work mates. Jack introduced them to his mom and sister.

"Happy Xmas" They chorused as they all shook hands.

"Now sit down lads" Sally said "And Ted you'll find beer and pop in the kitchen."

"I'll slip out and fetch a bottle of whiskey" Jack cried out.

"No you stay where you are I want yer ter meet Ben first."

"Where is he hidin'? Under the mat is he? Jack replied sarcastically.

"Now just you behave yourself, I don't want any nasty remarks while he's here, any how he comes across the yard.

As soon as Ben knocked on the door, Nellie ran to open it and greeted him. "If yer names Ben you're welcome, my names Nellie and a Merry Xmas."

"A Merry Xmas to you Nellie." He replied smiling down at her.

As soon as he came inside the room and say four boys he began to wonder who they were, until Sally introduced him. "These are my two sons Jack and Ted the other two lads are their work mates Alf and Bill."

"Ok, Sal, If I'd known I would have brought another bottle of whisky with me, never mind" he added "I think there's enough to go round, if not, I'll take 'em out this evening and treat 'em."

"Well thanks for the whisky Ben, I was just going out ter buy one, so its saved me a few bob anyway shall I open it now Mom?" Jack asked as he turned his back on Ben.

"It's better if you ask Ben!" Sally replied furious at his rudeness, but not wishing to make a scene, she went into the kitchen calling out "Yer dinner will be ready in a few minutes."

While Sally and Nellie where still dishing up their dinner jack poured out only four tumblers. Ben stung by his bad manners took an instant dislike to him. As soon as the four lads drank their whisky, Jack finally turned around and said "I'm sorry mate I forgot yer was 'ere, anyway here's yer bottle, yer can 'elp yourself, no doubt yer drink more than us."

"Yes" Ben replied, stung by the insult "Seeing I'm a grown man, I can take my liquor or anything you like to give out with your sarcasm."

"Oh! I really did ferget you was here" Jack replied slyly glancing at his friends.

Ben thought about calling him a liar, but he didn't want to pick a quarrel with him on his first visit, he thought there would be plenty of time when he would get him alone.

Jack was about to make another nasty remark when Ted nudged him "Not now Jack" he whispered "Yer know what Mom said."

"Oh all right" Jack replied with a sneer, shrugging off his brother's hand. As they all sat down to their meal, Ben ignored Jack and after gifts were exchanged the four lads left to end up in the Rose and Crown, leaving Ben, Sally and Nellie to clear away and wash the dishes. After the table was cleared, Sally said "Nellie will you slip across the yard to Tilly's and take her and Lizzie their presents, no need to hurry back I just want ter 'ave the chance to talk to Ben alone."

"Alright Mom" She replied and collected the two small gifts.

"Now Ben" Sally said as the door closed "Sit down I want to talk to you." He laid the tea towel on the draining board and sat down at the table, and as they sat facing each other she said "Ben, I must apologise for my son's bad behaviour.

"What was that? I didn't notice anything" he lied

"Yes you did, I heard every word he said to you about the whisky."

"Oh that! Forget it Sal, I have."

"I think he was just trying ter show off in from of his pals, Ben."

"Well anyway he's only young yet, he'll grow out of it when he's older.

But Ben thought, I'll soon tame him as soon as I can get my feet settled under this table.

Sally gave a big sigh before saying "I hope so, he can be very trying at times."

"Now think no more about it and lets finish the washing up before they come back and let me see that lovely smile, I want to talk to you about us."

She knew he was going to propose and once they had cleared everything away he made two cups of coffee and as they sat facing each other, he asked, "Do you love me Sal, if you say no, I'll go away and try to forget you."

Sally put down her cup and as he held her two hands she began to blush "But Ben" she replied "I've only known you a short time, and I like you a lot, but I was hoping we could just be friends at least for the time being, you must understand, it's not been long since my husband died."

"But I want ter marry you Sal, but you don't have to give my your answer now, I hope you'll think it over darling and give me your answer in a couple of days time."

"Alright Ben, I'll think it over and let you know."

"Promise love?"

"Yes, I promise, but don't say anymore I can see Nellie coming."

He put both his hands on her shoulders and after kissing her he turned to leave just as Sally's daughter came through the door.

As Nellie bumped into him she cried out looking up at him "Hello Ben, leaving us already?"

"Yes, my dear, I have a lot of paper work to catch up on. But I'll be back in two days time" he replied as he kissed her lips.

"Oh I forgot to thank you for me chocolates, me and Lizzie's mom thought they were delicious."

"I'll bring some more next time, know take care you yer mom and see that your brother don't upset her again." He added.

So he's noticed too, thought Nellie.

As soon as Ben went inside the Rose and Crown, Bill told him that Sally's two sons and their friends had been in but Bill had refused to serve them as they were too young.

"He's got a bit of a big head on his shoulders that lad of Sally's." Ben said.

"I wouldn't know Ben, Sally seldom speaks about her family when she's here, Any'ow, how did yer fare with Sally?"

"I told her how I felt about her and I asked her to marry me."

"That was quick you've only known each other a short time, any'ow what did she say?"

"She's going ter give me her answer in two days time, after she talked it over with her family. Now I must go up ter me room to do some paper work, I'll be down later for drink with the customers."

As soon as he sat down on the bed he thought about Sally. He had hoped she would have accepted his proposal there and then but now he had to wait for her decision.

In the meantime Sally asked her daughter if Tilly liked her gifts.

"Yes Mom, but Lizzie wasn't there, she's staying with her Auntie Ada."

"Very well Nellie just make yourself a cup of cocoa and you'll find yourself a mince pie in the pantry, I won't be long."

"Where yer going Mom?"

"Only to have a chat with Tilly."

"Will yer better slip yer shawl on, it's freezing out."

As soon as she knocked on the door she called out "It's only me Tilly."

"Come in Sal it's nice ter see yer and thank you for me present.

"Why didn't yer come and spend Xmas day with us? You know you'd be welcomed."

"I know Sally, but I heard your Jack was bringing his two work mates, and then there was that Ben."

"What yer mean that Ben?"

"No offence Sally it's just a saying I have, an expression, now sit yerself down and tell me what's on yer mind, I can see yer worried about something."

"Well Tilly, I've got a lot on me mind and you're the only one I can talk to about it."

"Is it about Ben?"

"Er- yes, he proposed to me."

"He what?" The two faced Romeo after asked me for lodgings she thought.

"He asked me to marry him."

"Well I am surprised, what did yer say? Did yer turn him down?"

"I told him I only wanted to be a friend and I told him I'd think about it when I'd spoken to my family, I've got to give him his answer in two days time!"

"But surely you don't love him enough to marry him! You've only known him a few weeks."

"I don't think so but I do like him a lot, but if I do marry him I feel I'm not being fair to my husband's memory."

"You can't live with that thought for the rest of your life. But tell me are you attracted to him?"

"Well he's good company and fun ter be with and we get on well together."

"Well if yer do marry him you'll know you have ter sleep together, would that bother yer Sally, or wouldn't it?"

"I really don't know, there's only been one man in my life, Tilly, and the thought of another man, to be honest would seem strange, but somehow I can't imagine havin' sex with another man."

"Well he must love you or he wouldn't have asked you to marry him."

"He did say he loved me and that he's a very lonely man since he lost his wife and his aunt whom he'd been living with."

"But what if your children don't approve of him, though you'll have ter consider them and yourself Sal. You're a very attractive women and you're not getting no younger like me, and if yer feel you like him enough to marry him, but discuss it with your family. But if you refuse him you may or may not regret it."

"That's the risk you'll have ter take." She added.

"You think so Tilly, you know I love my family, but at times they can be very trying, but I do feel I need a man to have around the house and to discuss future plans and things that matter most. If yer know what I mean?"

"Well Sal, if yer want my advice fer what it's worth you tell the children, tell 'em how yer feel an' see what they say."

"I don't think Nellie or Ted would mind one way or the other but it's different with Jack, he was very rude to Ben an' I don't think he'll approve."

"Whether he approves or not you must understand it's your life Sally and your happiness, because when they feel their wings sprouting and they start courting you'll be left on yer lonesome, so take the 'Bull by the Horns', as the saying goes and think things over before it's too late."

"Thanks Tilly, I feel much better now I've talked it over with you."

Sally thanked and hugged her friend saying she was glad she'd talked it over, she went back home to talk it over with the family. She couldn't still make up her mind until she slept on it.

*

That following day as they had finished their meal she decided it was now time to speak, to tell them what she intended to say and as they sat beside the fire, she gave a big sigh. "That was a big one Mom." Nellie cried out. "Anything on yer mind Mom?"

"Yes Nellie, I have something I want to tell you all." She replied as she sat facing them. "Ben has asked me to marry him."

Suddenly Jack shot out of his chair "You're joking!" he cried out as he glared at her.

"I'm not joking, Ben has asked me to be his wife."

"Oh God! I had a feeling this was going to happen when he kept eyeing you up and down pretending just ter be a visitor, yer tell him No! It's not on. You just ferget him, yer mad Mom if yer go through with it! I don't like the chap" he added. "And I can never accept a step father."

"Look Jack, if Mom thinks she wants to marry him, I don't think we should interfere if she loves him" Nellie replied.

"Shut up you!" Jack snarled anyway what's you're opinion Ted?"

"I agree with Mom and Nellie." Ted replied.

"There you are Mom, two against one." Nellie said.

"You shut up yer little squirt yer don't understand she can't love him!"

Sally kept quiet until she could see that her family where getting angry when suddenly she cried out, "Have you all finished? If you have I don't want to hear any more about it." Therefore Jack bounced up to bed when Nellie and Ted said "If yer love him Mom and you wanta marry him, it's up to you. So I don't think it matters what Jack thinks, he'll come round to your way of thinking later."

*

Next morning they each kissed their Mom before they left. Jack and Ted to work and Nellie soon after to school.

Two days later Ben came for his answer, when Sally said she had made up her mind to marry him. He took her in his arms and kissed her passionately.

"Oh my darling I really do love you and I know you'll learn to love me too in time." As he released her, he asked, "How did Jack and Ted take it when you told them?"

"Ted and Nellie agreed but Jacks' the obstinate one."

"But he'll come round in time love and I'll do my best to be a good husband and stepfather." But Sally and her family had a lot to learn in the coming weeks, and if she had been able to read his mind she would have been aroused to caution.

After a proper period, while Sally got herself ready for her new life, she tried her best to reconcile her older son to the situation the wedding was arranged. A car hired to take them to the registrar's office and as Jack sat next to his mother she noticed he was scowling. "Now Jack" she whispered "Don't forget your promise." He just shrugged his shoulders. Nellie also hoped he would keep his word. "Are you nervous Mom?" Nellie whispered.

"Just a little love." She replied.

"I wish it was me getting married, I'd feel over the moon."

"You'll have your day and I'd like to see you married all in white and married in a church like me and yer dad was."

Nellie wondered why her mom should mention her father on this day of all days, for she was looking so lovely in her new blue and lemon outfit and about to start a new life.

"Are you happy Mom, are yer sure you want ter go through with this?"

"Yes love of course I do! What makes you say that?"

"Just thinking Mom, have you brought the confetti Ted?"

"Yes." Ted replied, "Three packets."

"I don't want any." Jack replied still sulking.

"Please yerself." Ted replied unmoved.

As soon as Sally and Ben were made Man and Wife they stepped down into the street where they were showered with confetti from friends and neighbours.

As soon as Ted and Nellie showered them last, they both kissed their mother before getting into the car. Waving goodbye to everyone they set off to a hotel in the country where they were to spend the weekend on their honeymoon.

As soon as they entered their bedroom with its large bed and luscious drapings, Ben began to open a bottle of champagne and as he poured out two glasses he handed one to Sally. "To you my darling." He said smiling as they clinked glasses. "To you too Ben." She replied.

"Happy?" He asked.

"Yes Ben." She replied.

"Me too my darling." He replied as he topped up her glass again. After she drank it he pulled her onto the bed and began to embrace her and kiss her passionately. She felt do dizzy "I don't think I want any more champagne Ben."

"You'll get used to it darling after another glass." But she was adamant, but as he clasped her tightly he whispered into her ear, "Why don't you get undressed in the bathroom."

She had thought of nothing else since seeing that comfortable bed. Never the less, opening her case she took out her silky nightdress and toilet bag and went to prepare herself.

"Don't be long I'm waiting darling." She heard him call out. As soon as she was ready she looked at herself in the mirror, when she heard him moving about. After she put perfume under her arms and behind her ears, she felt ready to meet him. As soon as she entered the bedroom she was shocked to see him stretched out on the bed naked. She never expected this and as he waved the champagne bottle he began to slur his words.

"Don't stand there ain't yer ever sin a naked man before now cum and get in bed an' 'ave another swig."

"No! I think I've had enough and cover yourself up yer look disgusting."

"Oh nonsense it's our weddin' night my love."

There was nothing else for her to do but to refuse or try to refuse his mauling, as she crept in the bed and turned her back on him, but suddenly he tore her nightdress off and began to roughly fondle her, she was pleased he was too drunk to finish as he lay on top of her shortly after he turned over on his back and fell asleep.

She never expected anything like this, her late husband had always been considerate and gentle when he made love, but when Ben woke during the night he started to perform again, she thought he would never finish, in fact he was very rough at times and when she was about to fall asleep she would feel his hands wandering again over her body.

"Oh my god, not again!" she cried out as he began to climb on top of her again.

She was still sore and tired from his first bout of what he called lovemaking. But how could she refuse him without him getting angry, she only hoped he would finish quickly. She closed her eyes and pretended to enjoy it.

Next morning when she awoke she made up her mind to leave him. She was about to get out of bed when she felt him pull her back again. She pushed his hand away, "Leave me alone!" she cried out "I want ter get a bath and get dressed! I've had enough of your so called love making as yer call it."

"Why what's wrong?" He demanded.

"I don't want any more, that's what!" She replied angrily.

"But Sal my darling yer can't have too much of a good thing." He grinned as he slid his hand along her thigh again.

"You're disgusting! I don't want any more!" She replied as she slapped his hand hard.

"But I don't understand we're married now and I thought you wanted it as much as I did?" He replied.

"But we can't go on like this, you wanting it every night and morning!" She shot back.

"But my late wife was -."

Sally interrupted, furious at the comparison being implied, "Perhaps you late wife couldn't say no, so let's give it a rest."

"Oh come on love, be nice ter me."

"No!" She almost yelled out, "Enough is enough!"

"Oh please yerself" He snapped as he sprung out of the bed towards the bathroom, naked.

Breakfast was not due for another hour, in the meantime he washed, shaved and dressed and went down into the dining room. As soon as he'd gone Sally broke down and wept.

"Oh what a fool I've been to think that I could have learned to love a man so full of lust."

When she got home she put on a brave face. No one knew what had happened, she kept her secret. Now that Sally refused to sleep with him he began to show his true colours.

Two weeks went by when Ben came home worse for wear when he staggered up to bed. The next morning he slumped at the breakfast table in an awful mood. Everyone ignored him hoping that his temper would ease if he wasn't aroused.

"Any flakes wanted?" Their Mom called out from the kitchen.

"I could eat another piece of toast, Mom" Jack said.

"Toast coming up" Sally called out when Ben growled at him.

"I thought you'd had enough."

Jack glared at him, "What's it ter do with you?" he snapped, are yer counting em now? If you are I'll have another one!"

"Let me have less of your old truck! My boy!" Ben yelled back.

"Now, now, let's have no more quarrelling." Sally pleaded.

"He eats more than a navvy." Ben snarled.

"I'm entitled to eat what I like, I pay my whack."

Ted and Nellie looked across the table at each other, they had noticed the tension as soon as they all had sat down, but hoped it would seep away.

"Here's yer toast Jack." His mother said as she handed it to him.

"I don't want it now!" He snapped.

"Yer spoil him, Mummy's boy." Ben taunted

"She don't and I'm not a Mummy's boy!"

Jack was furious and so was Ted, who stood up sharply saying, "Come on Jack, let's go, we don't want Mom getting upset again."

"I don't want Mom upset, but how dare he criticise me in my own home! I can't stand the sight of him, far less his company."

"I don't know why our Mom married him." Ted commented

"Neither do I, anyway I'm not leaving home yet, but when I do he's going to be sorry."

As soon as they came indoors for their sandwiches and flasks of tea, their stepfather started again.

"I thought you'd run away Mummy's boy." He sneered.

This was more that Sally could stand, "Will you leave the boys alone!" She exclaimed.

"Well I won't be ignored by a snotty nose kid."

Suddenly Jack clenched his fist and was about to say something when his mother took his arm and told him to ignore the dig. She knew Ben was often in a filthy mood, for he'd been spending money at the 'Rose and Crown' like water on bottles of whisky and coming home at late hours. She also knew he was disappointed because she refused him sex night and morning.

As soon as the boys left for work and Nellie was on her way to school, she turned to Ben, shouting, "You should be ashamed of yourself acting like a jealous kid."

"Well I was right, wasn't I?"

"What yer mean you was right?"

"Well he does scoff more that all of us put together."

"Nonsense." She replied, "Anyway it's nothing ter do with you, he's almost a man and he's entitled to eat what he wants as long as he brings his wages home."

"Just as you say my love." He answered insincerely as bounced out of the house. Sally was shaking as she began washing up the breakfast dished, tears stung her eyes as she thought of her late husband, thinking if he hadn't died how happier they would have been. She was wishing now she had never married him, but it was too late now to do anything about it. Anyway she wasn't going to stand by and watch him browbeat her sons. But often she worried, wondering what would happen if Ben carried on sneering. So long as they ignored him she could put up with his tantrums. She wasn't afraid of him and could hold her own in the tongue stakes.

It was a very cold February morning when Sally did her shopping in the 'Bull Ring' market, when one morning, wandering between the stalls she saw Tilly making her way towards her.

" Hello stranger" Tilly cried our seizing her arm.

"Where yer bin 'idin' yerself?"

"Well Tilly I ain't had much time ter come and have a chat, but I'm glad ter see you, Tilly.

Her friend looked up and down and cried out "You've lost weight ain't yer Sal?"

"Just a little, but I find I have a lot more ter cope with now since I married." Sally replied as tears welled up in her eyes.

"Yer wanta talk about it Sal?"

"Yes Tilly, I've been meaning to tell you, but I kept putting it off hoping things would get better, but I don't want ter trouble you."

"No trouble what are friends for? Now if yer feel yer wanta tell me what's been happenin' there's no time like the present, so lets go inside the pub, we can't talk out here."

As they sat down Tilly asked if she wanted a drink. "Just a beer." She replied.

"You'll 'ave a whisky Sal it'll put some of them colours back in yer cheeks."

Sally would never think of entering a pub on her own but now she had met Tilly again, she began to tell her what had been happening during these last few weeks, but when tears ran down her cheeks Tilly cried out. "Come on now, Sal, lets hear wot yer trouble is, so get if off yer chest, and if I can help I will."

"I don't think you can now Tilly I don't think anyone can. It's too late now. I was a bloody fool ter marry him."

"But I thought you loved him?" Tilly asked aghast at the turn of affairs.

"I liked him a lot Tilly and I thought in time I would learn ter love him in time, but I can't be civil to him anymore. He's not the man I thought he was."

"But what made yer change yer mind?"

"Well Tilly, he's very lustful, he wants it night and bloody morning and every day of the week if I'd let him." Suddenly Tilly burst our laughing.

Sally wiped her eyes and cried out indignantly, "It's no laughing matter. When I refuse him he's really rude and not only that: Jack and Ted now even Nellie are beginning to notice things, he's even jealous of them and I'm afraid one day Ben will go too far and they'll come to blows. He's now sold his van and his business rounds and that, he tells me he's got a job part time as a barman at the 'Dog and Duck' and comes home some nights the worst for drink and starts sneering at the lads." Tears started to fall again as Sally's' tirade came to a choking end.

"Oh Sal I'm so sorry for yer, and I thought you was happy being as you never came to see me, yer know he still comes in the 'Rose and Crown' and tells us all that he loves you when we ask about yer."

"Tilly he's a liar and I can't trust him anymore whatever he says or does." She replied as her eyes filled again with tears.

"How about Nellie? What does she think about him?"

"She liked him at first but she avoids him like the lads do. If only I could turn the clock back Tilly."

"But Sally, why put up with him if you're unhappy, tell him to clear out. It's your house anyway."

"I told him several times, but he takes no notice."

"When he happens to come in the 'Rose and Crown' he never mentions anything to me."

"I think he'd be too ashamed if he told the truth."

"I'm so sorry for yer Sal and I thought you was happy, bloody men." She added, "They're all the same, only want yer for yer body!"

"Are you ever thought of marrying again Tilly?"

"Me? Not bloody likely! Once bit twice shy that's me, love and leave."

"Does Lizzie ever mention her Dad? Nellie often talks about her father, she often wished and so did I that he hadn't died so young."

There was a short silence, after Tilly said "Sally I hope you'll forgive - but I wanted to tell you this for fourteen years, but I was ashamed and scared - I was never married."

"But I always thought you was a widow?" Sal exclaimed.

"Well those many years ago when you found me crying near your home, I had nowhere to go only the work house, but you took pity on me and took me into your home, I felt too ashamed to say I was not married and pregnant."

"But why tell me now, you didn't have to. It makes no different to our friendship."

"I'm not bad really, but I like a mans company and if I find one I like enough I wouldn't marry him but just be content to live with him and bugger what me neighbours would say" She added.

"I wish I'd have had second thoughts instead of marry that lustful plausible lying bugger. But then my family wouldn't agree to me living in sin."

"There's no sin about it Sally, marriage is only a man-made law with just a piece of paper to show for it!" Tilly shot back.

"You sound bitter Tilly."

"I've every reason ter be, and yer know why. My Dad used to tie me to the bedstead and whip me with his belt when busy bodies told him they seen me coming out of the dance hall with a fellow. Often my Mother and my Sister, Ada, would stand and watch. That's why I ran away and fell for Lizzie's father Dennis Rabone, and when he took me to his sister's house, I later became pregnant with Lizzie. But when I found out he was married I ran away. That's the night you found me crying near your home. I felt too ashamed then to tell you and your family the truth, that was why I said I was a widow."

"Does Lizzie know?"

"Yes I've told her everything now, I left nothing out and I'm happy now I've got that off me chest before someone someday would find out and make it their business to tell her. Yes Sal, she understands now."

"Your secret will go no farther that me Tilly. I'll have to hurry home now Tilly, the boys will be home soon. I'll pop over and see you tomorrow.

"Alright Sal." She replied "And I'll be able to tell you more news and don't worry if there's anything or any way I can help yer know where I live."

They kissed each other as they went their separate ways.

As soon as Sally went indoors she noticed Ben with his feet up resting on the table. As soon as she asked him more. Ben didn't answer: he just slammed the door behind him and left.

Ben calmed down during the next few weeks. The brothers never spoke to him again, but Ben still had spasms of bad temper, which lost him his job.

A few days later he came home the worse for drink and said he'd lost his job.

Sally went wild. "Well, yer'll get no grub here till yer find one!" she yelled at him. "An' when yer've sobered up, yer can get out an' look fer one!"

But times were hard. There were not many jobs to be found. The only one he managed to get was a part time job at the "Bull's Head" cleaning the spitoons and sweeping up wet sawdust. This didn't bother him, as long as he got a meal, free beer and a few shillings. Now he was in his oil tot.

After closing time he would collect the glasses and drink up the dregs.

He seldom gave Sally any money, but she didn't need anything from him, as long as he kept his bullying for someone else. He didn't know she had a nest egg. She was very careful to save and hide away part of her sons' wages each week from his prying eyes, but she always fed her family well and took care of all their needs. They loved their mother. They also knew their lives would be happier and contented if their stepfather would leave. They knew no one else would put up with him. In sober moments he was quite a different person, but still moody, but these sober moments didn't last long. When he craved for drink, rows would start up again when he lounged about the kitchen dropping cigarette ends and ash all over the floor, after Sally had scrubbed it. Also the dirty habit that got on the boys' nerves, when he spat at the fire and missed.

*

One night, as the two brothers lay awake in their attic bed, Jack said, "Ted, we gotta do something about that old man." (They never called him by any other name).

"Yes, I've been thinking the same," Ted replied. "But what can we do, when Mom takes his part?"

"She don't, not really. She don't want us to get hurt, an' yer know he can be a sly old bastard at times."

"I know he hates us, Jack."

"Yes and we hate him too, but he'll never change while he's here sponging on us, so I've worked out what we're going to do. Then we'll leave her."

"But where can we go, Jack? We can't leave Mom here and Nellie with him."

"It'll only be for a short time and I think Mom and Nellie will be treated better if we get another job further away. Anyway, let's get some sleep. It's the holiday break next week. We'll look around for farm work. The money won't be like we've been earnin' but at least we'll be living in fresh air."

"Where yer plannin' fer us ter go?"

"Down south. There's plenty of farm hands wanted. Now let's get ter sleep, I'll discuss it with yer termorra."

A few days later they drew their wages and decided to get ready to leave. They knew their mother wouldn't be home until later, as she had taken Nellie and Tilly's daughter, Lizzie to the pictures. That same night, their opportunity came.

"Now, Ted, you watch through the winda an' when yer see him comin', we'll hide in the kitchen."

As soon as Ben almost fell inside the door, he yelled out, "Where are yer an' where's me supper?"

Suddenly he began smashing everything in sight, but he didn't get very far. The two brothers dashed out of the kitchen and began to lay into him.

"Yer drunk bastard!" Jack yelled out as he floored him. He added, "Mom aint here tonight ter part us."

Ben was too drunk even to retaliate.

As soon as Ted saw the blood running down Ben's face, he got frightened. "Jack! Jack! Don't hit him any more. Look at the blood."

"I'll kill the drunken bastard!" he yelled out.

"No, Jack, let's leave him. Just push him under the table an' let's go."

Jack put his foot against him and as Ben rolled beneath the table, they hurried to put a few clothes in a bag and left a note with their Mom's wages and to say they would write as soon as they found a place to settle.

When their mother came home and saw her husband lying in a pool of blood, she knew at once that her two sons had done what they had promised to do a long time ago. She was worried in case he was dead but, as she bent down to see, she noticed he was asleep and actually snoring. But when she saw the blood she got a fright. She rang for an ambulance in case he should die, and when a policeman arrived, he asked who had done it. Sally said she didn't know, but Mrs O'Leary, the Irish woman who lived next door, told him she had heard a lot of noise and seen the two lads running away. When the constable asked where they were, Sally said she didn't know.

In the meantime, the ambulance driver said, "This man's drunk! Otherwise there's nothing much ter cry about, an' I aint wastin' me time drivin' 'im ter the 'orspital. I'll just stick a plaster on his for'ead."

As soon as he'd gone, the policeman took out his notebook and asked again where her sons were.

As soon as she wiped her tears, she replied, "I don't know and that's the truth."

"Don't get upset. There's not much damage to cry about," he replied.

"I aint cryin' over him. It's me two sons who've run away through his drunken, cruel ways."

"Anyway, I may have to report this to the station."

"Yer betta read this note before yer report 'em," she sobbed.

"Mom," it read, "we aint ever cummin' back until you've got rid of the cruel, drunken pig. Take care of yerself. Especially watch out for our sister Nellie. We'll write when we get settled. Love from us both, XX."

After reading the note, the constable said there was nothing he could do to interfere in family quarrels, unless things got worse. She was to report to him at the station.

*

Since the boys had left, Sally would have nothing more to do with him. She took what she needed from her bedroom and settled to sleep with her daughter Nellie. Nellie was nearly fourteen now. She too missed her brothers and the more she saw of her stepfather, the more she despised him.

Sally would lie awake for hours. Tears filled her eyes when she thought what a mess he'd made of their lives, and wondering and praying that her sons were safe and well, hoping to hear from them soon.

Ben had often threatened what he would do if they came back. Each time he shaved he thought of the night they attacked him, and had the scar on his forehead to remind him.

"This is their home," Sally had reminded him, "and if they come back, you nor anyone else will stop them. And remember this: they're two young strapping men now and yer won't have one to deal with, you'll have two as well!"

"Rubbish! Rubbish!" he repeated as he leered at her. "They took advantage of me because I had had a few whiskies."

"A few? You liar! The bottle was empty you bought in the night before. Yer can't even tell the truth!" she added.

"Well it was my money that paid for it!" he exclaimed.

"That's another thing I'd like to know. Where yer get yer money from?"

"Ah, that would be tellin'," he replied, as he gave her a lopsided grin.

"Well you've had yer last meal here, until yer hand over. Otherwise, get out! If not I'll take yer ter court and get a separation."

"Yer wouldn't do that, would yer, Sal?" he cried out sheepishly.

"Well I'm warning you, Ben Twigg. If you don't stop pestering with yer tell tale signs, I'll do more than that! And what about this floozy you've been seen out with?"

"What woman? You're the only woman in my life, my darling."

"Don't you darling me, you - you plausible liar! I've been told by the neighbours you've been seen with some floozy and buying her drinks in the Bull's Head."

"Well, what yer expect? Yer wunt sleep with me anymore an' when I want it, yer refuse me, and now yer sleeping with Nellie."

"You can have a dozen women, for all I care, and the sooner yer pack yer bags and leave, I'll put the flags out."

"I'll leave when I'm good and ready!" he exclaimed as he walked out, whistling as he banged the door behind him.

*

"There's the postman, Mom. Looks as if he's got a letter for us."

"Good morning, Nellie," he greeted. "Letter for yer Mom."

"It must be from the boys. Nellie, get me me glasses off the shelf."

"What's it say, Mom?" Nellie asked anxiously.

"Yer can read it when I've finished, love," she answered.

"Dear Mom and Nellie," she read. "We're both doing well working on a farm, but if you need us we'll catch the next train home. You'll find the address on the next page. We'll be back home again soon and woe betide that swine if he starts agen. All our love to you and Nellie. Jack and Ted. XXXX"

Sally wrote back they were missing them both and that Ben had calmed down since they had been away and that she was seriously thinking of getting a separation and that she would write and let them know. Their mother didn't tell them about the other woman Ben was seeing, nor that he was staying out late at night. She thought she didn't want them to be upset. But as soon as she got her separation, it would be the time to tell them it was safer to come home.

*

Two days went by when Tilly called to tell her that Ben had had the audacity to flaunt his fancy woman in the Rose and Crown, where she was working.

"I told him what I thought of him and her, Sal. That I'd sooner lose me job than serve him, and if I was you, I'd come and show him up for the swine he is."

"No, Tilly, I aint interested whatever he does now. Anyway, I've been to the law court and stated my case. He'll have a shock when he receives his summons."

"Good fer you, Sal. All the customers know what sort of a bloke he is, and our neighbours Pat and George and Paddy O'Leary ignore him. But when they do throw out a bit of sarcasm, he's that thick skinned it's like water off a duck's back."

"Yes, Tilly, I know. But one of these days he's going to be sorry. I'm just waiting now for that day when I see the look on his face when he receives his summons."

"'as he ever struck yer, Sal?"

"No," she replied. "I wish he had, then I could have had him arrested. No Tilly," she added, "he's threatened lots of times, but he's too scared. He knows he'd get the worse end of the stick. Anyway he's too scared of my two sons since that night they beat him up."

"How are they, Sal? Do yer ever hear from 'em?"

"Yes, I had a couple of letters from 'em. They're doing well on the farm, but they say they're missing me and their sister and to let them know when I've got rid of him, they'll come home."

*

A few days later went by when Tilly came to tell her the postman had called, but finding no one in, he'd said he couldn't leave the letter. It had to be signed for.

"I expect it's the summons for Ben. Thanks for telling me, Tilly. I expect he'll call again."

"Is that that nosy barmaid from the pub?" he yelled out from the kitchen. She was about to answer when the postman came again.

"A letter fer you ter sign."

As soon as he read it, he threw it across the room. "If yer think yer can get away with this, you'll afta think agen!" he yelled out at her. "You're still my wife and you've gotta prove these accusations."

"I've got plenty of witnesses from the neighbours."

Suddenly he began to change his tune. "Don't do this to me, darling. I still love you," he pleaded.

"What you call love, Ben Twigg, is only lust, and I don't want any part of yer any more, so the sooner you leave here and yer fancy woman, the better it will be."

"Please, Sal, love, I'll give her up, darling, if you'll forgive me we can start afresh. I can change, I know I can, and I'll be good ter you and Nellie and Jack and Ted, if they'll only find it in their hearts to forgive me."

As soon as she saw tears in his eyes, she began to feel sorry for him. But she knew if she weakened now and gave him another chance, he wouldn't last long before he started his plausible lies and conceited ways.

"No, Ben, you've had too many chances and I can never forgive you, now that you've got another woman."

"She's only a friend, Sal, love. Nothing more."

"Don't lie to me! I know you sleep with her," she exclaimed.

"Well, what do you expect? Anyway, yer won't get very far when I tell the judge you refused me my conjugal rights! You'll quickly change yer tone."

"Anyway," she added, "is that what you call it? Wanting it every night and morning every day of the week, I was worn out. Now I don't want to discuss it any further. You got yer summons. I don't want anything more to do with you!"

"Very well, Sal. You'll be sorry you ever thought of doing this to me!" he cried out as he leered at her.

"You've soon changed yer tune, like yer habits!" she exclaimed. She knew he looked upset as he went back into the kitchen, but she knew she could never forgive him.

As soon as he came back out again he shouted, "I'm going now an' I aint ever coming back!"

"What about yer clothes?"

"I'll send for 'em later." As he walked towards the door, he tried to plead once more, "Darling, we was once so happy. Can you find it in yer heart to forgive me? I'll do whatever you ask, my love, if only you'll give me another chance."

"No, Ben, and that's final! You go to your other woman and try if she'll put up with yer and yer lustful ways. Now go!"

As soon as he walked out, she slammed the door behind him, then sat down and wept.

*

He didn't come back until three days later and worse for drink.

As soon as Nellie came home from school and saw he was packing his few belongings, she asked, "Where's me Mom?"

"'ow should I know? I'm leavin' 'er an' yew," he slurred.

Nellie didn't wait to answer. She ran across the yard to see if her mother was at Tilly's house. "Is me Mom here?" she asked as she went inside.

"No love. She left about five minutes ago. Said she had to go to the chemist before it closed. Yer wanta come in an' wait?"

"No thank you. I'll go back and put the kettle on. I know she'll want a cup of tea when she comes back."

While she was waiting for the kettle to boil, she thought Ben had just gone, but as she reached up to the shelf for the teapot, she felt him standing close behind her.

Suddenly he put his arms around her. "I'm leaving for good this time, Nellie. Would yer like me ter kiss yer before I go?"

"No," she replied, "Let me be! Yer breath smells!"

"Come on, don't be shy," he replied, as he held her closer.

She saw his eyes focus on her small breasts and belched as he said, "Yer a fine looking girl, Nellie love. Don't tell me you've never had a man kiss yer before?"

"No, never! Now let me be, yer a nuisance. Let me go!"

"Just a little kiss," he replied.

She tried to break away from him, but he was too strong for her. She wondered if she just let him kiss her, just once, he would release her, but she doubted it. Suddenly he pushed her against the wall and held her there. She was now scared. She knew now it was not only a kiss he wanted, as she saw his contorted face, ugly with alcohol and passion. He tore her frock. As soon as he let go and began to squeeze her breasts, she struck him with her two fists and kicked him between his legs. As soon as he yelled out and saw him double up, she ran across the yard to Tilly's.

She almost fell inside the room. When her school friend Lizzie asked her what was wrong, she burst out crying.

"Mom! Mom!" Lizzie cried out at the foot of the stairs, "Yer betta come down. Nellie's in some trouble."

"What's the matter, Nellie?" Tilly asked, "and why is yer frock all torn?"

"I want me Mom, Mrs Waldron. Can I say here till me Mom comes?"

"Yes, then p'raps we'll get some sense out of yer."

"I've done nothing wrong. It was him," she cried.

"Who do yer mean? Yer stepfather?"

She just nodded her head and, as the tears ran down her face again, her mother came. As soon as she saw the state her daughter was in, she cried out, "What's happened to you?"

When she told her what had happened, she yelled out, "Oh my God! I'll kill the bastard! But yer sure he daint interfere with yer? Yer know what I mean?"

"Yes, Mom, I do know what you mean. When he let go of me an' put his hands on me breasts, I managed to kick him an' get away."

"Has he tried anything before?" Tilly asked.

"No, Mrs Waldron," she replied. "But I never liked the way he always looked at me when Mom was out. But now he's threatened to cut my throat if I told yer."

"The best thing to do is ter tell the police, Sally."

"I can't do that, Tilly, much as I'd like to, but I don't want my daughter's photo splashed all over the front page of the News of the World."

"Anyway," Tilly replied, "you leave it to me, yer don't wanta go back yet. I want yer to stay here while I go over an' sort 'im out. And you, Lizzie, put the kettle on and make a pot of tea. I won't be long."

As soon as she walked in, she saw he was fast asleep in his chair and snoring loudly. She didn't bother to wake him up. She gently undid the buttons on his flies and pulled out his penis, and after pouring hot water over it, she struck it hard with the kettle and left him screaming.

As soon as the neighbours heard him, they came out of doors wondering what the trouble was but Tilly just walked away.

As soon as Tilly told her friend what she had done, she said, "Serves him right. P'raps he won't try to molest her again. In the meantime, would you mind if Nellie stays with you until after the court case?"

"She's welcome any time, aint she Mom?" Lizzie piped up.

"Yes. Yer betta get the bed ready, she can sleep with you, love. Do yer want me ter come back with yer, Sal?"

"No thanks, Tilly. It's more than he dare do to touch me."

But when Sally returned to her own home she saw he had already packed up and left.

*

The following night, as Tilly was serving drinks, Paddy O'Leary called her to one side and asked her what all the commotion had been about. When she told him about what she had done, he couldn't stop laughing. "What's the joke, Paddy?" George and Pat asked.

When Paddy told them, George said, "He wouldn't have got away with that, it worn't punishment enough for that little pervert. You leave it us. He wunt dare show his ugly face around here when we've finished with him. Now listen carefully," George whispered. "When he comes in don't ignore him, I've got a few bob. We'll fill him up with whisky and after I've slipped him a Micky Finn, he wunt know his arse from his elbow. Now this is the plan."

Nobody knew what they were planning; not even Tilly or the landlord. It was to be a secret between the three men.

They waited, it wanted just under an hour to closing time when Ben walked in the following night. The three neighbours were surprised to see him alone.

"Where's yer young woman ternight, Ben?"

"Don't talk ter me about women. I've had me fill right up to here." he replied, as he held out his hand beneath his chin.

"Cheer up, mate. Come an' have a drink with us," Pat asked.

"Good natured all of a sudden, aint yer, Pat?"

"Well it's me birthday," he lied. "I always treat on me birthday, don't I Fred?" he said to the landlord.

"Well in that case I'll have a whisky," Fred replied. "What'll you have, Ben?"

"I'll have a beer."

"But you always drink whisky. Come on now, cheer up, it's me birthday. Give him a double, Fred."

"Double coming up," the landlord replied.

"Mek it two, Fred. He looks as if he needs it."

"Cum inter a fortune, 'ave yer Pat?" Ben cried out.

"Not exactly. I always like ter be generous when it's me birthday, don't I Paddy?"

"Yer sure do, Pat me mate."

"Well it's the last call befower I put the towel over," Fred warned them. "The fog's coming down thick ternight."

"Well drink up and have one for the road, Ben," George said.

As soon as he fetched the last call, George slipped the Micky Finn into Ben's glass.

As soon as Ben's drink began to take effect, the landlord said, "That's yer last call, I'm waiting ter close up. Everyone else 'as gone, so yer betta hurry, the fog's gettin' thicker lads."

"Goodnight then, Fred," they chorused.

As soon as George, Paddy and Pat began to leave, Fred cried out, "Wot about him? Yer can't leave him here, he can't even stand!"

"He aint with us. We only treated him 'cause it was me birthday. Anyway, I expect his floozy will be coming for him."

As soon as the three of them got outside, they hid themselves behind the wall.

Ben was now too drunk to stand and when his legs gave under him, he cried out, "Where am I?"

Fred jumped the counter to help him outside. He was afraid of drunken men being seen on his premises after closing time; he'd been in trouble with the police before. He almost carried Ben and when he got near the door he managed to push him out and left him to find his own way home.

But Ben only got a few yards when he thought he'd lay down on the floor, and the fog was getting thicker.

"Did yer bring the barra, Paddy?" George whispered.

"Yes. Where is he? I can't see him through this fog."

"He's lying on the floor near the wall," Pat answered.

As soon as Paddy and George led the way, they picked Ben up and stripped him bare and lay in the barrow of horse manure. Ben was too drunk to know what was happening to him.

They left him there and, after throwing his clothes over the wall, they went off home, grinning all over their faces and vowed not to breathe a word to anyone.

Ben must have slept until dawn. When the local bobby found him, he was sitting up in the barrow, rubbing his bleary eyes. The fog had now cleared away. The constable didn't get too near for the smell. He blew his whistle.

As soon as the sergeant appeared with another constable, he took one look at the naked spectacle, held his nose and ordered them to wheel him off to the station.

Ben was put into a cell and sprayed all over with cold water. As soon as his clothes were found, he got himself dressed.

Next morning he was brought before the magistrate. When Ben asked for bail, after giving his name and address, Sally refused to come forward. He was tried and sent to prison for one month's hard labour for being drunk and disorderly and stealing the farmer's barrow.

That incident was the talk of the town. Splashed across the newspapers was his photo, name and address. "Benjamin Wilfred Twigg residing at Ledsom Court, was found asleep in a farmer's barrow of horse manure."

*

As soon as he came out of prison, he made his way home, hoping Sally would take pity on him and give him another chance.

But as soon as he came down the yard, the women leered at him and called after him and, as he hurried to put his key in the lock, he found the lock had been changed.

Dropping the key through the letterbox, he hurried away. Ben Twigg was never seen or heard of again, yet there were lots of rumours among the neighbours.

*

Jack and Ted Carter were two hard working lads. At first they got on well with the farmer, but Farmer Gray was a grumpy, decrepit old man, and always wanted more than the brothers could give, but they put up with his mean ways, until they found something better.

One day he was taken ill. When the doctor came he told him he had cancer. He knew he was going to die and when he told the brothers to put in extra hours and keep the farm going, he would leave them a sum of money.

"I bet he's goin' ter leave us in his will, Jack," Ted said.

"Don't yer believe it. He's got plenty of relatives and a couple of bastards ter leave his money to."

"Well, we'll have ter wait and see," Ted replied.

A few weeks later the farmer died and when the Will was read the farm and everything else was left to some widow woman and his bastard sons.

"What did I tell yer!" Jack exclaimed. "After sweating our balls off, he's left us nothing."

After the funeral the woman and her sons came to take over. They wanted the two brothers to work for twice the hours and less pay.

"Let yer bastards do what we've for a few pounds! We're leaving!" Jack exclaimed.

"But yer carn't leave now," her son replied.

"You heard what I said! More money and less work and we want it in writing."

"No!" their mother yelled out. "Yer better pack yer things and leave now!"

"Suits us, missus," they both replied as they walked into the shed to pack.

"What we goin' to do, Jack? Yer might have kept yer temper till we found another job," Ted said.

"We're going home first," Jack replied, "so let's hurry, Ted."

*

Tilly Waldron had been going steady with an elderly, attractive man for over twelve months.

Bill Penny owned a small confectioner's business in a quiet district three miles from where Tilly lived. He had often asked her to marry him. She was seriously thinking about it, but she didn't like to tell the publican she was going to give notice to leave.

Tilly had told Fred years ago the story of her life and why she had run away from home when she was barely eighteen, and who the father of her child was. But one morning she plucked up enough courage to tell him and explain why she wanted to leave.

"I'm sorry to 'ear yer wanta leave, but yer sure yer wanta marry him?" he replied.

"Yes, Fred. I've had sixteen years of this squalid district and now I've got this offer, I'm going to take it. Lizzie's growing up and I want her to have a better life than mixing with them ignorant O'Leary kids."

"I understand. Will you stay until I getta replacement?"

"Yes, Fred. Bill will understand. Anyway, I won't be getting married yet. When I do, I'd like yer to give me away, Fred."

"Yes, I'd like that, Tilly. But I'll be sorry to lose yer. We've had such fun together and you've always had a welcome smile for everyone and I'll be lucky if I get another barmaid like you. But don't forget me and the customers. We'll be more than welcome to see you and Lizzie any time, so don't forget the old Rose and Crown."

"I won't," she replied. "Now I must get on with me job before I start weeping."

During the next two days after giving Fred notice, she began packing some of her belongings.

When one morning there came a knock on the door, afraid to open it, she first looked through the curtain. When she saw who was standing there, she almost fainted when she saw Dennis Rabone as large as life. Suddenly she dropped the curtain, but she was too afraid to open the door.

As he kept knocking, several times neighbours came out on their doorsteps wondering who this well dressed man could be. Suddenly their tongues wagged.

"I wunda who 'e can be?" Mrs Mitchell asked.

"One of 'er fancy men yer can bet," Mrs O'Leary replied.

"Very likely," Mrs Freer replied.

"Cums ter summat now wen they call at the 'ouse."

"Well 'er can please 'erself, 'er is a widda," Mrs Flanagan replied.

Tilly heard every word they said.

They were gossiping away when Dennis Rabone walked across the yard and asked, "Could you tell me if I've come to the right address?"

"Who do yer want, sir?" asked Mrs O'Leary.

"Tilly Waldron. Does she live here?"

"Oh yes, yer've cum ter the right 'ouse. 'er lives theea an' 'er daughter, Lizzie."

"Thank you, it's my daughter I've come about. But they must be out, but when you see her will you tell her I called."

"What shall we say yer name was?" Mrs Freer asked.

"Tell her Dennis. She'll know who I am. Also tell her I want to see my daughter. I'll call again in two days' time at ten o'clock."

After he'd gone Mrs O'Leary cried out, "Sounds a grumpy feller! But I don't believe 'er's out. I'll goo over an' see." she added.

As soon as she knocked on the door, Tilly opened it wide for all the neighbours to hear. "Well, what do you want?"

"There was a bloke knockin' on yer dower. Sed 'is name was Dennis."

"So! What's that gotta do with you, yer nosy bloody old cow? And that goes for yer cronies too!"

"Keep yer bleedin' 'air on. Any'ow 'e said 'e's cummin' back in two days' time at ten o'clock an' 'e said -"

Before she could say more, Tilly slammed the door in her face, almost knocking her over.

As soon as she sat down she began to weep. She had almost forgotten he existed. She began to wonder how he had found out where she lived after sixteen long years. Also about Lizzie. The only person she could think of was her sister Ada, whom she had refused to let her adopt Lizzie when she was five years old. If only I can leave here today or tomorrow before he comes. Anyway, I'd better warn Fred in case he goes there.

As soon as she arrived at the pub, Fred noticed at once she'd been weeping. When he asked what the trouble was, she told him. "Yer sure yer don't wanta see 'im?"

"I'd sooner see him dead!" she replied bitterly.

"Wot time did yer say 'e was cummin'?"

"Ten o'clock Wednesday morning, so know-all Mrs O'Leary said."

"Leave it ter me, Tilly. I'll soon get rid of 'im."

"But I don't want you ter get in any trouble through me, Fred."

"Never you mind. 'e'll 'ave a shock wen I say who I am. Now leave this ter me an' 'ave this spot of whisky, and if 'e cums befower ten, just let me know. Now listen carefully to what I'm goin' ter do an' say," he added. As soon as he told Tilly what his intentions were, they both began to grin.

Wednesday morning came and at nine thirty Fred knocked on Tilly's door.

"Come in, Fred," she called out.

As soon as he entered he took off his coat, rolled his shirt sleeves up and, as he sat in the armchair beside a cosy fire, he lit his clay pipe. Then reading his morning paper, they both waited for the knock.

Dennis was fifteen minutes early, but Tilly was at the window on the look out. As soon as she saw him coming across the yard, she cried out, "He's here, Fred."

"Right, now yer know wot yer've gotta do," he replied.

As soon as he lit his pipe and pretended to read his paper, Dennis Rabone knocked on the door.

Tilly could see most of her neighbours standing on their doorsteps with arms folded, but she ignored them. As she opened the door wide she cried out, "What do you want?" She glared at him, waiting to hear what he had to say.

"Aint yer glad ter see me, darling? I've searched all over the country ter find you and my daughter. Yer can't believe how I've missed yer all these years. Now at last after all that time when you ran away from Emma's house, I've found you at last."

After Fred heard his plausible pleading, he cried out, "Who yer talkin' to, my darling, and close the door dear, it's draughty."

"Yer betta come inside! I don't want all the neighbours to hear!" she snapped.

As soon as he stepped inside the room and saw Fred smoking his pipe as he sat in the chair, Dennis cried out, "Who's he?"

"Wot yer mean, who's 'e? I'll 'ave yer know I'm 'er 'usband. Any'ow who are you an' wot do yer want?" Fred replied convincingly.

"I'm sorry Mister, but 'er sister daint tell me she was married. But can I see me daughter? I've come a long way to find her," he pleaded.

"You aint seein' nobody! Now clear orf from my 'ouse befower I kick yer arse out of 'ere. My wife 'as already told me all about you an' wot a lying rogue yer was to 'er, so I don't want yer ever ter see 'er or my stepdaughter!"

"She might be your stepdaughter, but she's my flesh and blood, and you, nor anybody else, is going to stop me from seeing her!" he yelled out.

Suddenly Dennis had a shock when he saw the size of Fred as he sprung from the chair and caught hold of him by his shirt front. "Now you listen ter me, Dennis Ragbone or wotever yer call yourself! If yer not outside of my 'ouse in two seconds, I'll throw yer out on yer bleedin' arse! Now wot's it ter be?"

"I'm going," he replied meekly. As he got safely outside the door, he called out, "But you nor nobody else can stop me seeing my daughter!"

"I'm warnin' yer! If yer ever try it'll be the worst for yer."

They both watched Dennis cursing and shouting threats as he walked away. As soon as he was out of sight, Tilly said, "Thanks, Fred. But what a performance! I don' know how I kept a straight face."

"Me neither," Fred replied as he began to smile.

"I'll be glad when the van comes for me few things," she replied.

"Do yer think yer doin' the right thing by marryin' this man yer call Bill?" Fred asked.

"Yes, Fred, I'm sure."

"Well yer old enough ter know wot yer doin'. Any'ow, 'ow yer fixed fer money?"

"Bill's over generous to me and Lizzie."

"'ow's she get on with 'im?"

"Very well, Fred. She's happy and I'm happy."

"Well always remember, if ever yer should need me, you'll always find me at me pub. Now," he added, "'ere's twenty quid as a farewell gift."

"Thanks all the same, Fred. You've paid me enough by this morning's performance."

"But I'd like yer ter tek the money and buy yerself a little somethink ter remember me by." As he placed the money on the table, she saw tears in his eyes.

She had been so happy working as a barmaid at the Rose and Crown and was sorry she had to say goodbye to her kind boss. But she had not only herself to think of, but the future for her daughter Lizzie.

Before he left, Tilly threw her arms around his neck and kissed and thanked him again, before he opened the door and left.

Now she had to go and explain to her friendly neighbour, Sally Carter.

"Come in" Sally called out when she saw Tilly at the door.

"I'm glad you're in, Sal. I thought you'd be out."

"Are you alright? Looks ter me as if yer been crying. Anyway, sit yerself down while I make yer a cuppa," she added.

As soon as they sat facing each other as they drank their tea, Tilly cried out, "He called today, Sal."

"Who?"

"That rogue, Dennis."

"Was that what all the commotion was about? I noticed all the nosy parkers on their doorsteps. Now come on, tell me what happened."

Tilly told her everything what had happened and when she told her how Fred had acted, Sally burst out laughing. "But that's not all, Sally. Me and Lizzie are leaving the district in a few days' time."

"But where are yer going?"

"I've never mentioned this to you before, in case I should change my mind, but now I'm sure. I want you to know that I've been going steady with an elderly gentleman who owns a confectioner's shop. He's a lot older than me and his name is Bill Penny and he's asked me to marry him."

"How long have you known him?"

"Just over twelve months."

"Do yer love him, Tilly?"

"I'm very fond of him."

"Enough to marry him?"

"Why do you ask that?"

"Well yer know how I fell for that waster Ben Twigg. I thought I was fond of him until I married him."

"Yes I know, Sal. It was a pity really you didn't wait to find out before you wed him."

"Anyway I had to get a bread winner from somewhere while me two lads and me daughter was too young to earn. Anyway we've seen the last of him, I hope. Now, what was you saying?" she added.

"Yes. I like him a lot. He's also a widower with a little girl four years old. She's a sweet, happy child and her name's Mary Ann."

"What about Lizzie?"

"Lizzie likes him a lot and little Mary Ann. I'm happy to say the three of them get on well together."

"Does Lizzie know you're going to marry him?"

"Oh yes, Sally. We've discussed this over between us. She's already given up that dirty job working all hours on a hand press. She's now serving behind the counter and Ben is pleased the way she's took to it. It's what she wanted. She's sixteen now and I'm glad she won't be mixing with them O'Leary kids any more."

"I know what yer mean, Tilly. I have to keep my eye on my Nellie now she's started to work. Anyway, she'll always have her brothers to protect her against that unruly tribe."

"I know tongues will start to wag when I've gone, but I can't get away from here quick enough. Don't get me wrong, Sal," she added. "I shall always think of you and Fred who have been the only true understanding friends I have ever known."

"Now wipe yer tears, Tilly, and I wish you lots of happiness. I suppose it will be a nine days' wonder when you've gone," she added.

"I daresay it will, Tilly, but the nosy parkers will soon forget when a new tenant comes, to find something to gossip about. But don't forget where I live if you ever feel you need me."

"Thanks, Sally," she answered. "And when the happy day comes, I'd like you to come to the wedding."

"I'll remember that and thank you, I'll look forward to it."

"Oh, and I forgot to tell you, Fred's going to give me away and I'm going to be married in St Mary's Church. I'll come and see you agen before the furniture van arrives. Now I must hurry, Fred'll be waiting for me to settle up."

As soon as she left, Sally's tears began to flow as she remembered that day sixteen years ago when she saw Tilly sitting weeping on a bench and told her she was pregnant and had nowhere to go. Sally Carter had taken her in her home and they had been friends ever since.

As soon as Nellie saw her two brothers coming down the entry, she ran indoors. "Mom! Mom!" she yelled, "our Jack and Ted are here!"

As soon as Sally ran out of the house and saw them, she threw her arms around them and kissed them. All the neighbours too came out to welcome them with open arms and handshakes.

As soon as they got indoors and hugged and kissed their sister, Jack suddenly cried out, "Where's him?" Their mother knew what he meant. "We've seen the last of him, I hope. But it's a long story, I'll tell yer later. Now get yerselves cleaned up. I daresay yer must be clammed, and Nellie will heat the pot of stew up while I get plenty of hot water from the brewhouse boiler."

After they had eaten and settled down beside a cosy fireside, their mother began to tell them the news.

"And if he dares to show his face anywhere near this district, neighbours will lynch him," she added.

As Sally's sons began to tell her why they had left the farm, there came a loud knock on the door. As soon as Nellie ran to open it, she saw their neighbour, Paddy O'Leary standing there.

"Who is it?" her mother called out.

"It's Mr O'Leary."

"Tell him ter come in! Don't let him stand out in the cold."

As soon as he came indoors he cried out, "'ello you two. It's nice ter see yer back 'ome agen. But my!" he added, "I wouldn't 'ave known yer. Yer grown up inter two 'andsome, strappin' young men."

"Go on with yer blarney," Ted replied cheerfully.

"That's no blarney, but it does 'elp sometimes. Any'ow," he added, "are yer 'ome fer good?"

"I hope so," their mother replied.

"Yes, but we've gotta find a job," Jack replied.

"Well that's what I've really come about," Paddy answered. "I'm still a charge 'and at the rollin' mill an' I know if I 'ave a talk with the gaffer, I know 'e'll tek yer both on agen."

"Yer think so, Mr O'Leary?"

"I'm sure. But now yer grown up yer betta call me Paddy. Any'ow," he added, "he wondered why yer both left in a 'urry, an' when 'e asked me, I explained the circumstances."

Suddenly remembering that foggy night when George and Pat and himself got Ben drunk and stripped him bare and put him in a barrow of manure to sleep it off, he burst out laughing.

"What's the bloody joke?" Ted cried out.

"Well lads," Paddy replied, still smiling, "it is an' it aint, but me an' me mates will tell yer 'ow we got rid of Ben, over a pint in the local."

"Yer on, Paddy," Jack replied. "I hope it's good. The joke I mean," he added smiling.

"Well yer betta see the gaffer in the morning. Now I'll afta goo or the missus will wonder where I am."

"Thanks agen for yer help, Paddy," their mother replied.

Next morning the two brothers were up bright and early. Mr Hopkins was pleased to see them and, as he told them to sit down, Jack at once began to ask if he could find them a job.

"If it's only a part time job, Mr Hopkins, until we can find something else, we'd be very grateful. Both of us."

"But why did you leave in such a hurry? Surely I needed some explanation?"

"We couldn't get along with that stepfather of ours and there was always rows and troubles in the home."

"Yes, I did hear something about it," he replied grinning. "News travels fast around this area."

The brothers wondered if he knew what the joke was about. Although they would both have liked to ask him, they thought it would be better to hear it from Paddy.

"Anyway I can manage to give you both your old jobs back full time, but it will have to be at the same wage as before you left, and if you work hard and obey orders, I will give you both a rise, say, in three months' time. Now go and explain to Paddy that you're both to start at a quarter to eight Monday morning."

After thanking him and Paddy, they sauntered along the street with their hands in their trouser pockets, whistling a tune, knowing now they were on their way home to tell their mother the good news.

Now, at last, the Carter family were happily united again.

Other Books by Kathleen Dayus

"Her People" published 1982 reprinted in 84,87,89,91 and 92.

"Where There's Life" published 1985 reprinted 1986

"All My Days" published 1998

"Best of Times" published 1991

"Omnibus" published 1998 reprinted in large print 1999

"Ghosts of Yesteryear" published February 2000